AF078458

FIVE MONTHS OR FOREVER

JAYE ROBIN BROWN

TWO FOX
FICTION

Copyright © 2022 by Jaye Robin Brown

All rights reserved.

No part of this book may be reproduced in any form or by any electronic or mechanical means, including information storage and retrieval systems, without written permission from the author, except for the use of brief quotations in a book review.

ISBN 979-8-9861769-0-1 (Paperback Edition)

ISBN 979-8-9861769-1-8 (Ebook)

The characters and events in this book are fictitious. Any similarity to real persons, living or dead, is coincidental and not intended by the author.

Front cover image by Bailey Designs Books

First printing June 2022

Two Fox Fiction, PO Box 481, Tryon, NC 28782

Chapter 1

HANNAH

The guest list glowed on my computer screen. To my right was a stack of cards, but instead of "Save The Date" they instructed our friends and family to "Cancel The Date Because Hannah And Lisa Are Not Getting Married So Find Some Other Exciting Plans." Of course, they didn't say this exactly, but the intent was the same.

My phone pinged. Lisa's plane was ready to board. Text messages from the airline had been a lovely thing when we were a couple, but now that we were done, this service would need to end. The trip to see her family was great for Lisa, but knowing the minute-to-minute details of my ex's life was no longer a good look for my frame of mind.

I was not flying off to a villa for a round of parties. Instead, I was stuck stitching up the loose ends of our conjoined lives. And if sending out notifications that the wedding was off wasn't bad enough, I also had to break the news to my daughter. Not about the breakup; she knew about that, of course. No, I had to tell her what I'd done. I had to tell her about the life-changing decision I'd made in a moment of heartache, wine, and soul-searching. It was a late-night choice that, upon reflection, could only be described as midlife-crisis-ism. Or crappy mom mode. Whichever was the more apt descriptor, it was too late to turn back now.

Maybe I had lost my mind.

She'd have every right to be furious.

It was definitely out of character.

But even though I felt guilty as hell, I also felt resolve. The tracking app on my phone showed Jordan was a block away. I took a deep breath and closed the computer. It was time.

"WE'RE DOING WHAT?!" Jordan's face turned the peculiar shade I liked to call Rage Against the Mom Magenta.

My carefully planned speech evaporated in the face of teen angst. "Jordan, honey, calm down."

"How can I calm down? You just told me we're moving next week, I'm switching schools, and I'm leaving all of my friends—the day after Christmas!"

"But it's the beach. We're moving to the beach." Guilt overrode my mom button. That was the thing about having been a single mom for most of Jordan's life. Our relationship sometimes blurred the line between parental and friendship. Even though I had crafted in-the-moment reasons for choosing Folly Beach—its proximity to Charleston, opportunities that came with living at a vacation destination, and a way to leave my overtasked teaching job—her freak-out made me feel terrible.

"The beach is for vacations. Not for moving to. I'm not going." She crossed her arms and stomped one foot.

And . . . mom button activated.

"Was there anything I said that sounded like a choice?" This was, of course, the exact wrong thing to say.

"My whole life you've told me that we are the choices we make. That I can choose to be anything. That our choices dictate how people respond to us and act around us. Which is it? Do I have choices or not?" Jordan balled her fists by her side, and one stray curl bounced into her eye before she blew it off her face. Vulnerability flowed over her angry edges.

I pulled her into a hug. "I meant all of those things. I believe all of those things. Unfortunately, you're only fourteen. That means my choices are yours too. Obviously, I'm going to have to deal with the fallout from this choice." I positioned her rigid body at arm's length so I could look her in the eyes. "But I'm hoping you can get with the program. I need a new outlook. Lisa gave us some money. She felt bad about us giving up our old house to move in with her and was generous."

Jordan wouldn't look at me, but I could tell she was listening.

"I need a fresh start, hon. You're young. You'll be okay. Can you do this for me?"

The tears building in her eyes were like tiny splatters of acid against my heart.

I immediately tried to figure out a way that would work for both of us. A way to get her on my side, if only long enough for my heart to build a callus or two. "Listen. How about this? Once we get there, we'll only have about five months left on the lease. If at the end of the lease you absolutely hate it, we'll move back."

She finally looked at me. "You promise?"

"I promise." My gut warred with the words. The thought of going back to my job, seeing Lisa around town, having to find a new place to live that wasn't the loft, all made me queasy. But this was Jordan.

"Five months?" She wrapped her arms around herself, but her shoulders relaxed.

I pulled her close again, smoothing another stray curl from

her eyes. "Five months." I nodded against her hair. "I promise."

But as I held her, every detail of the life we'd tried to create here came into brutal focus. Leaving didn't feel like running. It felt like purpose. And as much as I didn't want to ruin my daughter's life, I really hoped our move would be longer than five months.

I hoped it would be forever.

BLYTHE

Liquor bottles waved hello from the recycling bin at the curb as I pulled Chester into the driveway. The old Bronco was a hand-me-down from my belated grandfather, Papaw Fred, and I loved it. My sister, Ginny, could not understand why in the world I wanted to drive a beater when there was a revamped model on the market. The truth was, I loved this old wood-paneled thing with its crank windows and torn upholstery. It had character and seemed richer to me than any luxury automobile, despite what my sister and my ex thought.

The liquor bottles in the bin, though . . . they didn't bode well for what I might find inside the unit I'd been sent to clean.

Beach renters were typically families or nice couples with dogs, some messier than others, but the surprises weren't usually terrible. You could even check renter reviews if they'd stayed in other vacation homes managed by the network. Every now and then, however, Coastal Beach Rentals got someone new, and sometimes they were awful.

Cleaning wasn't my typical job, but the unit needed to be flipped and the usual guy had called in sick. Ginny had been hesitant to ask, but I'd told her not to worry, that I'd take care of it. I knew it was important because the next renter was staying for a while.

When Ginny had gotten the call for a long-term rental, she'd been surprised. Who started a lease during the holidays? But the woman's references had checked out. This walk-out, lower-level apartment, stuck in the middle of the island with no water view, wasn't a hot property, and the income during the slow months would be worth what the agency might lose in the spring months. And Ginny loved to make them money.

A chilly breeze, scented with ocean brine, got me moving. "Well, Blythe, no time like the present to see what's waiting inside."

I walked to the entry and punched in the master combination before opening the door. "Jesus. What a way to celebrate the man's birthday."

The rank odor of cigarette butts and spilled liquor wafted out to greet me. Christmas with nicotine. My favorite. Of course, any island property had a strict no smoking policy, but these renters had clearly ignored it. How hard was it to take four steps outside to sit on a porch chair?

Once inside, I got the full extent of the asshattery. A lamp had been knocked over, its harp broken at the base. A huge spill—what looked like red wine—was on the peach-colored sofa. Dishes were piled high despite the obvious checkout instructions to load the dishwasher and start it before leaving. I knew I'd be lucky if I could get the place cleaned up and smelling decent before the new tenants arrived. I didn't even want to see the bedrooms. I imagined that horrors were waiting for me there.

The prospect of getting out on my boat was looking slim. I snapped a couple of pics and texted them to Ginny.

Her response was quick.

Christ on a skillet, that's gross.

Bad tenants.

You gonna have time or you need me to come help?

My sister was a peach, but I knew she didn't actually have time.

Naw, I'm good. Just wanted to be sure you don't write a 5-star for these bozos.

I got praying hands and a kissy heart in return. Welp, no time like the present. I pulled on a pair of thick yellow rubber gloves after hitting play on a Brandi Carlile playlist. Indie tunes made cleaning less tedious. I opened a trash bag and started dumping plates full of cigarette ashes.

If my former colleagues at the architecture firm in Atlanta could see me now. Cleaning houses and being a handywoman for just over minimum wage by the good graces of my sister's boss. They were surprised when I resigned, but the Constance incident had been too much. I knew that, and even though nobody forced me to go, it had seemed like the right choice in the moment. Sometimes a person needs to hit the reset button. Especially when they've made a damn fool of themselves over a woman.

When Ginny told me the real estate agency was looking to hire a handyperson to help with the vacation rental side of the business, I'd surprised both of us by applying and then getting the job.

I missed my design work. I missed the creativity. I even missed a few of my coworkers. But the move wasn't all bad.

I'd found a sweet condo with a water view; I'd bought a boat; and I'd deepened my relationship with my niblings, as I liked to call my niece and nephew, because, you know, gender, construct, etcetera. I'd even convinced myself, on good days, that I never needed a relationship again. But as I dumped ashtrays and wiped countertops, the tiniest bit of discontent seeped through my pores.

Although this new existence I'd created brought me close to my family and the waterways I loved, something was still missing. Was it too much to wish for the kind of relationship my sister had with her husband? Was it too much to hope that there might be someone out there for me?

I thought about Constance and the pathetic, begging mess of a person I'd been at our end.

This led my thoughts to the biggest question of all.

If I ever could find someone worth the potential heartache, could I stop myself from being too much?

Or would I hit the repeat button again?

Chapter 2

HANNAH

Jordan hugged her best friend, Tilda, for the fifth time, tears streaming down their faces. "Text me every minute of every day."

"No, you text me every minute of every day."

Mother guilt was a heavy load, but the decision Lisa and I made, along with the generous deposit she'd put in my savings account, put the wheels in motion. I couldn't stay in Asheville. I didn't want to go back to work and explain to my colleagues the wedding was off. My true friends would eventually understand my rash decision.

When Lisa first suggested we call off the wedding, I'd been furious. But the more we talked, the clearer it became. She loved me and loved Jordan but didn't love parenting. Of course, it would have helped if she'd figured all of that out before we'd given up our long-term rental house and sold off our furniture to move in with her, but at least it came to light before things got legal.

The deeper we dove into our unraveling, the more I had to be honest with myself. Sure, I loved Lisa. She was a good person, but had I ever seen her as a real partner in my life with Jordan? The more I thought about it, the more I realized the answer was no. Lisa was beautiful, wealthy, and kind. The type of woman anyone would jump to be with—that's certainly what my mother would say—but what would it say about my priorities that, in my desire to finally have the married life I'd long dreamed for, I'd chosen someone out of convenience and steadiness rather than spark and a real love that included my daughter.

I told Jordan and my mom that Lisa had fallen out of love with me. That we had fundamental differences and I'd decided the single life I'd mapped out for myself all those years ago was my true path.

My decision to move to the South Carolina coast was one I'd had a harder time explaining. It was a gut thing. A whispering salt breeze that got under my skin when I'd opened up an advertising email from a vacation rental company's mailing list. I could rent something small and furnished before finding something permanent and use Lisa's payoff to change careers. I'd wanted to leave teaching for a while, and though I could choose to feel guilty about taking Lisa's money, she had pushed for me to give up our house. With the way rentals had skyrocketed in Asheville, I could never replicate what we'd had before her or with her. If things ended up working out for me, I'd find a way to pay her back, but for now I chose to see it as a fair arrangement. Especially since I'd done all the design work at the loft and everything was staying with her.

Jordan was harder. I tried to convince myself that the collateral damage from a big move would be less damaging to Jordan than learning that your mother's fiancée didn't want you around. Or that your mother was a hopeless romantic who apparently thought any arrow was true love rather than something to potentially duck.

Yet now I was faced with the very real consequence of my spontaneous and probably selfish decision.

"Jordan, it's time. Get in the car."

I stood next to the opened driver's door and smiled at Tilda. "You're welcome any time, T. Come visit us at the beach."

"I can't wait." She bumped Jordan's hip. "Surfing."

They giggled and hugged one last time, and then finally Jordan slid into the passenger's seat.

"You ready?" I pulled out of the loft unit's parking space for the last time, fighting hard to concentrate on our future instead of the life we were leaving.

"I hate you." Jordan scowled and popped in her AirPods before turning to slump against the window.

Normally, I might push, but today I let her have her moment.

My thoughts trailed off as we drove out of the mountains. Every now and then I'd glance over at Jordan. I knew Lisa was within her rights. Some women didn't want to parent and it didn't mean they were flawed, despite what she thought of herself. But I couldn't understand. Even when I figured out I was a lesbian, I still knew I was going to have a baby one day. A baby, a wife, all of the trappings of a heteronormative life, except, you know, queer af.

When no serious relationship materialized by my midtwenties, I decided to have a child through a sperm donor, on my own. Maybe I couldn't find the one, but I could at least have the child. And here I was, fourteen years later, forty and single after splitting from the woman my mother called "the catch of my lifetime."

That's where my mom was wrong.

The catch of a lifetime had pizzazz, fire, chemistry, AND

the solid, stable goodness that made parenting a teenager manageable.

My mom had it with my dad.

And I wanted it too.

Still.

BLYTHE

I'd just pulled the trash cans out to the curb when an older green Mercedes wagon pulled onto the street. I hoped it wasn't the new tenants. It was bad practice to still be at a unit when they arrived. Most renters liked to think they owned the place, even when they knew they didn't. The presence of the cleaning person was a sure turnoff.

But the car slowed and the blinker came on before I'd had a chance to get into the driver's seat. At this point, it'd be awkward to leave, so I waited.

A woman, about my age, and someone I assumed to be her teenage daughter got out of the car. I spoke before they could become concerned they were in the wrong driveway.

"Hey there, welcome. I work with the management. Sorry I'm still here. Just finished getting the unit ready for you. Welcome to the island."

It had taken every bit of five hours to clean the tiny apartment. I'd left all the windows open to blow out the stench of the previous renters. Washed all the bedding twice and had to wait for the dishwasher to run a second load and dry. It was finally ready and smelled like sunshine and citrus instead of cigarette smoke and liquor.

The girl had that sour look that came with puberty, but her eyes lightened when she saw the boogie boards and bicycles locked up near the door. Her mom had requested we have them waiting. "Do we get to use those?" she asked. Her voice was hesitant and made her seem younger than she looked.

"Yes, ma'am. They are yours for however long you stay."

"That's cool." The slippery beginnings of a smile edged out the corners of her mouth.

"See?" the woman said. "I told you this wouldn't be all bad."

Apparently, she'd said the wrong thing, because the girl

crossed her arms and rolled her eyes before huffing off to punch in the door combination at the lockbox.

"Sorry about that. She's fourteen and feeling every bit of it." She held out her hand. "I'm Hannah. And that ray of sunlight is Jordan."

I noticed her neat, unpolished nails before I held my own hand out to shake hers. The strength of her grip surprised me. "Blythe. Nice to meet you. I'm normally who you call if you have a fix-it need, so if the cleaning job isn't up to snuff, you can blame me." I dropped her hand, a self-consciousness settling over me, and I took a backward step toward the Bronco. "If you don't find everything you need, give Ginny a call at the office."

"Oh, I'm sure it's going to be great." Hannah glanced over at the open door of the apartment and then back at the trunk of the car. "I better get inside." She smiled, revealing dimples I could fall straight into.

My chivalrous side wanted to jump in and help her unload the car, but despite her charming grin, there was a tightness to the way she held her shoulders that didn't bode well for chivalry.

"Well, I'll get out of your way and let you get to it." Then, on a whim, or maybe it was the way her eyes looked so defeated, or maybe because I was too damn extra for my own good, I added, "If you ever, you know, need a mom-trick up your sleeve, I could hook you up with a pool day in one of our empty rentals. Once it warms up again. Your daughter might like that. My sister's kids sure do."

Hannah's eyes lifted, showing off lovely laugh lines. They suited her. In fact, now that I'd stood there a minute too long, I noticed how easy on the eyes she was, despite her defensive shoulders. *What the hell, Blythe? Get in your car and drive your ass away like you were supposed to thirty minutes ago.*

Hannah's stance softened. "You know, I may take you up on that." She paused, then added my name. "Blythe."

I liked the way it sounded coming out of her mouth.

After I left, I drove down to the far end of the island toward the lighthouse. One of our marsh houses was empty, and since it was too late to take the boat out, I'd take a break and sit on the dock for a bit. I stopped at the island grocery and grabbed a bottle of tea and a bag of salt and vinegar chips to tide me over until I landed at Ginny's house for supper.

Pilings held the vacation house high off the ground, and I skirted them to follow a gravel path to the wharf. It jutted fifty feet through the sound's marsh grasses to the open water of a boat channel. A couple of pelicans swooped by, skimming the top of the water as they searched for fish to scoop into their hungry maws.

A weathered wooden bench provided the perfect spot. Something about the woman—Hannah—stirred up my silly wishful thinking again.

I hadn't had a real relationship since Constance.

Constance had seemed so innocent. Fresh out of design school. Eager to work on bigger projects. Eager to get me in her bed. Which I'd done way too willingly. And for a couple of years, we'd been golden. A lesbian power couple of the design world. But then she'd leapfrogged right over me the first chance she got. Honestly, I didn't mind. I was proud of her. Happy to let her light shine brighter, because God knows she glittered. Even though I was a better designer, she had the star quality clients loved. I'd have given her the moon just to see her smile.

With Constance, I was the hottest woman on the planet. She showered me with starlight, and I jumped as high as needed to catch it. But then she started turning that light in other directions, looking for new rungs to climb on the corporate ladder. My jealousy skyrocketed to jarring proportions, and I compensated with colossal overeagerness that turned out to be a turnoff.

When I found out she'd slept with the project manager for one of the biggest downtown developers in Atlanta, I lost it. In the office. In front of everyone.

"Blythe. You're making a fool of yourself." She'd looked down where I had dropped to one knee, clinging to her pant legs. It hadn't been a pretty look.

Thinking about it still caused a ripple of queasiness. Or maybe that was the potato chips. Or maybe it was the feelings that caught me off guard back there in that driveway. Hannah. A palindrome. A solid name, the same forward and back.

A pod of dolphins broke the surface near the dock, and one of them eyeballed me. I swear the damn creature winked as if it knew I was having *thoughts*. Right. Ridiculous. A five-minute meeting with a tired single mom who obviously had her hands full with a teenager and was most likely straight was not going to be some miraculous meet-cute that changed my life forever. It would not erase my past wrongdoings.

I crumpled up the potato chip bag and shoved it in my back pocket, capped my unfinished tea, and headed for Ginny's. I was obviously delusional if I was communicating with dolphins and finding prophetic symbolism in names.

One thing was certain: No matter how much I convinced myself that I was totally and 100 percent happy with this new life I'd created, something deeper was calling me out. And I wasn't sure I could ignore it anymore.

Chapter 3

HANNAH

After Blythe drove off, I turned my attention back to unpacking the car, lugging everything into our new home. It hadn't escaped me that she was most likely a lesbian and very much my type. There was also the sun shining behind her, backlighting her into silhouette as if she were the freaking messiah. I might have even heard the sound of angels singing. But . . . the last thing I needed in my life right now was a woman. The ink was still fresh on the cancelled wedding invitations. The hurt—and remorse—still sharp in my heart.

"Look at this." Jordan's voice bordered on something like excitement, so I hustled down the hall to find her.

She was in one of the bedrooms, where an egg-shaped chair hung from a chain. It twisted back and forth as she pivoted on the cushioned seat.

"I'm guessing this is your room?" The bedrooms were basically the same size, but this one had its own tiny bathroom. If giving her this space made her excited, I'd happily give up the private bath. It was the least I could do after uprooting her whole life.

"Are you sure?" She looked at the bathroom.

"Yes. Absolutely. Go ahead and bring your things in, and please, use those hangers in the closet instead of your floor." I winked at her and smiled.

For a second, she forgot how angry she was with me and smiled back.

I left the room before she could curdle again and hoped that, by making simple concessions, I'd never have to face the promise I'd made to her about moving back if she hated it.

After I put away all the groceries and dragged my things into the other room—queen-sized bed, two nightstands, lamps with shell motifs, and a horrible color of pastel peach on the walls—I looked at my phone.

One message from Lisa. One from my mother.

I dealt with my mother first.

__I hope you rethink this catastrophe. Let me know when you arrive at your hovel.__

My response was simple.

We are here. Thanks.

Lisa's text was to the point.

__Let me know when you're settled. I'm sorry but really happy you're trying something new. My dad and stepmom are heartbroken the wedding is off. They loved you and Jordan.__

No update on the status of her heart. Wow. It made me feel less guilty about the expensive case of Stags' Leap I'd snagged on my way out the door. It was a vintage I'd never have afforded on a teacher's salary and could probably never afford again.

We're here.

Might as well confess.

I took a case of good wine, hope that's okay.

It was amazing how fast a text could come back at you from halfway across the world.

I hope you took the bottles of Cabernet you love. I can get more. Okay. Ciao.

There was no point in texting her back. Ciao was the same as goodbye, and with her it was the same as getting a final emoji reaction to end a text exchange. I put the phone down and walked the ten feet of hallway to the living room.

Whoever chose the awful shade of aqua-blue paint needed a few lessons on the color wheel. Even though the peach-colored sofa and love seat were technically complementary shades, the combination made my eyeballs hurt. The rest of the room consisted of a shabby chic dining table with chairs, three battered bar stools at the counter, and a large TV on a console filled with baskets of beach towels. It also contained Jordan, AirPods out, who'd helped herself to the fancy ice cream she'd chosen, her spoon diving straight into the carton.

"You said it was mine." Her full eyebrows—thanks, donor daddy—furrowed.

"I did." As a mother, I set decent boundaries and expectations. But sometimes, letting her eat ice cream from the carton wasn't caving, it was stockpiling goodwill. I knew if I told Jordan the whole truth about Lisa, she'd come around to my side more quickly and some of that anger would subside.

It would also hurt her, which I didn't want to do. And then there was my part of the equation. I would have married Lisa. Even though at my core—the quiet place deep inside—I knew our relationship was only so-so, I hadn't been the one to put on the brakes. I would have let my marital fantasy top our overall happiness and well-being. Which had me questioning myself.

But I wasn't ready to talk about it yet.

"Are you going to have room for dinner? I thought we could take a bike ride into town and grab something to eat. I'm not up for cooking tonight."

She shrugged but moved her legs from the couch to the floor.

"I saw a pizza place that looked kind of fun. We should take advantage of this warm day before the cold comes in again." I didn't wait for her to answer or argue as I pulled on my soft-shell windbreaker. To myself, I mused, "I wonder if they'd let us paint this place since we're going to be here for a while . . ."

"That'd be fun."

Though I wanted to scream with joy that my daughter had expressed a positive opinion about something I'd said, I managed to keep my mouth shut. "If they let us paint, what color would you want to paint your room?"

She stood up, put the lid on the ice cream, and carried it toward the tiny kitchen. "I don't know. Is white stupid? I liked how bright and clean everything was at the loft."

"Me . . ." I stopped myself from adding the *too*, knowing that it would be an entry for Jordan's refreshed retorts of "Well, why did we leave then?" I changed course. "Not stupid at all. White is beautiful and can look like it has color when the sun shines in your window. But we probably ought to let them see what solid tenants we are before we ask for the moon. Come on, let's go eat our weight in pizza."

Jordan smiled, and on our way out the door, she even leaned in for a sideways mom hug. I took it.

BLYTHE

Derrick and Isla were in the front yard when I pulled into Todd and Ginny's driveway. They left their new soccer ball—a Christmas gift from me—and came running.

"Aunt B!"

As long as the sun rose over the marsh, my sorry self would never tire of the exuberance from those two. It wasn't like I still lived in Atlanta and only saw them every other month or so. "Niblings!" I held my hands up for dual high fives, then raced past them to steal the ball. We passed, and dribbled, and bumped headers for a good ten minutes until I fell onto the dry winter grass, breathing heavier than I did a few years ago when Constance had me doing CrossFit. So yeah, I could stand to get back to some regular exercise, but life sure was more fun with relaxed standards.

"Come on, Beebs." Derrick—ten years old and already surfer cool with his swath of dirty-blond curly hair, languid brown eyes, and permanently tan skin—poked my hip with his toe. "You've got more in you. Coach always makes us run another lap if we quit too soon."

Right as I rolled up onto my side and cradled my head in my elbow, Isla threw her leg over me as if I were a horse. At eight years old, she was probably the most amazing child I'd ever laid eyes on, with her soft dark curls, medium brown skin, and ice-blue eyes that came from my and Ginny's side of her family—not to mention her way-above-average intelligence.

"Come on, BeeBee." She nudged me and did a little *cluck-cluck*. Todd's parents lived way out in Sumter and had racking horses. Isla had embraced her inner cowgirl as a toddler.

"Young people." I rolled over, but Isla stuck until I tickled her out of the saddle. "Your BeeBee needs to catch her breath. Her lungs are not as full of sunbeams as yours are."

"Daddy says you're as young as you feel."

"Wise man, your father. But he is also a natural athlete who isn't addicted to potato chips and long boat rides that only involve standing with a fishing pole."

As if I'd conjured him, my brother-in-law walked out onto their screened-in front porch. "You two leave that woman alone. Blythe, I cooked up a mess of collards and your sister's made gumbo with the leftover Christmas turkey and some fresh shrimp."

"Cornbread?"

Todd's big smile took over his face. "I told Ginny you'd want cornbread."

"Well?" I walked up the stairs to the porch, and he pushed a local brew into my hand. "You're not going to let my carb-addicted body down, are you?"

"Hope you don't mind I added jalapeños and some cheddar."

I pulled him over and plopped a wet kiss onto his cheek. "Your cornbread makes me kiss boys, Todd Scott."

My sister yelled from inside. "Boys plural? Is there something you're not telling me?"

The kids pushed the screen door open, and we let the innuendos fall mute. Not because my being a lesbian was a thing, but because they didn't need to hear about their aunt's dating life. I pulled out a chair at the kitchen bar and took a long draw from the bitter ale.

"How long did it take you to clean the unit?" Ginny shook a bit of salt into the gumbo pot.

"Five hours."

Todd's eyebrows rose. "For that tiny place?"

Todd had started at Coastal Beach Rentals, so he knew the properties. However, when an Alpha Phi Alpha fraternity brother started a commercial brokerage in Charleston and asked him to come in as a partner, he'd taken the career leap.

But before he'd quit, he'd met and married my sister, which was okay by me. Todd was a keeper.

"Yeah. Smokers. Partiers. They didn't even load the dishwasher before they left."

Ginny directed the kids to set the table, and they scurried around her grabbing silverware and place mats. "Well, they won't be getting a shining review from me. I don't understand some people. But I haven't heard any complaints from the new tenants, so you must have managed to get it back in decent shape."

"I did. Unfortunately, I was still in the driveway when they pulled up."

Ginny's eyebrows scrunched, but I held up a hand to stop her from fussing at me. "It was fine. Hannah—the new tenant—didn't seem bothered by it at all. She had worse things to deal with."

"Like what?" Todd grabbed a ladle and started scooping gumbo into the bowls.

"A teenage daughter."

Ginny glanced at Isla and muttered. "I remember how awful we were."

"We?" I snorted but kept my voice low. "I was golden. You were the one who made Mom walk ten steps behind you at the mall, you were so embarrassed to be seen with her."

"You did not." Todd turned to look at my sister, who raised her shoulders. He swatted her bottom with a tea towel.

"Didn't do what?" Isla had a radar for conversations she didn't need to be a part of.

"Didn't finish setting the table when your mama asked so nicely." I poked her in the side, and she squealed and danced away from me. I stood and took the platter of cornbread to put on the table. "I offered her a swimming day when the weather gets warm. The daughter, Jordan, is old enough to babysit.

Maybe you and the kids could supervise and see if she's the responsible kind."

"I want to swim." Derrick was a fish and could hit the water in temperatures that would make most people run for their heater vents. It was also true that we'd get decent days even in the dead of winter.

"We'll see." Ginny shooed him toward the table.

Once the plates were on the table and all were seated, Todd asked Isla to lead us in a blessing. My religious practices had waned over the years, yet something about this ritual was soothing. It was sweet to hear my niece's voice chirping, "God is great, God is good, let us thank him for our food."

"Amen," we all said in unison.

I looked around. This was the right kind of happiness.

Chapter 4

HANNAH

Jordan and I spent the first two days walking on the beach, exploring the little downtown area, and binging *Gilmore Girls* on Netflix while drinking hot chocolate. Sure, it was a tactical move on my part to show her how cool Lorelai and Rory were. Even Emily Gilmore, the grandmother, bore a resemblance to my mother, though the televised version had less bite than the real thing. It worked, a little bit, but the real thaw came from my promise to consider getting a cat, either here or back in Asheville. Jordan seemed resigned that I wouldn't come to my senses before her new semester started and had mostly stopped whining about it.

On the other hand, I'd gone from pissed to devastated to angry to heartbroken and back again. The absolute rightness I'd felt about quitting my job and running away from the reality of Lisa's revelation diminished with each passing hour. The breakup wasn't totally on her. But this move—it was totally on me.

I pulled up a job seeker's site on my laptop.

Food service, hotel service, basic administration jobs, jobs in sales, but nothing at all in the design field. At least not with an art education degree. There were teaching jobs, but the point of this whole endeavor was a complete and total change.

I searched area interior designers and surfed their websites for an entry-level job. Nothing.

I opened the budgeting spreadsheet I'd created and calculated our monthly expenses. I didn't want to spend everything Lisa had given us if I could help it. It'd be nice to hang on to some for a future home or condo purchase, but with the cost of my COBRA health insurance and the inevitable repairs on my beloved ancient Mercedes, my savings would dwindle fast.

If only I had a connection in the industry. Some way to get my foot in the door without having to go back for an additional degree. Not that I was opposed to that idea, but I had a daughter with her own college dreams looming in the not-so-distant future.

"Crap." I closed my laptop.

Jordan looked up from her phone. "What's wrong?"

Even though I wasn't ready to tell her the truth about the breakup, I could have an adult conversation about my fears. We'd been a unit for fourteen years.

"I'm not seeing the kind of job I'd hoped to find." I shifted on the couch. "And I'm worried this whole idea, coming down here, making you leave Tilda and go to a new school, was impulsive and that I'm not being a good mom. Please tell me you're going to be okay."

She ran her finger over an imperfection in the sofa's fabric. "I mean, yeah, it was kind of fast. But I guess I get it. Fresh start for you and all that. I'm sad, but I'm maybe getting excited, too. Living near the beach is cooler than I thought it would be." She glanced at my computer. "We're going to be okay, aren't we?" Then she looked around the tiny apartment.

I slid onto the cushion next to her and pulled her into me.

"Yes, baby. If I have to go back to teaching, I'll do that. Heck, I'd work at a fast-food restaurant if it makes the difference between taking care of you and not taking care of you. This little place is temporary, but it's nice being close enough to bike to the beach, isn't it?"

"Yeah, I guess."

I squeezed her tight. "Speaking of, let's go check out that bird sanctuary by the bridge. Get ice cream on the way home?"

Jordan nodded.

We grabbed our helmets and pedaled slowly down tree-lined streets that stopped only when they reached the ocean. On the marsh side of the island, we found the bird sanctuary and walked our bikes to the end of the long pier. A breeze picked up.

Jordan let me drape my arm over her shoulder. "Close your eyes with me."

She did.

Seagulls cried above the steady sound of traffic on Folly Road. Somewhere to our left, boaters called to one another as they maneuvered their trailers down to the boat ramp. The buzz of a motor sounded off to our right in the marsh. Other birds called from the trees behind us.

The air felt fresh in my lungs, and excitement once again replaced the dread I'd felt back in the apartment. My anxious heartbeat shifted to steady. A smile cracked, inch by inch, until I laughed out loud.

Jordan laughed in response.

I grabbed her hand and squeezed it. "You and me, kiddo. Before all else, you and me. I'm going to find a job. You're going to make super new friends. Tilda's going to come visit. And we're going to be happy. I promise."

Though I knew it wasn't a promise entirely within my

control, the affirmation filled my body with hope. Never again would I jeopardize my kid's happiness. It didn't mean I wouldn't eventually have another lover. In fact, the thought of actual physical intimacy seemed incredibly interesting. But I'd never let myself be duped into thinking I'd find the one again.

BLYTHE

The week had been good. Nothing more to deal with than a tenant who'd somehow jammed the lockbox and needed help getting into their rental. I'd spent the rest of the time enjoying the mild late December weather and trying to ignore the fact that New Year's Eve was looming. On one hand, I loved the ritual of a new year. It was time for reflection on what had been and a chance to reframe what was to come. Many people, including my sister, might be surprised to know that I kept a sort of journal.

Mostly it was a to-do list. Little check boxes next to what I hoped to accomplish on any given day. I also wrote down random things like the weather, how the fishing was, or if I saw something cool while out boating. But I also sketched. I dreamed of ways to build coastal houses that could withstand hurricanes. Structures that wouldn't be a blight on what little natural land was left.

When I'd left the firm in Atlanta, I didn't think about what I was leaving behind. Sustainability and green ideals were big talking points, but they meant something only if they were put into practice. I'd pushed for the firm to create a green division. It's what Constance had taken when she'd outmaneuvered me. But I would have happily worked under her if my jealousy hadn't been out of control.

In the end, I guess it worked out. The division never got off the ground in a meaningful way, and the last I heard, Constance had left the firm and married a music industry lawyer who kept her in Dom and plunging necklines.

So now I doodled and dreamed about building a home on the marsh. I'd create it out of materials reclaimed from damaged houses or ones that needed to make way for the rising tides. It'd be a testament to what a person with a little bit of time, and a whole lot of patience and vision, could do. I'd even gone so far as to rent a storage unit to stockpile materials when I came across a great find. And I was making headway. I had a pile of cedar shakes from one demo project. I'd raced to pick up the beams from an old barn that was being demolished. Each new find was like a beautiful piece of a puzzle that was slowly coming together.

And to be completely honest, I'd dreamed about doing the same thing for other people with similar visions. I couldn't refresh paint and fix doorknobs forever.

I pulled Chester into the parking lot of Williamson's. Lots of people went to big-box stores for their paint, but I liked this family-owned place. It was too bad Joel, the owner, had lost his right-hand guy, Zachary. He'd had a real flair for color that Joel couldn't match.

The bell over the door jangled and Joel looked up. "How you doing, Blythe?"

"Good. Caught some beautiful snapper yesterday."

"Boat of yours running good?"

"So far."

"What can I do you for?"

"Can you look up the trim and living room colors for the Bandy property on East Ashley? It's time for a touch-up and their leftover cans have gone gunky."

Joel typed the name into his computer and wrote down a few notes. I looked at the Purdy brushes and decided it was time for a couple of new ones, grabbing them off of the peg hooks.

"You want gallons?"

"Couple of quarts is good. One of each." I put the brushes on the counter. "Charge them to the agency."

Behind me, the bell jangled again. I turned, then froze. It was the woman, Hannah, and her daughter from the long-term rental. The sun streamed in from behind them, making the edges of their hair look like the gilt halos in Renaissance paintings. That damn winking dolphin popped into my mind, and some force managed to thaw me enough to form words.

"Well, hey there."

"Oh." She looked confused for a second before recognition took its place. "Blythe, is it?"

"Yeah. Hannah? And . . ." I smiled at the girl.

She looked at me, then looked at her mom, who looked at me again, which caused her to roll her eyes. "I'm Jordan." She turned to her mom. "She's from the apartment company, right? Can we ask?"

Hannah made a quick "no" movement with her head.

"Ask what?" When neither of them spoke, I laughed. "Come on, now, I'm not that scary. What do you want to know?"

Hannah glanced at Jordan again, then spoke. "Well, you've caught us at the start of a mission."

"Oooh, a mission. That sounds intriguing." Of its own accord, my muscle memory had taken over and put me into flirt-with-a-damsel mode. My smile quirked into what my brain assumed must look dapper, and my elbow propped me up against the nearby shelf in a "how can I help your mission, little lady" move.

Hannah, unfortunately, looked a bit horrified and took a step away from me.

Thank goodness her kid seemed oblivious to my flirtation fail and spoke up. "We were coming to get paint chips because the paint inside our apartment is butt ugly."

"Jordan!" Hannah gawked at her daughter.

"What?" Jordan shrugged. "It's true."

I chuckled. "What? You don't like bleeding peach and bang-the-drum blue?"

"No." Jordan shook her head. "It makes my eyeballs bleed."

Hannah laughed, and I relaxed. I hadn't totally put her off with my "Howdy doody, ma'am" maneuver.

"What Jordan is trying to say is that neither of us feels very calm with that interior. Fresh paint was only a bit of fantasy. We'd never paint without getting permission."

"Nothing wrong with a dream. But I'm not who you need permission from. The owners will have to agree to any paint jobs, and you'll need to go through Ginny at the management office for that."

"Do you think the owners will say yes?" Jordan asked.

I lifted my palms up and out to my sides. "Owners can be funny. What makes one person's eyeballs bleed is the pinnacle of design to someone else. But these owners are pretty absentee, and with a long-term rental, and a free paint job, it might be worth a shot. You planning on doing the painting?"

Jordan nodded. "I love to paint. I even like all the prep work to get a room ready."

Hannah ruffled her daughter's short dark curls. "It's true. She's actually really good."

"I like how new-looking it makes things." Jordan smiled and twin dimples appeared in her full cheeks, identical to her mother's.

"I tell you what. You two pick out your paint chips and put together a design board."

"You mean like Pinterest?" Jordan tilted her head in question.

"Yeah, just like that. It'll be easy for the owners to see your plans. Ginny can forward them the link and let you know if they have questions or disagreements. I will warn you, most owners are going to want it to be beachy in some way, even if it's not bleeding eyeball bright."

Hannah nodded. "We can do that."

Jordan edged over to the racks of paint chips and started

pulling cards. Even from where I stood, I could see she was headed in a more soothing direction.

"Well, I guess this was fortuitous, running into you. I appreciate it." Hannah held out her hand for a shake.

"Yeah, um, I'm happy to give Ginny the heads-up so it doesn't, um, you know, come out of the blue, or anything." I kept pumping her hand for a few seconds too long and then pulled mine back too fast before shoving it into the rear pocket of my jeans.

Hannah's eyes twinkled—they were a lovely light shade of brown that picked up the red in her short auburn hair—and I was pretty sure she was laughing at me.

But could I blame her?

I hadn't acted like this around a woman in a while. It knocked me out of my single-and-not-ready-to-mingle mindset.

I took a step backward and toppled into the display of rollers.

"Oh." She gasped. "Are you okay?" She reached to help me, and all I could think was, *Here I am, groveling at the feet of a woman one more time.*

I jumped up. "Fine, totally fine. Nothing to see here." I hastily straightened the fallen rollers, grabbed my paint from Joel, and practically ran out the door.

Chapter 5

HANNAH

Was it wrong to be flattered when Blythe got so flustered? I was obviously in no place to even think about women. But a woman flirting with me, even in the most awkward way, sure didn't hurt my self-esteem. And Blythe was attractive—ruddy-tan skin, ice-blue eyes, and a windblown head of salt-and-pepper hair. She had that soft butch look I loved but had given up on finding when I met sleek and sophisticated Lisa.

Oh well. Enough of that. I was not going to let fantasies take control of reason again. It was time to focus on myself, and Jordan.

"What'd you find?" I looked at the swatches Jordan laid out on the design table.

She pointed at the different soft coastal neutrals. "Living room and kitchen and hall, your room, my room, the bathroom."

The older man running the store approached us. "Want me to mix up some samples for you? My former employee recommended that folks paint the color on poster board and then tack the board up on the wall to see how they like it."

"Oh, that's a great idea."

Jordan handed him the swatches.

The man kept talking. "Did I overhear one of you say you love to paint?"

"That was me." Jordan's shoulders pulled back as she held herself, tall and proud.

He grinned, showing off a gold tooth in a face filled with joy. "Not many young ladies in the trade, but it's a good living if you communicate with your clients, clean up well, and do a good job." He looked at me. "What about you? You like to paint?"

"The painting is okay, but I don't love the prep work. Design, colors, composition, and organization. That's what I love."

He tapped on his computer keyboard but kept talking. "You good on the computer?"

"Sure," I said.

"Wouldn't happen to need a job, would you? Any friend of Blythe's is bound to be a good egg, and I've been high and dry since my man Zachary left for an opportunity down in Miami."

I started to tell him I'd only just met Blythe, but Jordan interrupted.

"Mom used to be an art teacher." Then she grinned at me and nodded in a silent "Go for it, Mom."

The man looked up again. "Name's Joel Williamson. If you were an art teacher, you must be good with color. I'm good at running the business and I know paint. But color and design are not my strong suit. In fact, I probably recommended your eyeball bleed colors." He chuckled. "But I'm serious. If you need a job, I'm desperate to find a new hire. You've got a trustworthy smile, and I can see by the colors you've picked out that you could sure help some of my clientele."

My brain clicked through a fast set of mental calculations. Though working as a paint store clerk had never been on my dream jobs list, the move would be in the general direction I wanted. Working here, I'd probably get to meet local builders who'd be willing to hire someone with only a knack for design rather than an interior design degree. I didn't aspire to be published in *Architectural Digest*, but I loved the idea of helping people with their overall decor. A job like this could be a stepping stone to the brand-new career I sought. One where I could be in charge, without having to deal with the endless bureaucracy that made my teaching career unsustainable.

It also meant I'd probably run into Blythe again, which, okay, was perhaps the tiniest bit interesting to me because who didn't want a bit of flirtation on the day-to-day?

I bumped Jordan's leg with my knee in silent mother-to-daughter excited body language before answering. "As a matter of fact, we're new to the area, and job hunting is on my to-do list."

"Sounds like fate to me. Tell me your name again?"

Such a polite Southern way of saying I hadn't introduced myself. "I'm Hannah Greenfield. And this is my daughter, Jordan."

"Well Hannah, and painter Jordan, pay's sixteen an hour for starters. Once you get to know the product real well, about a month or so, I'll bump you up to eighteen. It's not a lot, but our cost of living won't wreck you. After you've been working for me for three months and prove yourself steady, I'll put you on my insurance plan." He grabbed a business card from a drawer by the register and handed it to me. "I suppose you should shoot me over your résumé and let me call up some references just to be all official. That is, if the job interests you."

The minute he said insurance, my yes button had gone off. Insurance would be an excellent benefit even if the pay was low. I probably should tell him there was a chance I'd be leaving again, but I held on to hope that wouldn't be the case. Regardless, a paycheck would be nice. No matter how small.

"Actually, it sounds like it could be really fun. I'll email my résumé to you as soon as we get back to our apartment."

He finished mixing up our samples and slid them across the counter.

I pulled out my credit card to pay.

"No charge. Consider it an employee perk. Can you start Monday? Eight a.m.?"

My excitement waned a little. "Oh, that might be tricky. Jordan is starting at St. James and I've promised her she only has to ride the bus in the afternoon. I drop her off about that time. Would an eight-thirty start time be okay?" I hoped the time frame wouldn't affect his offer.

"Is only thirty minutes for lunch okay for you?"

I was the human equivalent of a horse, grazing through the day, so that wasn't an issue at all. "Not a problem. Sounds like a plan."

A couple of contractors came through the door, and Joel reached his hand out to shake mine. "See you Monday."

Once outside, I did a happy dance.

"Please. Stop." Jordan covered her eyes.

I stuck my tongue out but my feet stopped moving, saving her from teenage embarrassment. "A job. Your momma's got herself a new job."

Jordan mumbled as she reached for the door handle. "You could have kept your old one."

I chose to ignore her jab. She was smack in the middle of self-discovery, which meant being empathetic toward her mother—who'd just ruined her life—was not a realistic thing to expect. At least not yet.

Five Months or Forever

We ran to the office supply store for poster board, and then I drove Jordan past her new school so she could have a visual to take her through the weekend.

The charter high school was not keen on taking a transfer, but fortunately what Jordan lacked in cutting-edge cool—according to Jordan—she made up for in a dogged attitude toward school work and a passion for social justice. Her teachers had given her rousing recommendations, and the school here had made an exception.

That didn't stop me from noticing the furrows in her brow when I idled the car in front of the building.

"Hey." I patted her hand. "You're going to like this school. It's got a great reputation, and just think, you can go to the beach every single afternoon when you're done."

"Yeah. I guess. I miss Tilda, though."

"I know, hon. But don't you have virtual plans for New Year's Eve tomorrow?"

She nodded. "It's not the same."

My mind drifted to Lisa. She was probably going to some fantastic child-free New Year's Eve party with her father's friends in Italy. She'd kiss some handsome Italian man or woman under glittering lights. She'd dance, wear couture, and not think of us once.

I wish I'd seen it coming.

I wish I'd seen myself.

BLYTHE

Ginny was on the phone when I stopped by the office the next day. When she hung up, she blew out a deep breath.

"One of those days?" I asked.

"Yeah. New home on the marsh side and the owners are picky, picky, picky. I can't believe they're even willing to rent. They seem to want renters who don't eat, poop, breathe, or sit on the furniture."

"Speaking of owners, I ran into Hannah, the tenant at the basement unit. She and her daughter want to know if they can paint the interior. I told her it was worth a shot seeing as they're willing to do it themselves and pay for the materials. She said she'd send over some kind of Pinterest link to show what they had in mind. Would you be willing to run point on that?"

Ginny cocked her head. "Why do you have that look on your face?"

"What look?"

A smile bloomed. "Oh, I don't know. Kind of guilty. A little dreamy. This Hannah, what's she look like?"

"How would I know? I've only talked to her twice." But I did know. She was about my height, maybe a smidge shorter, five six or so. Short auburn hair with a feminine swoop of bangs, brown eyes, ample hips, dimples, a warm smile . . . okay, so I definitely knew.

My sister leaned forward. "She's got a kid, Blythe. She's probably straight."

"Lesbians have kids these days. Anyway, it doesn't matter. She just wants to paint, not be your sister-in-law."

Ginny tidied her desk to leave. "You're right. I shouldn't assume. Dating a mom would be new for you. You're super with my kids. I could see it. Let's invite her out for a drink. I can get the backstory out of anyone."

I was too old to be as embarrassed as I felt in this moment, but I wanted her to do it. Something about Hannah had me daydreaming all kinds of delicious scenarios.

Ginny was gregarious and charming and had a way of putting people completely at ease. But she was also cunning, which gave her an edge in real estate and a knack for reading beneath the surface. Before I even gave her the go-ahead, she was back on her computer, typing away. She read aloud as she typed.

"Greetings, Hannah. Blythe stopped by the office and gave me a heads-up about your painting project. As soon as you get the information to me, I'll give the owners a call. Since you're new in town, maybe you'd like to join us for happy hour? We're headed over to Tiki Surf around six-thirty. A little end-of-the-year celebration before I go home to hibernate before the real parties start. You probably already have New Year's plans. No need to respond. If you show, we'll be there. And since you've met Blythe, just look for her."

She typed the period with a flourish of her finger. "There. Let's see if I found you someone to kiss at midnight tonight."

"Ha. I plan on being under my covers and gently snoring by midnight."

Ginny waggled her eyebrows. "I bet you do."

"Oh my God. Why am I related to you?"

She smirked as she shut down her computer, grabbed her phone and purse, and pushed me toward the door.

But when she offered to give me a ride, I opted out. What if it actually went well and I wanted to stick around? What if Hannah was interested in women and a simple drink turned into something more? I'd need Chester to get me home.

A buzz of excitement started in my belly. The last time I'd tried to have a date was six months ago and it had not gone well. The kiss we'd shared had been awkward at best, and the woman had ghosted me not long after. Since then, I'd not even bothered. Being alone meant I never had to compromise on what I wanted to watch on the television.

Who was I kidding? Ginny was probably right and Hannah was probably straight.

I glanced at my reflection in the glass door. I'd put on fifteen pounds since the Constance incident and tended more toward carpenter pants than crisp chinos these days. Ginny could tell me I was a stone-cold silver fox all she wanted, but she was my sister and it didn't count. I looked tired. Okay, maybe a little sad. Probably a little desperate. Definitely a little ragged around the edges.

GINNY FOUND a tall table next to a heat lamp on the Tiki Surf patio at the same moment I convinced myself I was not worth the attention of someone as attractive as Hannah.

"Oh, God. No." Ginny laser-eyed me. The reflection of leftover Christmas light strings bounced off her pupils and made me feel as if I were shot through with red and green ice needles.

"What?" I plopped onto the wooden stool and grabbed a couple of in-the-shell peanuts from the bowl the server had set on our table. "Don't look at me like that."

"You've got the Eeyore look. Please do not make me give you the silver fox talk again."

Ginny had already ordered for us, and our server delivered a grapefruit and vodka in front of my sister and an IPA in front of me. I took a swig of the beer.

"Please do not give me the talk. You know it doesn't matter. Anyway, she's not going to show up. It's New Year's Eve and you sent her that message less than thirty minutes ago."

"Her apartment is literally less than half a mile from here.

She could walk it in less time."

"She's not coming. She has a kid. I'm sure she has a life."

Apparently, I was wrong.

Because when I looked up, there was Hannah poured into a pair of skinny jeans with her hands tucked into the back pockets and low-top green Converse on her feet.

"No way," I whispered.

"Is she here?" Ginny swiveled her head. "Where is she?" She located Hannah right as Hannah waved at me. "Holy shit, sis. She's hot. You could have told me." Then Ginny waved and beckoned Hannah over.

Which was good. Because I was frozen. Staring. Taking in the details. My sister was right. Hannah was hot. I hadn't noticed just how hot before because both times she'd been frazzled from long days of driving or dealing with her daughter. But watching her walk across the room toward us, the string lights twinkling overhead, her sweater falling in all the right places, I could feel my heart beating out of my chest.

How the hell was I even going to be able to talk to this woman?

Hannah settled onto the stool across from us. "Hi."

"I'm Ginny." My sister reached out her perfectly manicured hand and they shook. "And you know Blythe."

My hand did this strange little quick raise from the table, and my voice chirped out a high-pitched "Heya" like I was Canadian or something. I grabbed my beer and took a big swallow before I said anything else in random accents.

"Well, heya to you." Hannah mimicked my wave and then, Lord help me, she winked.

Which made my beer catch in my throat at just the wrong moment. I coughed out beer all over the front of my shirt, and if I thought I'd sounded ridiculous seconds before, now I looked ridiculous too. How I was going to talk to her should've been the least of my worries.

Chapter 6

HANNAH

I shouldn't have laughed. But it was ridiculously adorable the way Blythe got so nervous around me. I'd noticed it in the paint store, but her reaction to the wink confirmed it. Okay, so maybe I was messing with her a little bit. Maybe I was waggling my wings to see if I remembered how to fly. But I needed to back step quickly so I didn't seem like an ass.

"Here." I grabbed napkins from the dispenser on the table and handed them to her at the same time the server approached for my drink order. Which was good timing because it allowed Blythe some privacy for the cleanup. "Do you have a wine list?" I asked.

Ginny, the woman who'd invited me, put her hand on mine and patted it. "Oh honey, this is a surf bar. You're going to get the box stuff at best. They have great cocktails and tons of local brews, but I'd steer clear of the wine—if you actually like wine."

I laughed. "Noted." I didn't ordinarily drink much liquor,

but I wasn't a beer drinker either, so I left it to the waitress. "Something citrus-y, not super sweet, with vodka."

"Lemon drop martini it is." She turned before I could reconsider.

"How's the apartment working for you? Other than the colors?" Ginny asked. She was probably my age or a little younger. She had the same ice-blue eyes as Blythe—which made me wonder if they were related—but that's where the similarities stopped. She gave off professional wife, weekend soccer mom vibes, and she looked the part too. Her hair was shoulder length and definitely colored—no one had such a deep brown to blond ombre on their own. Long manicured nails painted in a soft nude color led my eye to the delicate but gorgeous sapphire and diamond band on her ring finger. I'd never paid attention to ring fingers before Lisa and I decided to get engaged. But now, I looked. Looking at hers made me a little sad. I'd been so close to realizing a lifelong dream.

I shook the fleeting emotion away, remembering I'd also been uncomfortably close to a lifelong mistake. "The apartment's great. It's going to be even better once the temps warm up enough for us to use the side yard and patio."

"And you have a daughter?"

"Yes, Jordan. She's fourteen."

"I'm not looking forward to that stage."

I glanced over at Blythe, who hadn't said anything since she'd squeaked out a hello, and she blinked, twice, those eyes of hers inviting a person to get lost in them, even if she did look a tiny bit freaked out. "You two have to be related." I looked from Blythe back to Ginny.

"We're sisters. Blythe didn't tell you that?"

"God, Ginny, there was no need."

Ginny's eyes grew round and wide at her sister's sullen response, and I could imagine what it was like when the two of them had been growing up. I diverted the conversation because obviously Blythe was having some sort of a moment. "You said you weren't looking forward to that stage? You have a daughter?"

"And a son. Isla's eight and Derrick is ten." She put her hand on Blythe's arm. Ginny was clearly a touchy-feely kind of gal. "Blythe here is the world's best auntie."

I smiled, hoping to ease any sort of embarrassment Blythe was feeling. "That's sweet. Jordan only has honorary aunts. I'm an only and she's an only and her father isn't in the picture."

"Oh, so what happened to him?" Ginny leaned in closer.

"It's too long a story for cocktail hour. Besides, I don't want to bore you with the details of my life."

"That's why we're here. We know each other's stories. You're fresh meat. Tell us everything."

I didn't want to be rude, but I also didn't want to tell them everything. Jordan's personal details were her own, and we had reached an agreement about how much I could or would share once she'd gotten old enough to understand how her parentage made her different from her friends. In Asheville, where there were so many donor kids, it was no big deal. Here, it might be.

"Well, I won't bore you with that old story, but I will share my news. Thanks to Blythe, I have a job."

Blythe finally seemed to snap out of whatever she was battling internally. "Thanks to me?"

I sipped the lemony martini the server had set in front of me. It was too good. "Unintentionally on your part. Joel, at the paint store, hired me. In fact, he said, and I quote, 'Any friend of Blythe's has to be a good egg.' I didn't correct him, but I did send him some additional references and my résumé."

Ginny drew back in her chair. "The paint store? Really?" Then she seemed to catch hold of herself. "I'm sorry, that sounded judgmental."

I nodded and smiled. "Maybe a little, but I get it. It's not a job I ever would have considered for myself, but the opportunity landed in my lap and, I don't know, it seemed right somehow."

Ginny leaned forward and glanced at her sister before whispering dramatically. "Don't tell me, you're another one leaving their big corporate job to come find simple, soul-fulfilling, every-person work in a small town."

She had no idea how close to the mark she was. Though it wasn't *my* corporate job I was fleeing. But I was curious what she meant. "Another one?"

"This one." Ginny flicked her thumb at Blythe. "Packed up and left her big job in Atlanta to fix doorknobs for me at the beach."

"Oh." I took another sip of my cocktail. "What'd you do in Atlanta?"

Ginny shut her mouth, though I could tell it was killing her not to jump in and speak for her sister.

Blythe cleared her throat and swept her hand back across the close-clipped part of her hair. "I was an architect."

Well, shit. Her cute level just soared through the ceiling. An architect. A soft butch architect with ice-blue eyes and a kind heart. My curiosity level ramped up a notch.

"Was?" I took two more sips of my martini in quick succession, and before I realized she'd even done it, Ginny had ordered another round, though I noted she got grapefruit and club soda, no vodka, for herself.

Blythe shrugged and sipped her new beer. "I needed to get out. Things got . . . well, I won't bore you with my old story either. I'd made decent financial decisions and was able to step away."

I bookmarked her copycat answer but didn't remark on it. "You stepped away permanently?"

Ginny gathered up her purse. "God, I hope not. She's majorly talented. She designed my house. You'll have to come see it sometime. Bring your daughter. My kids will annoy her,

I'm sure, but they'll also idolize her. They think teenagers are the real deal."

"You're leaving?" Blythe sounded panicked as she noticed Ginny gathering her things to leave.

"Yes, love. Todd and I have a hot date making homemade pizzas with the kids and talking about what we want in the New Year." She stopped and looked at me again. "Where's your daughter tonight?"

I shrugged. "Teenager. I am no longer fun. She's on a Zoom call with a bunch of her friends, having an hours-long party. She's loaded up with crappy pizza and her favorite snacks."

"Hmm, maybe teenage years don't sound that bad after all. You two have fun." She winked at her sister, then waved to me. "Don't be a stranger."

When I turned back to Blythe, she was staring after her sister the way a kindergartener looks at their mom on the first day of school. Was I that awful to be around?

BLYTHE

I couldn't believe Ginny. I mean, I knew she did this because she wanted me to learn more about Hannah, but she'd basically gotten nothing out of Hannah. And now here I was, on New Year's Eve, with a strange woman whom I happened to be increasingly attracted to, hammering beers like I was sixteen. But I was so nervous.

Hannah cradled her glass in her hand. "If you have someplace to go, don't feel like you need to babysit me. I'm only a few blocks away." She looked around. "I think I better get something to eat before this vodka wreaks havoc on my brain cells." Hannah smiled in her warm way, and I noted again how utterly adorable her dimples were. When she started to summon the server, I spoke up.

"Uh. No. I, um, don't have anywhere to be." Oh, good Jesus, Blythe, could you sound any more pathetic? Where is your inner player? "If you want, I'll have dinner with you." Better. "I know a place that has excellent tacos and Thai-inspired sandwiches if you like that sort of thing. Plus, it would be quieter." I gestured toward the band that was setting up on the corner stage of Tiki Surf. "It's going to get loud here in a minute." I almost felt normal.

Hannah dropped her hand and leaned forward, her sweater gapping so that I got a glimpse of a swell disappearing into a lacey black bra. Straight lingerie? No. Lace didn't rule out sapphic tendencies.

"Perfect," she said. "Let me run to the restroom and then I'll be right back."

I noted she didn't carry a massive purse. Instead, she had one of those phone cases that also held a credit card and a few bills. Practical. My eyes followed her until I caught myself and forced them to look up at the sky. But I kept seeing those shapely curves mirrored in the building storm clouds.

When the server returned, I picked up the tab. It wasn't a date, but Hannah was new in town, so treating was simply being polite. That's what I'd tell her anyway. I grabbed my jacket off the back of the chair and walked over to wait for her.

When she came out, she smiled at me and I felt that flutter of excitement. The one I'd convinced myself I never needed to feel again. It was all I could do to act nonchalant. "I got the tab. Think of it as a welcome and congratulations on your new job."

"You didn't have to do that. I'm getting dinner, then."

"No way. Didn't your mama ever teach you not to look a gift horse in the mouth?" I held out my arm for her to walk ahead of me on the narrow path out of the bar.

"Hah." She looked over her shoulder. "I've worked very hard not to take many of the lessons my mother tried to teach me. I love the woman, but she's the opposite of nice."

It was the first personal thing she'd shared all night. Maybe I'd have better luck than my sister did.

"And your dad?"

We were walking side by side down Hudson Avenue. There was no traffic, and this was the kind of place where cars were used to pedestrians milling about. They'd slow and drive around us.

"He passed away about ten years ago. A stroke. Probably the stress of living with my mom."

"Where did they live?"

"Birmingham, Alabama. My mom is still there."

The low rumble of thunder sounded off to the west. Hannah glanced up. "Do you think it will storm?"

I looked around. "Hard to know. Lots of storms come at us from the west. But sometimes the ocean breeze pushes them back and they don't make it to the shore. Are you an Alabama fan?"

Hannah grimaced. "I'm embarrassed to tell you, because it makes me kind of a bad lesbian, but I'm not into sports."

Did my heart just stop? I think my heart stopped. Hannah said she was a lesbian.

Before I could respond, she sighed. "You're judging me. I can tell. Is it the sports? Or the gay thing?"

I needed to get my shit together, and quickly.

"Uh, the sports thing, totally. But I'm glad you're not a Bama fan. I'd have to renege on dinner."

"Well good. Glad that's settled." She glanced over. "I kind of guessed the lesbian thing was a nonissue."

I opened my arms wide and did an awkward jig in the street. "Is it that obvious?"

"Well . . ." Hannah tilted her head and put her forefinger to her chin. "I hate to make assumptions about anyone."

"Same, though I'll admit, your paint store job makes a whole lot more sense now. But why Williamson's and not Home Depot?"

We turned toward the restaurant.

She pivoted toward me, her hand shoved into her back pockets again. "Believe it or not, the paint store job is not because I'll be running into all of the lady-loving community but because I love interior design. I used to be an art teacher, but kind of thought, with this move, it'd be a good chance to pursue a new career. Joel's job offer seemed like a step in the right direction. I have to thank you again for the leg up. Even if you had no idea you were helping me out."

"That makes sense." I tamped down the tremor of warning. The last time a woman had used me as a leg up, it had ended badly. Constance hadn't wanted me for me, and the soul scars of being used instead of loved still caused echoes of pain.

But Hannah was not Constance. Just because she was new in town and seeking a new career didn't mean anything. Besides, Constance, unlike Hannah, never ever admitted that she'd used me, inadvertently or not, as a stepping stone on her career path. "Design is a great field."

Hannah blushed. "Oh, I don't think I'll be able to call myself a designer. Don't have the degree for that, not like you. I'd be okay with decorator, and for now, color specialist."

We arrived at the restaurant. It was almost empty and quiet enough to have a decent conversation. A few locals sat at the bar, talking to Matilda the young bartender, but the tables out in the garden were pretty empty. I led us to one at the far end, where we'd have privacy. Hannah looked around, taking in the Tiki torches and the strings of Edison bulbs hanging between draping live oak branches.

"This place is awesome." She pulled the antique folding chair out to sit in. "It's one of the things I love about Folly, gorgeous trees all the way up to the sands of the ocean."

"Have you seen the Angel Tree?"

She shook her head. "No, what's that?"

"This gorgeous old oak. They say it's at least four hundred years old. About thirty minutes from here. You'll have to check it out. There's a little museum and a fence to keep it protected."

"That sounds like something I'd love. Jordan too. Maybe you could show us one day?"

The way it came out of her mouth was so natural. Like we were old friends, and our hanging out was the way of things. I wanted to pull out my calendar and pick a day, but I worried it would come off strong. "Yeah, sure. For sure. Um, one more drink? With food, of course."

She smiled and shifted in the chair. A small emerald stud glinted from the edge of her upper ear, the shade of green a perfect color against her skin. "Only one. I don't want to start the New Year with a hangover."

Matilda stood by the table ready to take our order. "What's

this I hear? Isn't that what New Year's Eve is for? Party till the break of day?"

I leaned back in my chair to look at them. "I'm old. Those days are done."

Matilda shook their head. "Bullshit, Blythe. You're total cougar material." Then they smiled at Hannah. "You've made a wise choice with this one." They bumped my shoulder with their hip as if we were in cahoots. "Now, what can I get y'all?"

Jesus. Was the entire community dead set on embarrassing me into an early grave?

After we'd ordered a smorgasbord of tacos, another beer for me, and some alcoholic ginger beer concoction for Hannah, Hannah leaned in. "Seems like you have a fan."

I glanced across the plant strewn garden to the bar. "Matilda? They're twenty-four. I could be their parent. Baby queers are not my thing."

Hannah raised her eyebrows. "Oh, but you know how they identify?"

"They tell anyone who will listen." My voice raised slightly before I noticed Hannah laughing. She was teasing me. I let my shoulders drop again.

Matilda returned with our drinks, and we grew silent for a moment as we each took a sip.

Then, at the same time, we spoke, "So, tell me about—"

I finished mine with "—life in Asheville" and Hannah finished with "—about leaving architecture."

She stayed quiet and waited and because my stomach was in knots and she had this weird way of both making me nervous and putting me at ease, I started blabbing. And once I started, it didn't seem like I could stop.

Chapter 7

HANNAH

I'd dodged a bullet by asking Blythe about her decision to leave her career. Though she didn't seem willing to tell me much about her final days at her firm, she was obviously passionate about architecture. My mind drifted as she started into a blow by blow about the commercial projects her firm had handled. I thought about Lisa and the wedding we would have been having in six weeks. How could I talk about my life in Asheville without bringing up that salient tidbit?

"I'm sorry, this has got to be boring." Blythe swiped the side of her hair, a move I was beginning to recognize as a nervous tell.

"Oh, no, I'm sorry. You were talking about how commercial projects weren't really giving you the opportunity to design sustainably. I was listening, but I was also thinking I ought to check in on Jordan."

"Shit, right. Sorry. I should have thought about that."

"Stop. You're fine. Let me check my phone." I turned it

over from where I'd set it facedown on the table and shot off a quick **You okay?** text.

I got a thumbs-up in reply as our tacos arrived.

"Thank you." I smiled up at Matilda. "These smell amazing."

"Best on the beach." They gave us each a roll of silverware. "Another round?"

"Better not," Blythe said. "I have to get myself home at some point."

A younger, childless me might have jumped all over that with a "Go ahead, have another, you can crash on my couch if you need to." Blythe didn't know my sad story, and if there was ever a time to throw my cares to the wind and have a night of New Year's Eve fun, this was it. But those days were gone.

"A water for me."

Matilda shrugged. "Suit yourselves, but it's a long way till midnight."

They walked off, and a less comfortable silence settled. What had started out as drinks for two potential new friends had turned into something that almost felt like a setup—and a New Year's Eve setup came with the weighty implication of midnight. I wanted to say something, make a joke about it, but then wasn't that presumptuous?

The sky settled my dilemma as a flash streaked in the distance, followed by a low rumble. The wind picked up, making the various wind chimes hanging around the restaurant's garden sing nervously.

"Guess that storm is coming in." Blythe looked up and around. "It's too bad." She grinned at me and, damnit, inconvenient flutters vibrated in my chest. I could totally crush on this woman if I wasn't dealing with the aftermath of a broken relationship and almost marriage. Why couldn't it be a few months down the road —some respectable amount of time for thoughts of romance?

"Why's that?" And there I went, being all coy, asking her to answer the question when I could have ignored her comment and brought up something else.

"Because I'm having a nice time. The company's attractive and the conversation is easy." Blythe lowered her eyes and dove into one of the tacos. It was cute and shy, and I could tell it probably took a lot for her to say that. But she wasn't wrong, about the conversation anyway, and it wasn't like she was asking me out or anything. There was no harm in being kind.

"Agreed. It's nice to have a friend in a new town." I took a bite of my food, knowing we'd need to eat quickly for me to make it home before the storm moved in. I didn't emphasize the word *friend*, kept the delivery casual, but hoped she'd pick up on the implication and not push further.

We finished our food, split the bill, and headed back toward Blythe's Bronco and my house.

"Will you go over to your sister's after this?" She'd said she was going home, but maybe she was seeing someone. Flirtatious with a side of awkward shy could be her shtick.

Blythe shook her head. "Naw. To be honest, I like staying home on New Year's Eve. It's amateur hour. People who don't drink much all year round get overfaced with champagne and choose to drive. I'd rather be cozy on my couch, reading a book, and falling asleep early." She blew a breath out at the sky. "Oh boy. I'm really selling myself, aren't I?"

I bumped her with my hip as we walked down the road. Okay, that was a move. I knew it, but my body took over of its own accord. It'd been so long since I flirted and had it reciprocated. My relationship with Lisa lost its spark early and I'd puttered along, convincing myself the stability was worth more than sex. But here was Blythe— so damn cute in her self-effacing way—and, hello, butterflies. She was practically the human equivalent of a teddy bear, and who didn't love one of those? "Honestly, staying in sounds perfect. As soon as

Jordan was born, going out lost its importance. I do love the promise of New Years and the rituals of New Year's Day, though."

We got to the bar we'd left earlier. A raucous crowd danced on the patio, undulating in unison, while the band blasted surf music.

Blythe smiled. "You don't want to listen to one song? We could hang out here." She slid closer and bumped me in return. Blood rushed into my face, and I hoped my body wasn't emitting visible shimmers of energy in response to her casual touch.

The sky responded to my unexpected reaction with a crackling bolt of lightning that splintered across the dark clouds. This was quickly followed by a collective "whoa" from the bar crowd as we stopped next to Blythe's car.

I did want to listen to one song. I could pretend I was young and unencumbered, that Blythe would wrap her arms around me and that we'd sway along to the music while the storm crackled around us. I'd be able to forget about my not-wedding for a night and maybe Blythe would have some fun too.

But I was not a girl anymore. I was a middle-aged, single mom who'd been recently ditched by her fiancée. As much as I was inconveniently attracted to Blythe, the timing was piss poor.

"I better head home. Jordan will probably get freaked out by the storm."

"Okay. See you around?" Blythe's arms hovered near her sides like she was unsure whether she should hug me.

"Definitely." I stepped in, but kept my head purposefully turned away to receive her hug.

She gave me a big squeeze—a real hug. Not the pat-pat of nervous huggers. It was a welcome and an invitation and an appreciation. I desperately wanted to stay there and push myself completely against her, but instead I slow-counted to five before reluctantly stepping back.

She cleared her throat and looked everywhere but at me.

A plop of water landed on my head. The raindrops started to multiply. "I better run."

"You sure I can't drive you?" She met my eyes.

I shook my head and started drifting toward the sidewalk. "Thanks again. Happy New Year, Blythe."

She slow-blinked, then lifted her chin and grinned. "Happy New Year to you too, Hannah."

I waved once more, then turned and ran toward home.

BLYTHE

I woke up thinking about hugging Hannah. Which is no surprise given I'd gone to sleep thinking about it. But thoughts were going to get me nowhere. It was officially a new year, and if I ever wanted to hug Hannah again, I had to step boldly into it. I was not the same Blythe. Just because Hannah was the new girl in town, looking for an intro into a new career and a new community, didn't mean she was going to walk all over me. And it didn't mean I would lose all reason and get attached too fast. Constance was three years ago. I'd had a whole lot of lonely weekends to think about how I wouldn't be if I ever got the chance at another relationship.

The marsh appeared as my remote-operated blinds rose inch by inch. The year's first sunrise was something I didn't want to miss. I wondered whether Hannah was a morning person like me.

When the sun was high enough above the distant trees to see its round glow, I rolled over and padded in sock feet to the kitchen. I put grinds in the pour-over and heated up water in the kettle. Once it boiled, I poured the water slowly over the coffee and inhaled the rich smell. I wondered whether Hannah liked coffee as much as I did.

A few years back, I decided to do the things on New Year's Day that would set my focus for the year. This year my plan was lunch and football with Ginny and family, but first a morning boat ride, then a visit to my storage shed to mentally catalogue my treasures. But now, I kind of wanted to add Hannah and Jordan into the day. Granted, it was probably a dumb idea. Though I'd established she was indeed a lesbian, there was so much I didn't know. I mean, it didn't seem as if she was in a relationship, since she arrived solo, but I knew people's lives were not always what they seemed. And even though it definitely felt like she'd flirted here and there last night, I also got some strictly friend vibes.

But good Lord almighty, that hug was electric. The minute my arms went around her, I knew she was someone special. She didn't shy from a real hug. She let me hold her longer than many people would. And she'd felt amazing. I could have kept her there all night.

Maybe inviting them over to Ginny's for traditional New Year's lunch would be a low-key way to explore this. It wouldn't be like a date. She'd said she liked New Year's Day traditions, and even though she wasn't into football, maybe she'd be into the food. Jordan could meet Isla and Derrick, and even when you were a teenager, sometimes it was fun to run around and kick a soccer ball or jump on a trampoline.

I texted Ginny.

Would you mind if I invited Hannah and Jordan over to your place for lunch and the game?

I knew this was going to open up an intense text stream, but I had no choice if this was my plan.

OMG you devil. And of course. What happened? Tell me everything!

A pause.

Holy shit. Is she THERE?

I texted back an eye roll emoji first. Then:

No, she's not here. Nothing happened. She's nice and new in town and says she likes New Year's Day traditions.

Uh-huh. Whatever, sis. You don't make invitations lightly. But yes, yes, please invite them. Todd always cooks for an army. His brother's coming with their kids, so there will be other kids Jordan's age. Let them know. It might help your cause.

Will do. See you later.

She sent back a string of hearts.

That's when I realized I didn't have Hannah's number. Which put me in a conundrum. Bug my sister to get it from the office, which would give her another chance to obsess over my personal life, or swing by to see if they were home and deliver the invitation in person. Neither seemed optimal. Why hadn't I gotten Hannah's number last night? I wondered whether there was a way to conveniently need to fix something at the unit.

Even though I hadn't decided what I was going to do, I took a little bit of extra care getting ready. I clipped and filed my nails. I washed and blow-dried my hair. Even though the salt air would mess it up again, at least it'd smell clean. I put on a pair of clean charcoal gray Carhartts and a super-soft blue plaid flannel that Ginny and Todd gave me for Christmas. It made my eyes look good. My black canvas pea coat was the perfect weight for today's temperatures. I finished off my look with a pair of black socks dotted with little hound dogs and my deck shoes. When I was done, I surveyed myself in the mirror.

Even if I couldn't shed those fifteen pounds or the wrinkles around the corners of my eyes, at least I looked clean and respectable. Rather a jaunty handywoman, if I did say so myself. I grabbed the keys to my boat and storage locker and headed out the door.

Driving over the bridge, I made my decision. I would go over to their place first, while I still had the nerve to do it and before I talked myself out of it. A food truck was parked near the library, no doubt trying to capitalize on so many businesses being closed for the holiday. As I neared, I saw which one it was. Perfect. Donuts. I'd stop in with a box of fresh, warm donuts. Because that was the neighborly thing to do. And it was on the way to the marina.

Once I had the box of treats in hand, I drove to Hannah's apartment. My dashboard clock said 9:03 a.m. Still early. I knew she hadn't been out late, and if she'd been a teacher, chances were . . . she was up? My heartbeat ratcheted up as I slowed to turn into her driveway. I came close to driving on but thought of the hug. I pulled in and turned off Chester's engine.

Okay. I'd walk to the door and tap lightly, and if no one answered, I'd leave the donuts on the front stoop.

When I got to the door, I straightened the hem of my shirt and arranged the collar before reaching up and rapping on the curtained glass once, then two quick taps. I took a step back and waited.

The curtain pulled back slightly and Hannah's face, creased with concern, peered through the glass. The concern disappeared and was replaced with a curious smile. Then the door opened.

"Blythe?"

She stood just inside with one bare foot pressed against the calf of her other leg. She wore an oversized flannel nightshirt covered with penguins in ski gear. The top buttons were undone low enough to show the promise of cleavage. I glanced down at the donut box but ended up looking at her lone foot on the floor, noticing the high delicate arch complemented by perfectly pedicured toes in a barely blue polish.

"Um, yeah, hi." I shoved the red box forward. "I brought y'all donuts."

A groggy voice came from inside. "Donuts? Who brought us donuts?"

Hannah opened the door wider. "Why don't you come on in? It's a little chilly."

I stepped just inside the door. Jordan sat up from where she'd been lying on the couch. Her dark curly hair was flat against one side of her head, but her eyes brightened when she saw the box in my hand.

"Remember me? Paint lady?" I lifted the donut box and held it out while she jumped up and took it from me.

"Yum." She cracked the lid as she carried them to the table

and grabbed one covered in pink frosting and sprinkles before she even set it down.

"Napkin, child. Don't be a slob."

Jordan mumbled something at her mom but grabbed a napkin and plopped onto a bar stool.

"Yeah, so I won't stay long. I'm headed out to my boat. Ginny wanted me to invite y'all over for Hoppin' John and turnip greens and pork chops later. You said you liked New Year's Day traditions. Full disclosure, for us that means watching the Sugar Bowl. But Todd's brother's family will be there and he has a son and a daughter who go to St. James and the food is always delicious."

"Oh." Hannah reached up and pulled the placket of her nightshirt closer together. "That's really nice, but I . . ."

Through donut crumbs, Jordan spoke. "You have a boat?"

I nodded. "Yeah, y'all are welcome to come for a ride, and then you can follow me over to Ginny's for lunch later if that interests you."

Suddenly, Jordan seemed totally awake. "Mom, please, can we? Maybe we'll see dolphins! I want to be able to post something cool from New Year's Day."

Hannah's hand clasped tighter at her neckline. "We don't want to intrude on their family gathering, hon."

I wanted to put Hannah at ease. I also hoped I could get her to say yes. "No intrusion at all. We love company." Then, in a move that might be considered slightly underhanded, I appealed to Jordan. "And I guarantee I'll find you some dolphins to post on your social if y'all come for a boat ride."

Maybe it was a little low to get to Hannah through her kid, but it'd been a while since somebody got me daydreaming about them. Besides, it was always cool when a young person got excited about nature, and if I wanted to get to know Hannah, that for sure meant getting to know Jordan too.

Chapter 8

HANNAH

Spending New Year's Day with Blythe was not what I had planned. In fact, I'd been planning to avoid her for as long as I could. I worried if I told Blythe the whole truth of why I'd moved to Folly Beach, she'd see me as a charity case, or worse, think there was something wrong with me. With Jordan.

I did want to get to know her. Was it so bad to want a little attention? Especially from someone as kind and interesting as Blythe? There was also that stupid vision from when I'd first laid eyes on her that had sparked every single true-love-forever fantasy in my lonely lesbian heart. Where was a ten-foot pole when you needed it?

Except . . . Jordan. How could I say no to her? Five minutes before Blythe had knocked, she'd been sullen, frowning, and complaining about the move. Now she was wide awake, donut crumbs on her chin, with the sparkle in her eyes I loved. All it would take to keep that sparkle going was for me to say yes.

The decision was easy.

"Okay. We'll go. If you're sure it's not a bother."

Now I had two pairs of sparkling eyes flashing at me as Blythe's whole face brightened. "Awesome. I'll wait outside so you two can get ready."

I rode in the back seat. Jordan, riding shotgun, peppered Blythe with questions.

"They sleep while swimming?"

"Yep. One or two members of the pod will swim alongside the sleeping dolphin and keep an eye out for predators or obstacles. Other times they just kind of float and sleep all together. It almost looks like they're standing."

"That is so rad." She turned and looked over the headrest. "Did you hear that, Mom?"

"I did. Pretty cool." My heart did a ridiculous double flutter before I could stop it. Lisa had conversed easily with Jordan too. This wasn't a sign of anything.

Blythe turned down a road marked with a marina arrow and then parked the Bronco in a gravel lot. Lines of boats moored to docks extended perpendicularly from a concrete sea wall.

Jordan bounced next to her as we walked toward the water. "This is awesome." She reached out with her phone and took a selfie, then took a bunch more pictures of the boats. "Which one is yours? Is that it?" She pointed toward a really large boat that looked as if you could live on it.

"Negatory. You need to downscale that vision a bit. We're over there." She pointed in the direction of a much smaller speedboat, which looked brand new and fancy to me.

Jordan didn't care. "Sweet."

I walked slightly behind them, which gave me an opportunity to watch Blythe. As she talked and laughed with Jordan, the laugh lines around her eyes deepened. Someone, once in my life, had called them kindness wrinkles, and although that didn't fit everyone, it seemed to fit Blythe. It was an attribute I may have overlooked too often in my younger years.

Once onboard, Blythe instructed Jordan and me to hold the boat steady.

"Keep holding those cleats while I get the motor started." She cranked it up, and we let go as she reversed out of the slip and motored slowly toward the waterway and the marsh.

Out on the water, all my worry about this decision slipped away. It felt fantastic, even with the chill, to be breathing in the salt air and feeling the wind on my face. This was nothing I would ever do in Asheville but it was everything I wanted in my new life.

When Blythe pointed out dolphins to Jordan, and Jordan clambered to the bow to watch them swim in lazy circles around the boat, I smiled. "Thanks, this is amazing."

Her return smile was shy. "I'm glad you're enjoying it. Seemed like a good way to start the year."

She held my gaze, and this time I was the one to glance away. How in the world was this possible? She had literally been waiting in the driveway when we arrived to start a new life. Was it some sort of sign? When the wrong door closes, the right door opens kind of thing?

I shook the thought away. Nope. Nope. Nope. Of course it wasn't a sign. Things like this didn't happen in real life. Everyone had a story. Everyone had baggage. Including me. Especially now.

"Do you want to drive?" Blythe's voice carried above the wind.

"The boat? Absolutely." I stood up to take my place behind the steering wheel.

Jordan turned from where she was perched on the bow and held her arms out as if she were Rose from *Titanic*. "This is awesome!"

"You want to speed her up and freak out your kid?" Blythe grinned, and those delicious blue eyes twinkled.

"Oooh, you're devious." But I laughed along with her.

Blythe put her hand over mine and showed me how to push the throttle forward and catch a little air over the waves.

If I were in a movie, this would be the part where I leaned back and she wrapped her arms around my waist. She'd rest her chin on my shoulder and the swell of orchestral music would begin. But I wasn't in a movie. Though this little fantasy I'd created between real thoughts was fun, it was entirely unrealistic.

I slowed the boat down and gave the wheel back to Blythe. "So fun. The speed. The waves." I looked out to the marsh. "All of this." It was true. Thinking about Blythe was helping me not think about Lisa— an excellent way to start the new year.

"Anytime."

After we'd come in from the water and parked the boat, Blythe drove us back to the apartment. "I'm happy for y'all to ride with me over to Ginny and Todd's."

"That's okay. I want to shower and get cleaned up. Why don't you text me the address? We'll find our way over there shortly." I gave Blythe my number, and she typed it and a text with the address. My phone vibrated in my hand, and I added her as a contact. Then I held it up. "Got your digits. Thanks again for the treats, and the unexpected boat ride." I would have hugged her but Jordan was at the kitchen counter, her legs pulled up to her chest as she wolfed down a chocolate-glazed donut.

"No problem. It was nice to do that for y'all. And super fun to watch Jordan get so excited about seeing that pod. She's a good kid." This she said loud enough for Jordan to hear.

Jordan scrunched her face at Blythe, and Blythe mimicked it back.

Lisa would be yelling at Jordan not to eat another donut and to put her feet down like a civilized human. Blythe was making faces at her and trying to bounce her off the boat.

God, I was such a lesbian sometimes, marrying us off in my fantastical head. For all I knew, this was simply Blythe's way of being. Maybe she was a huge flirt. That server, Matilda, seemed happy enough to hit on her.

I waved bye as she got into her Bronco, then I turned. Jordan was staring at me.

"What?"

"You have a weird face."

I touched my cheek and felt the guilt from my secret fantasies. "What do you mean?"

"Blythe's cool. But you don't *like her* like her, do you?" Jordan stood in the hallway, her hands pulled up into the sleeves of her fleece hoodie, hugging herself.

"No, sweetheart. Of course not."

"Okay. Good. Because that would be strange. We were supposed to be getting married, to Lisa, in February."

Hearing her say that broke my heart. Jordan had come up with the whole "we were getting married" thing, referring to me and her marrying Lisa. Because up until Lisa, it had been a lot of Mommy Does Dating and not so much Mommy Gets Serious. And the marriage was about us marrying Lisa. Or it should have been. But Lisa hadn't seen it that way. And Jordan didn't know that.

And I wasn't about to tell her.

BLYTHE

Ani DiFranco's "32 Flavors" blared from my speakers, and I sang along as I headed back over the marsh and away from Hannah. I felt good, super good, as I pulled into the lot of the storage units. This stop was my attempt at setting intentions for what I hoped was shaping up to be an excellent year.

The padlock came open with a click, and I rolled up the heavy metal door, the scent of salvaged lumber greeting me. "Ahhhh." I walked in, running my hand along the big beams. Everything looked in order, no rain had gotten in, and I saw no evidence of bugs. This ritual kept me grounded. Helped me remember I was not only a fine handywoman but also a creative. Someone with the vision to build things from the ground up. I slowed my breathing and softened my gaze. I sat on one of the beams and held my palms upward.

Now, I was not any kind of New Age believer, but something about this simple act of turning palms toward the sky provided an opportunity to listen. Whether it was my subconscious, God, the universe, or a muse, I didn't know. Whichever it was, the gesture somehow allowed subconscious thoughts to spring to the forefront that could never get there when I was driving around town, running from rental home to rental home.

As I slowed my breathing, I pictured the perfect marsh lot, with a long deck, my boat moored at the end. I imagined myself standing, looking toward the water, then slowly I turned back toward the land. The house I'd built in my mind changed a bit each time. It had started as a simple square fishing shack with an awe-inspiring porch and deck system. Then it had morphed into a lot filled with live oaks and a home built into the branches with rooms joined by walkways above the ground. After a period of obsessing over the endless possibilities of tiny homes on trailers, I'd envisioned my own recycled version. Today, however, as the house sprang up in my mind, it was slightly larger—two stories—with my salvaged cedar shakes covering the exterior. A tree rose from one corner of the deck, and a long covered lanai spanned the upper and lower stories. There was only one reason my mind was imagining something this large. Other people were living with me. Warmth spread through my body. A family . . . this home was a family home.

"Damnit." I stood up abruptly, shaking the vision away. I knew what my subconscious was doing, and she was going to get me in trouble. She was going to tumble me down a path toward Hannah at lightning-fast speed, and I was going to end up giving everything of myself only to lose it all again in the end. And it'd surely scare Hannah half to death. The woman hadn't even finished unpacking her bags. Oh, hello, I'm Blythe's subconscious and I think I want to make you my dream-house wife.

I closed up the storage unit. I needed to play it cool. Not be so obviously interested. Jesus, I'd shown up on New Year's Day with donuts after one hug. Without even calling. Hannah was a mom, and I knew from my sister that mom life trumped everything. Why would I assume she even had time or would be willing to go on a date?

On the drive to Ginny's, I talked myself off a ledge. I hadn't made a fool of myself by showing up. They'd seemed genuinely happy on the boat. They'd agreed to come over for the afternoon. Friends. We were friends. I was not going to make any sort of move. She knew I was a lesbian. Once she'd been around for a while, she'd know I didn't have a partner. I could play it cool.

At least that's what I thought until she stepped out of her car in Ginny and Todd's driveway and smiled. The image of that damn dream house plastered itself to the inside of my eyeballs.

She held up a bottle as she and Jordan approached. "I brought wine."

"Not necessary, but I'm sure it will be appreciated."

The door behind me creaked open and Todd's face appeared. "Hey! You all made it! Welcome, welcome. Don't make them stand outside in the cold, Blythe. Come on in."

I held the door open and let them pass in front of me, noting the fresh smell of whatever lotion Hannah used. Todd took the bottle Hannah held out and read the label. "Oooh, you don't play. This is an excellent vintage. We would have been fine with the cheap stuff."

"It was gifted to me, and it seemed wrong to drink it alone."

"Well, we sure won't say no. I'm Todd, by the way. Ginny's husband. And you must be Hannah. And you must be Jordan. C'mon, let me take you to the back and introduce you to Jacquie and Tedrick, my niece and nephew. Now you'll know people when you get to school on Monday."

Todd led Jordan away, and I was left standing with Hannah. She watched them leave.

"He seems great."

"The absolute best thing that ever happened to my sister." The sound of football filtered in from the great room down the hall in front of us. "Shall I lead the way?"

"Wait."

I stopped midstep, my foot hovering before I set it back down.

"Yeah?" Was she going to tell me something? Like she wished we'd kissed last night? Or how even though we'd just met, she was developing feelings for me? Everything went still.

"Ginny said you designed the house. Aren't you going to tell me about it? Show me your mad skills."

Though it wasn't what I hoped she was going to say, I was flattered. "Sure. I always start with the land and the compass points. I want to maximize light and any view, minimize the heat of the summer sun, and create a natural flow and function for the end user. For this house, I situated east to west to give them this great long, dogtrot-style hallway to capture the breeze from front porch to back during good weather."

"Blah, blah, blah, blah, blah." My sister traipsed into the hall swinging an empty wineglass. She grabbed Hannah's forearm. "This house is beautiful and I love my sister, but she will talk your damn ear off about design decisions" She turned to me. "You haven't even brought this woman in and given her a drink? What kind of Southern woman are you?"

"Belle gone bad?"

"Well, there's some truth."

Hannah grinned. "Oh yeah? How bad? What family secrets am I going to learn today?"

"You're going to have to stick around to learn our secrets." Ginny winked at me as she linked her arm with Hannah's and led her toward the kitchen. "And I'm determined to wheedle some out of you today as well."

I walked a couple of steps behind them, enjoying Hannah's easy way with my sister. She didn't seem intimidated, and their laughter was light. It had never been like that with Constance. Ginny hated her from the minute they met, and vice versa.

This felt different.

Chapter 9

HANNAH

I was relieved to see Jordan laughing and looking relaxed out on the back porch. There were two other teenagers and the younger kids. I poked my head out to make sure she was okay.

"Hello?"

All five faces looked up at me. Four of the five smiled, and I got the "Please don't let my mother say something stupid" look from Jordan.

"I'm Hannah, Jordan's mom. You okay, hon?"

"I'm fine."

Ginny's daughter, the youngest, piped up. "We're watching a dance tutorial so we can do it, and Tedrick's going to put it on his account because he's internet famous."

My daughter turned pink in the cheeks, and I wondered if she might end up with her own crush after today. The boy in question grinned at his cousin. "Am not." He had short twists and a prep meets surfer style with a stark white button-down shirt over board shorts and a pair of Timberlands.

His sister, her petite face swallowed by a giant pair of gold wire-rimmed glasses, shushed him. "You are too. You're the only person at St. James who has over twenty thousand followers." She looked up at me. "He does parodies of old movie scenes but from the Black perspective. And he looks like *that*, so all the ladies follow him." She then turned to Jordan. "Do not fall for him. It's all style and no substance."

By the way Jordan was slowly trying to sink into the porch sofa, I figured I better back on out of there and let her handle it on her own. I could grill her about Tedrick later, when she was receptive to sharing.

I sat in the armchair near the end of the couch where Blythe was already seated.

She handed me a glass of the wine I'd brought.

"Thanks." I took a sip, and the memory of when Lisa and I first had this vintage popped in my head. It was early days. We'd gone out to a new farm-to-table restaurant known for local ingredients and excellent wine. I knew she'd been showing off for me when she'd ordered it, but we both loved it and I'd been impressed. She'd wooed me with fancy dinners and elegant evenings and things that I'd never been able to afford on my teacher's salary. Maybe I'd fallen for that as much as anything else. Single parenting was intense, and though my mom would help out with only a few questions asked, letting Lisa round out the financial edges of my existence had felt easier somehow. To be fair to her, she'd never minded. She knew I worked every bit as hard as she did, only for way less pay, and honestly I think some part of her wanted to be a caretaker. The problem was, she only knew how to do it with material things. Not her time. Not her affection.

Blythe shifted to face me. "Everything okay out there?"

"Out there?" I lifted my chin toward the back porch, making sure Blythe was referring to the kids and not my interior thoughts. "Yeah. They're making dance videos."

"Oh yeah. Tedrick has some kind of channel thing he does."

"So I heard. Jordan seems smitten."

Blythe's face filled with warmth. "He's a great kid. You don't have to worry."

"I'm not. Jordan's got a good head on her shoulders. A little crush never hurt anyone." I might have held eye contact a second too long. Blythe looked down.

Ginny came in from the kitchen, followed by Todd's brother and his wife. The moment I'd created ended, and conversation turned toward a new grocery store that had opened and the traffic on I-26. I sipped my wine and listened, enjoying the easy banter between family members. This was exactly what I'd dreamed of. Acceptance and comfort and the easy camaraderie of people who loved one another for who they were, at every age and stage. It was something Jordan and I had tried to create with found family, but we'd only had moments that felt like this. What would it be like to grow up and grow old surrounded by this kind of easy love?

Every now and then I'd cast a glance toward Blythe. The moments when I caught her looking at me, she'd look away quickly. I'd been worried about Jordan and Tedrick, but I was no better.

Todd called us to lunch, and as the group filed toward the kitchen island to fill up plates full of greens for money and black-eyed peas for luck, I hesitated and asked Blythe, "Um, where's the restroom in this gorgeous house you designed? Will you show me?"

"Yeah. Sure." Blythe led me back toward the light-filled entrance to a door. She opened it and flipped on the light, then as she turned to let me by, I tripped on the area rug and fell into her.

"Oh." She reached her arm around my waist to keep me from face-planting and I held my wineglass aloft, managing not to spill. We were close. Close enough for me to notice the fine, light hairs that ran along the edge of her jawline. Close enough to feel the warmth of her slight belly pressing into mine. Close enough to . . .

"Blythe? Hannah?" Ginny was calling from the other room.

"Shit." I took a quick step back.

Blythe looked as flustered as I felt, but she had the foresight to peel the wineglass out of my hand. "Let me take this to the table for you." She hesitated another second, but I didn't wait to see what might play out. I stepped into the powder room and shut the door.

Inside, I rested my hands on the sink. What the hell was that? I had been within inches of kissing her. I'd wanted to kiss her. My insides felt hot and my thighs were tight and quivery. I turned on the water. It was cold coming out of the faucet, and the stinging brace of it as I splashed it on my face helped deliver me back from fantasy land.

By the time I'd finished using the bathroom, I'd gotten my wits about me. We'd leave as soon as dinner was over. Blythe didn't know I was fresh out of a relationship, so there was no reason for her not to flirt. I knew better though.

At the table, the adults passed around a basket of rolls and cornbread. Blythe was already seated, my wineglass at the empty place next to hers. Of course.

Todd pointed to the kitchen island. "Load up a plate so we can say grace."

Grace. I was going to need some grace to get myself through a meal seated next to Blythe. My body was having some sort of orgasm-deprived meltdown being near the first attractive lesbian I'd met in my new town. That's all this was. My libido knew I was single. Nothing more.

"Hands, please." Ginny raised hers and grasped Todd's hand on one side and his brother's on the other. Of course, this meant I had to grasp Blythe's hand in my left and Todd's on my right. Ginny bowed her head and in her rich coastal drawl began a prayer. "Dear heavenly Father, bless us for this bounty and this gathering of family and new friends. We trust in your guidance and hope that the path you lay ahead of us in this new year is filled with your mercy. Amen."

I mumbled "Amen" with everyone, though technically my Jewish heritage meant Jesus was probably immune to my prayers. Which, good, maybe? Because I wasn't thinking about the bounty and gathering as we held hands. I wasn't even thinking about family and new friends. I was thinking about mercy, as in, Lord have mercy, Blythe's hand is strong and warm and I'd like her to run it from the top to the bottom of my naked body.

When the prayer ended, Blythe gave my hand a soft squeeze and her thumb passed over mine in a gentle caress before letting go. Any chance I had of sitting still through the meal ended as my body fired signals to my groin in a way that happened only when attraction was off-the-charts strong.

"Are you okay?" Blythe's smile was knowing. Not that she knew what was happening in my pants. But she knew we'd had a moment back in the hall. There was confidence in her eyes that hadn't been there before.

Fuck. I wasn't supposed to be doing this. Not at all.

BLYTHE

I leaned next to Hannah's car window and propped my elbow on the opening. "Thanks for coming over. You sure I can't convince y'all to stay for the game?"

We'd had a moment. When she tripped into my arms, the energy lifted the fine hairs away from my skin. I'd felt it again when she'd sat next to me. I'd felt it when I'd taken her hand. I'd seen her slight shiver when I'd gently grazed my thumb over hers. But now she was running away, getting out of here as fast as she could. I couldn't believe I'd already blown it.

"Tomorrow is Jordan's first day at a new school. We're going to go home, settle in, and have a quiet night. But we really appreciate the invitation."

Jordan leaned over to talk out of her mom's window. "Yeah, thanks again for the boat ride and everything. That was awesome."

Okay, maybe I was overreacting. That all sounded legitimate. Hannah did have Jordan with her, so it wasn't like anything could be done about our sizzling energy in this moment.

"Well then, Happy New Year. Drive safe. Good luck at work, and school, tomorrow. First days all around." I patted the roof of the wagon and took a step back, watching them pull out of the driveway and head down the road.

When I retreated to the porch, I could hear my family yelling at the football game, which didn't bode well for our team. I popped onto my phone and did a quick search on social media for Hannah. The page I found was so secure, I couldn't even see who her friends were. But we were friends now, weren't we? I pressed the request button, then shoved my phone back in my pocket before heading inside.

. . .

Five Months or Forever

THE NEXT DAY AT WORK, Ginny had a long list of to-dos for me to tackle. We were taking advantage of the slow rental season to do some bigger projects. When I scanned the options, I noticed I'd need to do a little caulking and painting at a couple of homes. Hannah hadn't accepted my friend request, and texting her felt kind of desperate since I'd shown up at her house uninvited. Going to Williamson's was 100 percent in my normal scope of duties. If I showed up just before lunch, maybe I could convince her to join me. Friend to friend.

It was a workday, so I wore my handywoman usual—worn, paint-splattered cargo pants, a Coastal Beach Rentals T-shirt, and my steel-toed, work boots. As much as I wanted to put on a wrinkle-free button-down and a tidier pair of pants, I'd stand out like a sore thumb to my sister and anyone else who saw me. Playing it cool was the name of the game.

The bell jangled on the door of the paint shop as I pushed in. Joel was at the counter, ringing up another painter. At first glance, I didn't see Hannah. Then I found her, sitting cross-legged on the floor near the wood stains, stacking small cans into neat rows.

"We've got to quit running into each other like this."

She looked up quickly and tilted her head. "Maybe you're stalking me."

My heart froze. I could see how she might think that. Showing up out of the blue. Friending her. Being here. Crap. Was I already being too much?

She broke into a smile and laughed. "Take a deep breath. I'm teasing. I don't think you're a stalker. You're not, are you?"

"A stalker?" I raised my shoulders a smidge. "Not in a bad way. I did legitimately come to get paint and caulk. But I also came in hopes I could take you to lunch on your first day." A new year. A bold move. Ginny would approve.

She unfolded herself and stood up from the floor, then dusted her hands off on the back of her jeans. "That is super sweet. But I only get thirty minutes because of Jordan's school schedule. Not enough time to go out anywhere. I brought a sandwich to eat when things slow down between customers."

Joel finished with his transaction at the counter. "Don't distract the help, Blythe. She's only just arrived."

"I was going to take her to Duck's for the view and a softshell crab sandwich if she'd let me, but I hear you're scamming her out of a real lunch hour."

"I didn't say that." Hannah sounded horrified. She stepped toward Joel. "I'm thrilled with our arrangement."

He adjusted his readers as he opened the cash register. "Don't forget, I know this one." He pointed in my direction, then winked. "I'm kind of hankering for some crab cakes myself. Tell you what. I'll let you have that hour today . . . if you bring me back a platter." He pulled a twenty out of the drawer and handed it to Hannah. "Deal?"

"I absolutely don't expect this. I have a sandwich." Hannah wouldn't even look my way, and suddenly my bold move seemed as if it might have been a big mistake. Of course, she would take her first day seriously, and here I'd come in asking favors for her from her new boss.

"Go. You should try the food. I won't be happy with anything but Duck's crab cakes now that I'm thinking about 'em. If you work half as hard this afternoon as you worked this morning, I'll have gotten my day's worth from you . . . plus a little. Go on. Take a break. Eat something delicious."

She pocketed his cash and finally looked at me. "Guess you get to take me to lunch."

Once outside, I rushed to open Chester's passenger door for Hannah. "I hope you'll forgive me for that move. My intention wasn't to do harm with your boss."

She turned to face me before getting in. "Intentions are interesting things, aren't they? I guess yours worked out this time."

Five Months or Forever

As I walked to the driver's side, my confidence drained away step by step. There'd been a lot to unpack in her tone. And she was undoubtedly a little upset with me, even if things had worked out with Joel. But she'd still agreed to go. Which gave me approximately one hour to work my way through this with her.

Chapter 10

HANNAH

I'd only been kidding when I'd asked Blythe if she was a stalker. I didn't think she was, but between yesterday's unexpected donut delivery, her online friend request—which I'd cautiously ignored—and now this unexpected turn of events, there wasn't a lot of ambiguity left in her intentions.

When Blythe apologized for the third time, I figured I'd put her out of her misery. "It's fine. I promise. Tell me about where we're going for lunch."

She let out a relieved sigh. "It's called Duck's. It's a great little hole-in-the-wall. Boats pull right up to the docks and sell seafood to the market there. The restaurant out back was started by a friend of Todd's. They have six regular items on the menu, but they do them really well. Soft-shell sandwiches are a seasonal special. Figured you shouldn't miss out on one."

"That's nice, thank you."

Things grew quiet again between us, and I noted how Blythe rolled her hands on the steering wheel. I'd upset her with what I'd said outside Williamson's.

"Look, I didn't mean to get short with you back there. This was just, well, a lot."

She blew out a breath. "Yeah, I get it. Intentions are worthless if they're not received correctly."

"Blythe. You seem like an incredible woman. And I'd be lying if I told you I didn't find you attractive. But my intention is friendship. Nothing more. I've just moved here. I have a kid. Things are complicated." I took a breath as she held hers. "Look, I apologize if I'm being presumptuous, but I feel like maybe I've given you the wrong impression."

We pulled into the parking lot. Seagulls squawked and rose off the pilings as the car crunched over the oyster shell gravel.

She cut the engine and turned toward me. "I'm the one who should apologize. I get that I've been kind of in your face with my appearances and invitations. And . . ." She looked down, and color rose to her cheeks. "I guess I had the impression we'd shared a moment or two. But it's been a while since I dated, so my instincts might be off. And to be honest, my instincts are kind of shit anyway." She looked into my eyes, her face growing serious. "I did pull out my signature move though."

I tilted my head, trying to figure out what she was talking about.

"Donuts. Delivered uninvited at the crack of dawn."

"Really? That's your signature move?"

Her eyes crinkled, the laugh lines illuminating her smile. "Naw, that was my first time. But maybe I should hang on to it. What do you think?"

"It is hard to go wrong with donuts." Damnit. Now that I'd told her I couldn't, wouldn't, shouldn't, my inner thirteen-year-old was lighting up with girl crush fireworks all over again because she was adorable and funny and just a woman excited about the potential of a moment or two with me. Talk about stirring up all sorts of warm and cozy feelings. I glanced away so she wouldn't read too much into my smile.

"Come on." She unbuckled her seat belt. "Let's get lunch. As friends."

"Cool." Now that I'd settled things with her, I instantly regretted it. We *had* shared a couple of moments. She wasn't wrong. But friends were still messaging to find out what the hell happened with me and Lisa. Students and colleagues were begging me not to let my semester leave of absence turn into a permanent absence. Plus, there was my promise to Jordan. There was no guarantee we'd even be here for long.

My stomach growled. Lunch. That's all I needed to focus on.

The day was warm enough and the breeze still enough that we could sit out on the pier without freezing. I took a bite of the sandwich she'd recommended. Chewy French bread, a spicy remoulade sauce, tart dill pickle slices, and a soft-shell crab, fried to perfection. "Oh my gosh, this is divine."

"See? I wouldn't steer you wrong." Her phone buzzed and she turned it over. "It's Ginny." Blythe read the text and her face lightened.

"Good news?"

"For you." She turned her hand and gave me a thumbs-up.

"Oh yeah?"

"Owners agreed to let you and Jordan paint. Said they'd even pay for the materials."

"That's amazing! Jordan's going to be so excited. And they'll pay? That's extra nice."

Blythe took a bite of her sandwich and nodded as she chewed. The guy behind the counter carried out a to-go container with Joel's order. Between bites, we talked about the water birds, the boats, the tides, and how to catch the best seafood. Blythe's love for the area obviously ran deep, and it was a beautiful thing to listen to her talk about the local ecosystems. "You have a gorgeous way of painting this area with your words."

"Oh yeah?"

And there it was again, that shy uplift of her eyes. The slight smile giving away her happiness at what I'd said. My insides warmed knowing I was the one to put that expression on her face. I cleared my throat. "I guess I should get back to work."

As we tidied up our table and threw our garbage in the bin, she looked out to the river. "It's much easier to show someone in person, you know? But I supposed inviting you guys out for another ride on my boat might send the wrong intention?"

Was it wrong that I was thrilled she didn't give up on us so easily?

"Jordan would be super excited."

We walked toward the parking lot.

"And you?" Blythe walked backward so she could face me.

"Blythe." I raised my eyebrows and pursed my lips.

"I know, I know. You don't have to answer that." She turned toward the car. "I'll take you back to work, and we can have Joel gather the materials for your project and put them on the tab for the realty company." She stopped when she got to the passenger door. "But can I ask you one thing?"

"Of course."

She opened the passenger door for me and stood with her hand on the top of the window frame. "Do you really find me attractive?"

I set the to-go box on the floor before turning back to look at her. My face went hot. I had said that. What the hell, I wasn't dead. We both liked women. What was wrong with a little harmless flirting between friends?

I looked up and took my time answering. My gaze went from the top of her salt-and-pepper hair, to her blue eyes, to her smiling lips, to the slight swell of her breasts, to strong hips that led to athletic thighs, down to her no-doubt-she-was-a-lesbian steel-toed boots. Then I looked back up and shrugged. "I guess you're okay."

With that, I reached out and grabbed the door handle and climbed into the passenger seat. I tamped down the urge to laugh out loud before pulling the door shut.

When Blythe climbed into the driver's seat, I was still chuckling.

"You're that funny, huh?"

"I'm hilarious."

She paid me back, her eyes skating over my body, locking with mine, then when I blinked, she lowered her gaze to stare at my lips. "You're not only hilarious," her voice lowered an octave. "But I also find you very attractive and damn if I don't want to kiss you, despite everything we talked about at lunch."

I stopped laughing. My breath grew shallow and still. The same connection we'd had at Ginny's house was back, but now we were in an even smaller space. I was a mouse. She was the snake. Or maybe it was the reverse. Either way, I froze.

Blythe leaned toward me, she even hesitated, a question in her eyes. Was this okay? I'd told her the intention was friendship. I knew I should put out my hand and stop her. I knew she was going to kiss me and *just* friends didn't kiss. But I couldn't bring myself to stop her. I couldn't stop myself. The feeling in the car was alive and I needed this moment. It'd been too long since I'd felt powerful or appreciated. It'd been too long since I'd felt wanted. I wasn't sure I'd ever felt this buzzy with anyone before.

Her hand found my waist as my lips found her mouth. It started slowly. Light nice to meet you's. Upper lips to lower lips. Whispers of breath. Then her other hand went to my hair and I scooted closer. Mouths opened, hellos turned to hey there's turned to *oh*, hello's, as our kisses grew in intensity. When she pulled my body toward her, and slipped her palm against the skin of my back, I broke away, fighting against the rapid stream of my heartbeat.

"Damnit." I stared out the window and caught eyes with one of the cooks as he winked at me, then made a lewd gesture. "We shouldn't have done that."

"But we did. I did." Blythe looked shocked, which, given my little speech at lunch, wasn't a surprise.

"You did. We did. I did. Damnit." I brought the base of my palms to my eyebrows and pressed.

"It seemed like we intended to do that. You know. Since we talked about intentions."

I dropped my face into my hands and mumbled through splayed fingers. "I meant all those things I said earlier. About it being complicated. And there's Jordan."

"I like Jordan."

"But that's complicated too."

Blythe started the car. "Okay. Maybe we should talk about it?"

I rubbed my temples. "You know what? It was just a kiss, right? Does there really have to be an intention?"

Blythe's expression shifted, and I knew her answer before she said it. "I mean, for me, yeah. It's kind of how I operate. I wouldn't have kissed you if I wasn't interested. I got the impression that underneath all those things you said, you might be too."

I sighed. "How about you drive the long way back to the paint store. There's some stuff you need to know."

BLYTHE

Hannah disappeared into Williamson's with the list of apartment-painting supplies I'd hastily scrawled onto the back of an old envelope. I'd be lying if I said things hadn't gotten awkward on the drive back. She'd given my brain a lot to unpack.

The kiss. Her history. The wedding that would have taken place in a few weeks' time. A woman named Lisa in Asheville. There hadn't been a lot of time for Hannah's explanation, no matter how slow I drove.

My brain was torn. In one half, I was flying. She'd kissed me. She'd let me kiss her. It had been sweet and hot and unexpected. I slammed on the brakes at an almost-missed stop sign because my brain couldn't stop replaying that kiss.

Adrenaline flipped the switch. The other side was all reason and self-protection. She wasn't ready for me. I had no interest in being the fire to someone else's frying pan. That wasn't where I was in my life. I'd done the hookup thing. I'd been the next best thing. I'd been the not-quite-right step on the ladder. And I was finished with all that.

For me, it was either something that could end up as a long-term partnership or nothing at all. Plus, there was Jordan. I didn't want to be messing around with a woman who had a daughter, unless it was respectful and serious. There was no way this was going to turn into a booty call situation.

Damnit mother clucker to hell and back. I'd done this to myself, and all Hannah had done was respond to my flirting. Probably a booty call was exactly what she needed, and I'd practically begged her to throw herself at me with my Southern chivalrous garbage. She didn't know I was daydreaming about getting wifed up and having an instant family.

I pulled into the driveway of my next repair job and looked at my phone.

She'd sent a text.

I'm really sorry. I shouldn't have done that.

What I wanted to write was "But you did. You kissed me. And I liked it."

Instead I wrote, **Yeah, probably not. Sounds like you have things to sort out. I'm sorry if I came on too strong. Didn't mean to overstep.**

It didn't look like she was responding, so I gathered my tools and headed inside to fix a couple of loose doorknobs and a toilet that was running nonstop. The problem was, she'd lit a fire inside me that had been comfortably smoldering beneath deep ash. I'd stopped fantasizing about a one-day wife. I'd grown comfortable with the occasional date with my vibrator or a steamy erotic novel on my e-reader. I'd even held off the occasional temptation to see if baby queer Matilda had a slightly older friend I could hook up with.

The doorknob I was unscrewing fell loose and hit my kneecap. "Damnit." I dropped my screwdriver onto the floor and rubbed the tender spot on my leg, then stood up and paced around the house, pulling my short hair up by its ends out of frustration. A week ago, I'd been fine. Happily single, expecting nothing else. But today . . .

My phone rang.

I walked over to the kitchen counter where I'd left it, not knowing what I was going to say. "Yeah?"

"Um, excuse the tone. Hello to you too." Ginny was rightly annoyed with my abrupt greeting.

I leaned forward onto the counter and looked at a couple throwing a ball to their dog on the beach outside the window. The dog chased it into the choppy waves of the January sea and bounded back out. His enthusiasm and energy reminded me why I was yet to actually go through with a dog adoption, something I'd been thinking about since moving here. Something that was probably a lot steadier than trying, once again, to have a relationship.

"Sorry. I just had a heavy doorknob land on my knee."

"Ouch. But that's no reason to be rude."

"You're right." I didn't want to get into the whole Hannah situation. "What do you need?"

"I have a surprise for you."

"Okay."

"Remember the couple I was telling you about that bought a parcel of lots facing Clark Sound? Soon-to-be retired professors from the D.C. area?"

"Vaguely. Oh wait, did they buy those three lots in the bend? Kind of a protected cove?"

"Exactly. They just popped into the office to say hello. They're here to check on their land and gather information about builders. And they have an interesting proposal."

"Which is?" I loved my sister more than anything, but she could spool a story out until sunrise if you let her.

"They want to trade one of their lots in exchange for general contracting and home design."

"That's nice land."

"It is."

I waited for her to say more, but when she didn't, I broke. "So, who'd you recommend?"

"You, dumbass. I know you've been looking for the perfect lot, and the one they want to trade is a bit more challenging geographically, but that's the kind of property you love. It's private and has a killer west view to the marsh."

"I'm not a general contractor."

"Technicalities. You're a licensed architect. I'm pretty sure you could easily get a contracting license. And you know enough about building to oversee subs."

Before lunch, my mind would have been flying, thinking

this was an enormous sign. That the family house vision I'd had was based on premonition and here was the next step of the journey, landing in my lap. Now that I knew more about Hannah's story, cynicism crept into my thought process.

"You're not saying anything. Blythe, hello? This is good."

"Yeah, maybe. But have you forgotten I have a job? And it's not like I have a ton of residential property to show in a portfolio."

"Good gravy. Would you shut up? I took them to my house. They loved it. They're flexible with their time frame because they're still working in D.C. What they want is someone trustworthy to work with at a distance. Someone who won't bankrupt them by making stupid mistakes. They're excited to meet you. Can you drive out to their land now?"

"Now?"

"Now. Do I need to come and get you myself?"

The reality of what she was telling me sunk in. A lot to build my dream home on. And all I needed to do to own it was the thing I loved to do anyway.

"Text me the address. I can finish here tomorrow."

"Good. Stop by later and let me know how it went."

I gathered up my tools and headed back to Chester. When I shut the door, my phone buzzed with a text. This time, it was Hannah.

Could I buy you a drink after work? Give us a chance to talk a little more? You didn't overstep. I probably misled you.

I stared at the screen as if by reading each letter individually a crystal ball might appear to tell me how to proceed. With caution, I thought. Even though we had chemistry—that was indisputable—nothing that she'd told me made me feel comfortable about proceeding. I would fall for her. I would need more from her than she could give. And I'd end up right back where I'd been when I'd flown off in a jealous rage at

Constance. That was something I planned never to repeat, even if it meant I'd be celibate the rest of my life.

Sorry. Can't tonight. It will have to be another time.

Once I'd hit send, I threw the phone facedown on the passenger seat and put Chester in reverse.

Tonight, it was land before ladies.

No matter how delicious the lady's kiss was.

Chapter 11

HANNAH

I stared at Blythe's return text, surprised—and maybe a little relieved. But I couldn't blame her for saying no. Not after what I'd pulled at lunch, not after the revelation of my very recent breakup history. Honestly, I guess I respected that she didn't just tell me it was okay and push ahead. It let me know she wasn't a player. Which, sure, was maybe a little disappointing in its own way, because if she was, then there might be a way to scratch this fresh itch she'd roused in my sensual soul.

The school bus pulled up in front of the paint store, and Jordan appeared. I hated to make her take the bus, but Joel was already being gracious enough letting me come in thirty minutes late so I could drop her off in the morning.

"Hey, kiddo. How was your first day?"

Her cheeks took on the cheerful pink glow she had whenever she was happy about something but maybe didn't want to share. "Good."

"Did you see Tedrick and Jacquie?"

"Yeah." The dam broke. "People saw the dance video we

made, and it was wild. It was like I was popular or something. I was getting high fives and stuff in the hall, and they were calling me 'Slide.'" She did a slide move to demonstrate.

I laughed. "Well, that's good. I guess? And your classes?"

She hoisted her backpack a little higher on her shoulder. "Same as anywhere. Boring. Long. But I like my geometry teacher. He's cool."

"Thank god for donor daddy and the math he passed on to you."

She rolled her eyes, and I motioned for her to follow me to the stockroom, where she could hang out until I got off work. In a bid to keep things positive and in the we're-not-moving-back camp, I remembered my news. "Oh, guess what?"

She let her backpack tumble onto the break table. "What?"

"We got permission to paint the apartment. That box is our supplies. Double-check to make sure I got everything we need."

"For real? That's awesome."

The disappointment I'd been feeling since texting with Blythe diminished. My kid was happy. And honestly, that's all I really needed in my life.

Once we got home, I fixed a supper of grilled cheese sandwiches and tomato soup. It was the perfect cold weather meal, and the weather had done just that, taken a turn for the cooler side. Which I guess was to be expected in January, even if we were at the beach. Jordan had me sign some stuff for school and then disappeared into her room to call Tilda.

I opened my laptop and deleted the mass of junk emails, answered a few questions from the teacher who was filling in for the semester, and then popped over to my social account. Blythe's friend request was still there. Now that she knew the whole truth, I'd accept the request. She'd be able to see everything. The recent seriousness of my relationship with Lisa was the only thing I'd wanted to hide. The rest was me. And if she didn't like my politics, sense of humor, or occasional off-color memes, then so be it.

I clicked the accept button.

And immediately went to her page. We actually had a few friends in common, which, given the interwoven nature of the lesbian community, wasn't really a surprise. Nobody who was a close friend, but still, points for future conversations. If there were going to be any.

I scrolled down. She obviously didn't spend much time on her page. There were a few announcements of various design awards. Some videos of interesting architectural homes. It looked like she'd taken an interest in tiny houses eight or nine months ago, then seemed to move past it. A few family photos with Ginny and Todd and their kids, but no women in the past year.

I dug deeper. Eventually I found someone. A stunning redhead who was dressed to the nines in every picture, most with Blythe. She was tagged in a couple of them too. Constance O'Donnell. I clicked through. Not a lot that was available for a random stranger to see, but from what I could piece together, she'd moved on to a higher-powered version of Blythe with a bit more swagger. An attorney for the hip-hop recording industry. Someone who'd apparently draped her in jewelry and wanted even deeper cleavage in her dress choices.

Which made me go back to the pictures of her and Blythe. There was no doubt that Blythe absolutely rocked a tux or tailored suit. But to me, the Blythe who showed up in paint-splattered work pants and a worn pair of boots was the way sexier version. What did Blythe like? Was this woman her ideal type? I knew I was feminine, but I didn't go out of the way to get done up. My nails were sometimes manicured. My hair was short for convenience. I barely wore makeup. My boobs were pretty good for someone who'd breastfed a kid, but they did not vavavoom like Constance's.

I closed my laptop. My online snooping freaked me out more than it answered any questions.

Someone knocked at the front door.

I stopped at Jordan's room. "Are you expecting anybody?"

She shook her head. As I walked down the hall, I wondered if I'd find Blythe standing there again. Maybe she could have that drink after all.

Disappointment and curiosity mixed as I pulled back the blinds to find a delivery person instead of Blythe. They held a large box and smiled when they saw me. I cracked the door, keeping the chain latched, just in case.

"Hello?"

"Sorry I'm so late, but I had a hard time finding the place. I need a signature from . . ." They looked at the box. "Hannah Greenfield."

"That's me." I unlatched the chain, took the proffered pen, and signed.

I got the box inside and looked at the return address. Jemima Boutique. I sat down hard, the air rushing from my lungs as if I'd been slammed into a concrete wall. Lisa must have given them my forwarding address. I knew what was inside but wasn't at all sure if I was ready to open it. It had been a sample and was nonrefundable, especially since it had been fitted to my body.

Jordan appeared. "What's that?"

"My wedding dress."

"Oh." She sat down next to me. "Are you going to open it?"

"I think I should drive it straight to a donation shop."

"I want to see it again."

Jordan had gone shopping with me. She loved watching *Say Yes to the Dress* videos on YouTube and didn't want to miss the moment with her mom. We'd had a great time, laughing at the oversized Cinderella gown she'd talked me into trying on, cringing at the plunging mermaid with the open sides, and both of us in total agreement on the flowy A-line with the simple, strapless, beaded bodice. Now I would never wear it.

Jordan got a pair of scissors from the kitchen and carefully cut through the packing tape. Inside the box, the dress was wrapped in layers of blush pink tissue paper and tied with a grosgrain black ribbon. A sprig of lavender released its scent into the apartment. She glanced at me.

"Go ahead."

She eased the bow apart, then lifted each side of the tissue paper. The dress lay beautifully in the box, a promise of ever afters.

I stood up and reached for the edges of the bodice, then pulled the dress up and out as if I were facing myself on the dance floor. A sigh whispered out of my chest. "It's still pretty."

Jordan came to my side and put her arms around my waist, nuzzling against me. "I'm sorry, Mom."

I gently draped the dress over the box and took her into a hug. "Are you sad about Lisa?"

I felt her shoulders lift. "I mean, yeah. She was nice. But it felt like I always got in her way. Especially after we moved into the loft. It's a lot less tense with just you."

I kissed the top of her head, and she looked up.

"Don't take this the wrong way, but you guys didn't seem super lovey-dovey ever. Not the way you described Lala and Gramp's marriage. She spent a lot of money on us, but it didn't seem like she wanted to hang out much."

I pushed her out at arm's length. "Are you calling me a gold digger?"

"What's that?"

"Someone who dates somebody for their money."

"God, Mom. No. Not like that. You had a job. You didn't have to worry about *her* money. Like when Auntie Tess left that one girlfriend of hers because she emptied the savings account."

I dropped my arms and really looked at my daughter. She was turning into an adult before my eyes, including this incredibly insightful bit of thought. Because even though Lisa's personal epiphany about her needs was the flame that burned us out, maybe the first spark came from the lack of one in our relationship. We'd found stability and consistency in each other and moved forward based on that. When really, we both needed more.

BLYTHE

I drove away from my meeting with the Smith-Itos and immediately texted Ginny.

Hey! You busy?

It had gone really well. Joseph was an economics professor, and his husband, Hiroshi, was an art history professor with strong ideas about design. Hiroshi was a huge fan of Bruce Goff, Bart Prince, and Gaudi. We'd hit it off immediately, even though my designs and visions were a tad staider than those iconic architects' designs.

When we'd talked about the land, I knew I wanted the job, regardless of whether the lot was part of the deal. They loved sustainability and thoughtful building practices. They wanted it to be extremely energy efficient and clever in its use of resources.

My phone buzzed.

Sorry sis, my hands are full with Isla and Derrick right now. Can you call me later? I do want to hear about it, I promise.

I was disappointed, but I understood.

No problem.

What was I going to do with all this excitement? We hadn't signed a contract yet, so it wasn't a given. But they seemed as thrilled to have me as a neighbor as I'd been about the lot, which was perfect. I was hopeful.

I decided to drive toward Charleston to eat some oysters, have a beer, and watch women's soccer on the big-screen televisions at the Slippery Pearl. Hannah came to mind. I'd turned down her offer of a drink after work, but I wondered whether I should text her now. The phone's clock read 7:45 p.m. It was too late to bug her. Or was it?

The phone felt weighted in my hand. I knew I was being overeager. I knew she wasn't in a place where she could fall back into a relationship. She had kissed me, though. That meant we had something, didn't it? Besides, I was excited, and she was fun to be around. She was a dream chaser, too. She'd understand this rush I was feeling.

I noticed she'd accepted my friend request, so I took a quick minute, before driving off, to poke around her profile page. She'd been totally honest. Only a couple of weeks ago, she'd posted that the wedding was cancelled and that she hoped everyone would understand her going silent for a bit. Which she had. Nothing about her move. Nothing posted since then.

In previous posts, I saw Lisa. She was a stunning woman with shoulder-length black hair cut in a bob, deep olive skin, and an athletic build. It looked as if she was involved in some sort of pharmaceutical business. Dressed smart. More on the feminine side than I was. They certainly made a beautiful couple. I wondered what had gone so wrong.

My snooping continued as I found photos of a gorgeous loft apartment with incredible art and furnishings. Loads of snaps of Jordan and Hannah at various protests and marches. Teacher-related articles, birthday wishes from friends—Hannah was a Libra—and happy group shots of Hannah, her colleagues, and students. There was nothing tangible to put me off except for the timing of her most recent relationship. But the intangibles were huge. She had a daughter, and even though I had no personal problem with kids, I could only imagine how huge it would be for Hannah to decide to get involved with someone. She wouldn't make that decision spontaneously.

A motorcycle blasted down the street behind me, knocking my thoughts back to center.

As much as I wanted to see Hannah. As much as I wanted to know more of her story, to find out what had gone wrong with her relationship, it felt like I should give her, and myself, some space. Because the timing of that relationship and my tender heart did matter to me. How could she possibly be ready for what I needed?

AT THE SLIPPERY PEARL, I sat at the bar and put in my order for a raw dozen and a pale ale. Gia, the regular bartender, set it in front of me. "How's things, Blythe?"

"Not bad."

"You ever see Kiki?" She cleared the glasses from the bar next to me and began wiping it down with a rag.

Kiki was my last fling. A voluptuous, bold, blonde woman who was the heiress to a department store fortune. We'd had amazing sex, but she was too performative and too loud, in the bedroom and out.

"No. Been keeping busy at work."

"You want to go out with me and my wife and a friend of ours?"

"A setup?"

Gia walked to the end of the bar and grabbed the plate of oysters from the waiter standing there. She brought them back and set them in front of me. "It can be. Or it can't be. Her name's Jody. We grew up together. Hadn't seen her in years, but she found me online after she heard I was queer. She moved here last year." Gia turned around, grabbed her cell phone from a cubby underneath the bar, and showed me a picture.

An attractive woman with close curls and a beautiful smile was sandwiched between Gia and her wife at a different bar.

"Good looking." I shook the Tabasco bottle over my oysters and squeezed a lemon wedge so that the juice ran over each one. The shell was cold as I plucked the first one off the ice.

"Smart too," Gia said.

"What's her deal?"

Gia put her phone back. "She's single. Separated two years ago and decided about six months ago she was ready to start dating again. She's run up against the liars and the cheaters and asked us to keep an ear to the ground for sane, eligible women."

"You sure I'm qualified?"

Gia smirked. "I know you're sane. And her type. Are you seeing anybody?"

Now there was a question. I'd been kissed. Hannah wanted to talk to me again. I was definitely interested in her. But if it was another dead-end street, why would I turn down the opportunity to meet a beautiful woman who knew what she wanted and didn't give me the Constance/Kiki vibe from her photograph? If nothing else came from meeting Hannah, it was the knowledge that I wasn't ready to go to the grave single. I wanted the wife life.

But . . . I couldn't bring myself to commit.

"I'm not seeing anyone." This was technically true. "Does she have kids?" This question sprang from a deeper thought. Dating a mom, especially a single mom, meant you would never come first in the relationship. I hoped I was mature enough to handle that scenario, but what if I wasn't? Then who'd be the one to break hearts? Maybe a totally different path than Hannah was the right path.

"She doesn't have children." Gia cocked her head. "I wouldn't think that would matter to you either way, knowing how you go on and on about your sister's kids."

I shrugged, not willing to share my musings. "Can I think about it for a day or two?"

"Of course. And like I said, no pressure. Just let us know if you want to hang out. We can do something in town, or you could swing by our place for a drink."

A group of women sat down at the far end of the bar, and Gia excused herself to take their orders. I watched the Canadian women's team drill a ball toward the goal as I made quick work of my oysters. There was really only one way to work this out in my head.

I pulled out my phone.

If you still want to chat, I'm free most of this weekend.

I was actually free all weekend but didn't want to sound totally pathetic. Putting it off until the weekend also gave me, and Hannah, some space and distance from the kiss. I pulled out my credit card, and Gia rang up my tab.

"You got our number, right?"

"I do. I'll let you know either way."

"Jody's cool. I promise you'll like her."

I signed the ticket and made sure to leave a solid tip. As I walked out the door, my phone vibrated against my leg.

Hannah.

Want to help us paint? I promised Jordan we'd do at least her room and bathroom. I can't commit to anything else until we're finished, but I absolutely want to chat.

The "absolutely" won me over. That and the opportunity to impress Hannah with my mad painting skills.

Chapter 12

HANNAH

Working at the paint store turned out to be way more satisfying than I could have imagined. There was a rhythm to it that felt as familiar as a school day. Contractors first thing, designers midmorning, housewives and project painters in the afternoon. There were regulars and people who didn't feel like driving all the way over to the Lowes or Home Depot. The part where it differed from a school day was the lack of paperwork and bureaucracy, and for that, it was worth every dollar less on my paycheck.

The front door bell jangled. I popped my head up, hoping it'd be Blythe. But, like every other time I'd come to attention at that sound, I was disappointed. It was Friday and there'd still been no sign of her.

I sighed and sunk my chin into my hands. My brain was a strange land these days. It enjoyed getting another chance to see the dress. It mulled over the reality of my breakup. Sadness swirled in too. Though I knew we'd done the right thing by calling the wedding off, it didn't stop me from feeling a bit lost.

Five Months or Forever

I was forty. Mom to a teenager. Yet I still held on to the stupid dream of real love. The real partnership I'd convinced myself existed even as I'd pursued one grounded more in groundedness than mutual adoration.

Which is where Blythe came in. I'd kissed her and confessed about Lisa, and she'd disappeared. Now I couldn't stop thinking about her. About the serendipity of her being in the driveway of our rental. About how the minute our lips touched, my body had shimmered with recognition. She'd felt like fire and family and everything I'd ever wanted. I thought about her twinkly eyes, the way she joked with the people she loved, and how her heart exited her body and flew above the water when she captained her boat. I wanted to run to her and fall to my knees and ask her to marry me, to love Jordan, to make a home. But what if I was wrong?

This was some stupid shit if ever there was stupid shit on the face of the planet, but I also had a feeling. I'd never had a feeling about Lisa.

Jordan was right. A pragmatic decision didn't equate with lovey-dovey, to use her words.

Apparently, I was a bigger romantic, dreamer, fairy-tale princess than I realized. Because here I was, less than two weeks into a new life and already freaking out that I'd lost the chance to connect with my potential soul mate. And seriously—soul mate? I barely knew Blythe.

"Jesus. Get it together."

"Did you say something, darling? People sure have called me worse." The painter, who wasn't Blythe, hooked his thumbs under the straps of his coveralls and belly laughed.

I hadn't realized he'd placed himself next to me to look at the display of scrapers.

"No, sorry. Talking to myself."

"I figured. But whatever you've got going on in that head of yours is going to have to wait. Joel told me you're real good with colors, and I promised the apartment manager I could do something like this." The man pulled a wrinkled, glossy magazine page out of his pocket and flattened it before handing it to me. "You think you can help get me sorted out?"

It was a relief to take it from him and have something to focus on besides myself. "You got it."

The rest of the day sped by. At four-thirty the bus dropped off Jordan, and at five we were packing up to head to our apartment.

"You ready to paint?"

"Yes. Goodbye peach and blue. Also, I'm starving." She held up an empty chips wrapper and shook it at me.

"How about some burgers on the way home? Let's try out that place we pass every day. The parking lot's always crowded, so it must be good."

At the restaurant, we were seated righted away. As we walked across the room, a voice called out. "Hannah! Jordan!"

We looked. Ginny's husband, Todd, was there with the two kids.

"Look, Mom, it's Derrick and Isla and their dad."

We walked over to say hello, and Todd instructed his kids to scoot over on the bench. "Join us. Ginny has to work late, but she'd be very upset with me if I didn't extend some hospitality."

"Oh, we wouldn't want to interfere."

Jordan decided for us and plopped down next to Isla, who was showing her something on her game tablet.

"Are you sure?" I asked.

"Of course. We just ordered some cheese fries to start." He waved at the waiter, who brought over two more menus and waters. "How are the first weeks of job and school?"

"Good. We both seem to be settling in. And this weekend we have big plans to repaint our apartment."

Isla looked at her dad. "I want Jordan to come with us to

GeeGee and Geepaw's tomorrow." She turned toward Jordan. "Do you want to come ride horses at the ranch? It's so much fun."

"Oh." I shook my head ever so slightly in Jordan's direction.

"That's a great idea, Isla." Todd turned. "We'd love for Jordan to join us. My parents have six or seven horses. I can't ever keep up. Didn't get the riding gene myself. But Isla loves it. Derrick likes it. And we always have a bunch of good food and good fun. You're welcome too, of course."

Jordan's eyes had gone puppy dog wide and her face was lit up with excitement. "Mom, can I?"

"What about our painting?"

"But, horses! Can't we paint on Sunday?"

About that time, my phone buzzed. I took a glance. It was Blythe.

I'll stop by tomorrow about ten if that's good. Help you paint, then maybe we can grab some lunch.

My busy brain calculated on the fly. I looked at Jordan and tried not to let guilt override this quick decision. "If you help me get things prepped tonight, then I'll get started with the painting tomorrow. Sunday, it's homework and whatever else I tell you to do."

She jumped out of her chair and hugged me around the neck. "You're the bomb."

No. I was more like an explosion about to jump out of my own skin.

Somehow, I'd managed to have an opportunity to talk to Blythe alone. In the comfort of my own four walls. With Jordan's curious ears and eyes off on an adventure.

Now this, if there was such a thing, was serendipity.

BLYTHE

I didn't pick up donuts on the way over. Figured I'd come on too strong from the start and now it was my turn to be low-key. When I turned onto Hannah's street, I saw her getting out of the car like she'd been out somewhere and was returning. I pulled in next to her.

She waited for me as I turned off the engine and climbed out.

"Hey." Her smile seemed expectant.

"Did I get the time right?"

She pushed her bangs off to the side, and I noted the fading tan line on her ring finger. I couldn't believe I hadn't noticed that any of the times we'd hung out.

"You sure did. Ginny didn't tell you?"

"No. Tell me what?"

She motioned for me to follow her to the door and talked as she let us inside.

"We ran into Todd and your niece and nephew last night at Bull & Brew. They invited Jordan to go to the ranch, and horses totally trumped her desire to paint. I was just dropping her off. I hope that's okay? That she's not here?"

The ramifications of what she said sunk in. We were at her house. Alone.

"Um, yeah. Do you still want to paint?"

She flushed and looked away. When she spoke again, her voice came out in a slightly higher pitch than before. "I mean, that's up to you. We did do prep work, but I don't want to force you into manual labor. I figured we could have a cup of coffee and chat, then you could get on with your day."

If we were to just sit and chat, I might end up doing something I'd regret. Painting seemed like a good activity to keep us focused and give us an opportunity to clear the air.

"You know what? Let's paint. I'm all coffee'd up. When we

get the first coat done, I'll take you for a boat ride. I was hoping to get out and look at this one particular piece of land from the water to get another viewpoint. If Jordan's gone to the ranch, they won't be back for a while."

"Are you sure you don't mind helping?"

"I don't mind a bit. Where are we starting?"

She pointed to the room behind the kitchen with the little bathroom. "Jordan's room. She's got it taped and ready for us."

Hannah was nonchalant as she chatted about her work week and how lucky she felt to be working for Joel. If she could be so relaxed, then I could be too.

We worked easily, sanding the patches Jordan had filled the night before, brushing primer onto the trim. But as the morning slipped past us, I couldn't stand the elephant in the room any longer.

From the bathroom, where I crouched on the floor painting trim on the cabinet, I spoke to the unspoken thing hanging between us.

"Why don't you tell me about Lisa?"

She released a heavy sigh. "Okay." I heard her shift positions. "I met Lisa three years ago. I was chaperoning for the queer youth prom, and she was on the board of the organization. We flirted and danced and then she disappeared. But a week later, I got a phone call at the school where I taught and it was her, asking if she could have my number so she could invite me to dinner."

"And obviously you went."

"Obviously."

I rose from the floor and moved into the bedroom, where she knelt next to the casing. Sunlight settled over her body, accentuating each beautiful curve. I cleared my throat. "Things must have been pretty great for you two to decide to get married."

She shrugged and glanced in my direction. "They weren't

bad." Her hand paused as she turned fully. "I don't want you to think Lisa is a bad person. She's not. It wasn't a cheating situation or anything like that."

I moved to the final bit of trim on the doorframe and tried not to stare at Hannah. I wanted her to feel that she could tell me anything—even though she obviously wasn't telling me everything—and gawking probably wouldn't help. "How did Jordan take it?"

"She was sad. Also, weirdly insightful about the entire situation."

"Must be fun being her mom."

Hannah rewarded me with a crinkled nose and dimples. "It is. We've been a duo for fourteen awesome years now. I can't even wrap my head around the fact that she'll be leaving for college in a few more."

"Yeah, I bet."

"Did you ever consider having kids?" Hannah's tone held something I couldn't quite quantify.

I ran the brush at an angle, cutting in at the corner of the doorframe. "Me personally? No. I'm not built for it. Besides, Ginny did it for me. I get all the fun of being the cool aunt without the cravings for pickles and ice cream."

I finished my trim work and wrapped the brush in wax paper before opening the gallon of wall color and giving it a good stir. The roller soaked up paint as I rolled it in the pan. "Nice color." I smiled to try to lighten the intensity of the conversation. Hannah didn't need to hear about how desperately I'd dreamed about marrying Constance and either having or adopting a child.

Or maybe she did.

"I never wanted to be pregnant, but I did dream about adopting or having a child with my previous partner. She wasn't into it though."

"Seriously?"

I kept rolling on paint. "I mean, yeah, some women don't want kids. Or they're not ready."

"Or the reality is not the same as the idea." There was an edge to her voice.

"Yeah, I guess. In my case, it's way too late to have a baby." I didn't want her to get the impression I was against kids, only that it had never worked out.

She stood up and set her brush in the tray. Her face held a soft smile as she wiggled her legs to shake off any stiffness. "I'm really glad you came over today."

I paused. "Oh yeah?"

"Yeah." She walked over and sat gingerly on the edge of the bed, the plastic drop cloth crinkling beneath her. Her shoulders slumped. "I'm going to tell you something I haven't told anybody."

I stepped closer. It felt like I should be near her for whatever she was going to confess.

She patted the spot next to her in response to my hesitation. "Sit."

I did.

She took another deep breath. "Lisa called off the wedding because she figured out she didn't want to be a parent."

"Oh man. Poor Jordan." I moved my hands from my thighs to the bed and then back again, trying to place them so they wouldn't bump Hannah.

"I haven't told her the whole truth. I don't want her to blame herself."

"Makes sense." She was so close I could feel the warmth radiating off her arm. I wanted to comfort her, to wrap her in my arms and hold her through this confession. "You must be hurting though."

"I am and I was. Both. When we first decided to call off the wedding, I blamed the breakup purely on Lisa's response to parenting. I think . . . ." She paused and looked up toward the ceiling, and I noticed her smooth skin below her jawline. "Well, I think that was a convenient thing to focus on." Hannah looked at me, and the crackle of energy I'd been tamping down roared back to life.

I swallowed and bounced my heel against the floor. "What should you have been focusing on?" My voice came out huskier than normal, giving away what was going on inside my body.

She looked toward the floor, but I noticed the way her breath quickened, and a shy smile grew on her lips. "I think I should have been focusing on my needs. Finding what I want."

This time I practically whispered. "What do you want?"

She shifted her arm slightly, and the damned energy pinballed the minute she brushed against me. Her breathless "Oh" let me know she felt it too.

It was all the encouragement I needed. I leaned in, and when she looked back up, I moved forward, my own heart accelerating. "Maybe this?" I asked, and without waiting for her answer, I pressed my mouth against hers, ignoring everything I knew about my own needs.

Chapter 13

HANNAH

The second Blythe's lips touched mine, my thoughts disappeared.

I knew I should stop. She'd already made it clear that casual wasn't her thing. But she was an empathetic and kind listener, and she was warm and soft, and an incredible kisser, and god, the same feeling of familiarity and rightness was sending me into the stratosphere.

"Is this okay?" Her arms pulled me closer, and I mumbled something affirmative as I tipped my head backward to give her all the access she needed to the nape of my neck. Her lips were warm as they gently traced my skin, and I let my body melt into the press of her. I belonged here.

Our kisses intensified. Blythe shifted as I moaned softly. I clutched at her shirt, pulling her toward me and falling back. She followed willingly. The weight of her, as she pressed the length of her body against the length of mine, opened up depths of desire I didn't even realize I contained anymore.

We kissed in slow motion. We kissed deeper. I looped a leg

over hers and arched upward, my hands spanning her strong back in an attempt to get even closer. I wanted this woman under my skin. What was so wrong about wanting this in my life?

Her hand traveled down my T-shirt. As her thumb circled through the fabric, my body went fire hot. "Oh, please, yes."

Her eyes brightened and a smile parted her lips as she saw how my body responded to only the slightest touch.

I wanted her to ravage me. I wanted her to slide her hand down inside my jeans and feel what she'd created in only a matter of seconds. I wanted our bodies to meld until we could no longer separate where she began and I ended.

"Hannah," she whispered.

I tilted my head back and my eyes fluttered open. Her smile was gentle, but her eyes wicked. I took in a ragged breath as she reached beneath my shirt. Oh, good god, I did not want this to stop.

But . . .

Jordan's childhood stuffed octopus, Legs, stared at me from under the drop cloth where she'd tucked him out of harm's way.

"Blythe." I put my hands on her shoulders and gave a half-hearted push.

She looked up, her breath whispering across my skin. "What? Is everything okay?"

I reluctantly moved myself into a more upright position, letting my shirt fall into place in the process. "No, I mean yes, it's very good. But . . ." I pointed to Legs.

She immediately understood. "Right. Jordan's room." She held out a hand and pulled me up into her arms before turning and walking me backward toward the hallway.

Once there, she pressed me against the wall, kissing me with such ferocity that my knees threatened to buckle. I pulled her hips against mine and held her there, feeling the delicious pressure of her body.

Blythe whispered, her voice husky with need. "Your room."

I put my hands on her forearms and walked her back, then turned and grabbed her by the wrist. Two steps across the threshold and the anchor dropped, dragging me to an abrupt stop. What the hell?

Then I saw the cause.

My wedding dress. Hanging in front of my closet. I'd placed it like a piece of art, working up the will to take it to the donation shop. "Shit," I whispered.

Blythe's expression was raw as she stared at the yards of white silk. "Is that . . . ?"

"Yeah."

Blythe dropped my hand and took a step back. "Right."

"Blythe. Don't get freaked out." I mirrored her backward steps out of my room with my own moving toward her.

Why had I left the stupid dress out in plain sight? If I'd simply hung it in the closet or put it back in the shipping box, I would be naked by now. With this kind and incredibly hot woman, who'd dropped on my doorstep like a gift for the New Year.

She shook her head and put up a hand, asking me to stop. "That's a lot to take in."

"I know. I'm sorry." I stayed put, suddenly self-conscious about how easily I'd thrown myself at her.

She stepped fully into the hall away from me. "A few years ago, I could have ignored that dress. I'm not that person anymore. Hannah . . ." She crossed her arms, then dropped them to her side. "You're not ready for me."

I looked away, crossing my arms over my chest. She was right. Hearing the words cracked open a wound that hadn't even begun to truly stitch together. I felt like an ass. She'd been so clear about her needs, and by letting her kiss me the way she did . . . well, it was disrespectful.

Because no matter how much I daydreamed about having a partner who wanted me and Jordan, how would I trust that possibility after what had happened with Lisa? And with me?

She kept talking. "Like I said, hookups, or rebounds, don't interest me. No matter how much the chemistry sizzles."

I wanted to latch on to the second comment and fly it to the moon, but I kept silent and listened.

"Then there's Jordan. I like her. I don't want to piss her off by moving in on her mom when her mom is still thinking about the wedding that never happened." Blythe shrugged. "I'm sorry."

"No, I'm the one who's sorry. If it's any consolation, I'm extremely attracted to you. Your pheromones made me lose reason and respect. I mean, not blaming your pheromones, but my response to them."

Blythe dug her hands into her pockets and lifted her shoulders. "Yeah, well, my sister says I have immense sex appeal."

I smiled. "Your sister's right."

"I won't tell her that."

"Can we try to be friends? With boundaries?" Part of me couldn't believe this conversation was even happening. Not with where we'd been just a few moments ago. But I didn't want to lose Blythe completely. Not when I'd just found her. She was awesome, and I did want to be her friend.

I wasn't a teenager. I could control myself.

"Boundaries can be hard for me, but yeah, we can try."

I felt the shift. Some wall dropping between us. But could I blame her? Better to let her go gracefully. At least I'd have five minutes of heat to dream about at night.

"You know, you don't have to stay and do this. I'll finish up. I'm sure you've got things to do and you've already helped a ton."

"I don't mind, and I promised you a boat ride."

I'd already figured out Blythe was a giver. Now it was my turn. "Save the boat ride for when Jordan's around. She'd love for you to take her out to stalk dolphins again. I've got this."

Blythe nodded. "She's going to be excited about her room." Then a deep breath. "I'm sorry I can't be the kind of comfort you need right now. We'll stay in touch?"

I put my hand on my hip. "Well, duh. You are my only friend here. And you can't avoid Williamson's forever."

She laughed. "True. Okay then."

There was a bit of hesitation, probably both of us deciding what our goodbye should entail.

Blythe decided. She raised her hand. "I'll see myself out. Keep painting."

When the door shut behind her, I slumped against the wall. Destiny and timing didn't always see eye to eye.

BLYTHE

I called my sister.

"Are you home, or did you go out to the ranch?"

"Home. How did you know about the ranch?"

"Long story. You want to meet me at the marina? Take a ride with me and go look at the lot from the water?"

I'd be lying if I tried to convince myself I wasn't down in the dumps. Less than an hour ago, my hands were exploring soft skin and I was ready to fall into a woman's bed after many months of drought. Hannah's wedding dress turned on the cold water, quenching the flame she'd lit inside of me. Her reality was exactly what I'd worried about. But damn, I still wanted to pull that shirt over her head and wriggle her out of her jeans. She'd been everything I'd imagined and so much more.

It still wasn't enough for me to walk straight into a broken heart.

"You sound weird." Ginny was always perceptive when it came to me.

"I could use a friend."

"I'll meet you in ten."

True to her word, Ginny pulled her Lexus in next to Chester. She popped out of her car and grabbed a cooler out of the back seat. "I came prepared."

"Come on. We can talk on the boat."

Once we were out on the water, a hard seltzer in my sister's coozie and a cold IPA in mine, I told her some of the story.

"But you like her?" Ginny smiled. "I knew it!"

"Yeah, I like her. But she's not available. And by the time she is, she'll have figured out that some part-time architect with a lack of financial drive is not what she's after."

"Why do you always sell yourself so short? High-powered jobs and flash lifestyles are not what all women are into. That's just Constance in your head. Okay, so Hannah's not ready, but it sounds like you are? That's good, Blythe."

I arced the boat across the sound and slowed as we neared the shoreline of the lots. "Good? How could that be good?"

"Good because you have some clarity. You've been kind of lost since you moved back. Like you're going through the motions. Like something is missing. I don't want this to come out the wrong way—"

"If you start a sentence that way, there's a high likelihood it will." I pulled back the throttle till we were barely moving, and I searched the shore for the group of live oaks I'd noted at the edge of the properties.

"What I was going to say before you so rudely interrupted me is that as much as we adore having you over all the time, it has got to be boring hanging out with us. Especially after having lived in Atlanta for all those years. I remember the texts you would send me and the photos from parties and brunches and hanging out with all those gorgeous women. You need to get back out there. Find that woman who's going to love you like Todd loves me. You're worth it, sis."

"There." I pointed to the shoreline.

Ginny turned, and her attention shifted to real estate for a moment. "Which would be yours?"

I motored closer, careful to stay out of the reeds and shallow water. When I was as close as I could get, I cut the engine and dropped the anchor. "There. To the right of that group of trees." I pointed out the hump of land in the center that was the ideal home site.

"It's perfect." Ginny shaded her eyes to take it in.

We were quiet for a moment, sipping our beverages, feeling the gentle rock of the boat beneath us. A plover flew overhead, and we could hear the sound of someone playing Spanish guitar on the shore. Ginny's words soaked in.

"Thanks for saying all that. Before."

My sister stretched her legs out on the cushions and covered them with a beach towel I kept in the boat's storage cubby. "I meant it. And I'm sorry things didn't work out with Hannah. I like her."

"Yeah." I sighed and finished my beer. "Me too. Apparently not meant to be."

LATER, after Ginny and I went for tacos, I went home and got on my computer. I scrolled through pictures of adoptable dogs and looked at smiling faces and goofy faces and crooked tooth faces with names like Pluto and Annabel and Zeus. But when I got to a picture with the name Larry, I stopped.

"Huh." He was at a shelter not far from me. On a whim, I filled out the interested adopter application and didn't even hesitate when I hit send. This guy would be ready for commitment, and maybe that's all I really needed.

Afterward, I pulled up the plot maps for the lots and loaded them into my design program. I spent a couple hours mapping out the Smith-Itos' potential home site, with notes on why I thought it would work best. I'd had an email from them this morning expressing their interests in initial proposals and thoughts. They'd even offered to pay me for my time since we hadn't committed to the swap yet, which was the kind of respect for creativity I appreciated.

Inevitably, my mind drifted back to Hannah. I thought about how I'd kissed her and how she'd kissed me. My body clinched in response to the memory. I was glad she still wanted to be friends, and I appreciated how she understood I didn't want a one-off experience. The real truth was, I had no idea how I could have boundaries with a woman like that. She'd entered my body and mind like a full memory—past, present, and future. How was I supposed to let that go?

But Ginny was right. It was time to get off my ass and get

back out there. If it wasn't going to be Hannah, why not at least dip my toes in the water? I'd never find someone if I only went to work, my sister's, and out on my boat alone.

I found Gia's number in my phone and shot her a text.

I can come hang out sometime. But not a setup. Just a hello.

She texted back quickly.

Sounds good. It may be a few weeks though. We're headed away on vacation. When we get back, I'll invite a couple of other people around, so it won't be awkward.

Pretty sure it would be awkward no matter what, but at least it'd get me out of the house and out of Ginny's hair for a night. Who knows, maybe this Jody woman and I were fated? There were worse things than being set up by friends.

Like having to maintain boundaries with a woman who otherwise seemed like the answer to your prayers.

Chapter 14

HANNAH

That night, I stood in my doorway watching Jordan sleep. She'd been exhausted and smelling of horses when she returned, but exuberant as well. Now, she lay in my bed with her hands curled up near her face and her breath coming in soft snores. Poor thing had been through so much for me. It seemed like she was doing okay, though it was still early days.

The disappointment I'd felt about Blythe drifted away. It was time to focus on this new life. Once Jordan went to college, I could start dating again. The wedding dress hung where I'd left it.

Start a life. Find the right wife.

Damnit. What was the matter with me? The stupid dress was reciting poetry. I took it off the door and shoved it in the closet. Then I went out to the couch to fall asleep in front of the television and definitely not think about Blythe, a new life, or the right wife.

The strength of the paint smell subsided by the next morning, and Jordan moved back into her room. We'd tackle more next weekend and the weekend after that. As long as we had some time to enjoy it before the end-of-semester decision drew near.

In the evening, we were gearing up for Monday—each of us exhausted from our weekend adventures—when the phone rang. My mother.

"Hi, Mom."

"Were you ever going to call me?"

"We've been painting our apartment and it's taken our whole weekend."

Jordan perked up from where she was finishing up some homework on the sofa. "Is that Lala?"

I nodded and she stood up so she'd get a chance to talk to her grandmother. The one extreme point of gratitude in my life was that all the judgment my mother flung at me was nonexistent when it came to her granddaughter. She was grateful she had one. When I came out at sixteen, she figured she'd never have a grandchild, because lesbians having babies wasn't as much of a thing back then.

"Jordan wants to say hi." I was always more than happy to hand the phone over and avoid the grilling and commentary I was bound to receive.

"No. Not yet. There's something we need to discuss."

"Ooookay." This sounded dire.

"I'm planning a visit."

"When?"

"Three weeks."

"What?" I looked around. The place was a mess, between our half-finished paint job, half-finished unpacking, and general laissez-faire.

"I want to see where you're housing my grandchild and have a look inside your brain to find out what the hell happened to make you call off your wedding so suddenly. I don't trust your mental health."

"Mom." I blew out an exasperated breath. "My mental health is fine. It always has been."

Jordan put her hand to her mouth to cover her laughter.

"There was the aftermath from that girl in college."

"Can we not dig up ancient history? I'm forty years old. The mother of a teenager. With a job. And a retirement account, no matter how paltry. We're fine. I had therapy for that episode and graduated." I took a breath. "Are you staying here? We're in the middle of painting, and this place is tiny."

"Dear Lord, no. I've booked an oceanfront home. You two can stay with me for the weekend and we can visit. There's even a hot tub and a heated pool I convinced them should be opened for me."

"You mean for Jordan."

"Put her on the phone. I'll see you soon."

I handed the phone over, and once her grandmother filled her in, Jordan immediately started firing questions back. No wonder she didn't gripe much about the move lately. Horseback riding her second weekend, an oceanfront condo in the near future . . . Coastal life agreed with her. At least I hoped she saw it that way.

OVER THE NEXT FEW WEEKS, work was steady. Joel gave me more and more responsibility helping customers with design needs. I'd even been flattered by a real designer who'd whispered to him, loud enough for me to hear, "How you manage to always find the best people, I don't know. Careful, or I may steal her from you." I knew she was only being kind, but it made me think about the one-day possibilities for beyond the paint store.

The awful part about the passing weeks was the lack of Blythe. Even though she'd promised not to be a stranger, she was clearly avoiding me. She'd been in the store only once, and

I'd been elbow deep in paint swatches with an elderly man who kept calling me "sugah." All she'd done was lift her hand in a wave as she pushed out the door. I couldn't bring myself to text her. Not when I was the one who'd suggested boundaries, whatever the hell that meant.

Thursday, around four, a Mercedes much newer than my own pulled into the parking lot of the store. I recognized my mother by her giant Chanel sunglasses. Unlike me, she was petite and wiry. She still colored her hair, but it was almost more burgundy than auburn. Her last face lift was starting to drift south but I wouldn't mention it, even if it was something she'd jump to comment on if it were one of her friends.

I glanced at my reflection in the glass of Joel's office door and pressed down a stray hair that was standing up near the crown of my head. There was nothing I could do about my lack of lip gloss. The door bell jangled.

"Mom. You're here." I walked out from behind the counter and gave her a kiss on the cheek. She always smelled like Chanel No. 5. It didn't matter if she'd just run a half-marathon—which was something she used to do occasionally—or was dressed for the opera, the woman always wore her perfume.

She looked around. "This is quaint."

A shuffling came from inside the office, where Joel was working on the books, and he emerged. "How do you do? You must be Hannah's mother." He held out a hand. "Joel Williamson."

Mom turned on the Southern charm. "I do hope my Hannah is making good use of herself and not being a problem for you."

"She's a gem. I'm real glad she wandered in that day."

Mom fluttered her eyelashes. "Well, that is genuinely good to hear."

I don't know how she did it, but the woman could reduce

me to an eleven-year-old in a matter of minutes. God, I hoped I wouldn't do that to Jordan. "Mom."

"What? He paid you a compliment. It's good to hear."

How could I explain that it was all in her tone and insinuation? I didn't have time though, because Jordan's bus pulled up out front.

"Jordan's here."

Mom turned. "She has to take the school bus?"

"It's not a problem. I drop her in the morning. She'll be driving soon enough."

Jordan pushed into the store. "Lala!" She plopped her backpack by the door and ran into Mom's outstretched arms.

"My jellybean." Mom pressed a kiss onto Jordan's curls and pushed Jordan back to assess her. "You look beautiful."

I smiled in response to the look on Jordan's face as she welled up with her grandmother's compliments. She was often hard on herself, but if her grandmother said it, she believed it.

"Thanks." She squeezed Mom again.

A customer walked through the door.

"Mom, why don't you take Jordan with you to check in to the house? I'm not off for another forty-five minutes. It will give you two some time to catch up without me. But be sure to text me the address. I'm going to run home first and grab the bags we packed. We can show you the apartment later."

"All right." She waved at Joel. "Lovely to meet you. Just let me know if she starts behaving badly and I'll whip her into shape."

"Mom. Go." I pointed to the door while Jordan giggled.

Five Months or Forever

BLYTHE

My adoption application for the animal rescue had finally been approved after an arduous few weeks of waiting, a home visit, and checked references. When I met Larry, there was no doubt. I brought him home immediately. It was a solid life choice. He was a warm body in my bed and an excellent companion. Too bad it wasn't as easy with women.

He loved the truck and begrudgingly accepted the harness and leash after I explained it was the only way he could come to work with me. I'd even taken him out on the boat with his own little life jacket, which he adored. I'd taken a ridiculous number of pictures of him and shared one on my social, my first post in ages. Hannah had commented, saying Jordan would be jealous. I'd have to figure out a time to take him by to meet her, but I was having a hard time figuring out how to be near Hannah without a double pheromone problem. The one day I'd seen her at her job, it was all I could do not to pull her away from a customer and take her somewhere for a good long kiss.

"Come on, Larry." I let him follow me out to Chester. We were off to get a pool up and running for a client who'd paid big bucks so they could have both the seasonal hot tub and the heated pool. In February. On the Atlantic. We might get a day or two of springlike weather here and there, but for the most part it was chilly to swim outdoors. To each his own though.

The house was not far from downtown on East Arctic Ave. It was relatively new but not like the huge monstrosities built when the owners tore down the smaller homes for bigger and better. I liked this particular home—it had good vibes.

I cranked the cover off the pool and checked the chemical

levels. Larry lounged on one of the deck chairs, the ocean breeze making his fur lift in the wind.

"Well, boy. This is your new life. I hope you like it."

A car door thunked from the parking area. Larry yawned and stretched out his furry front legs. Unlike when I met Hannah, this client had asked for someone to be at the home to let them in, citing concern they wouldn't be able to figure out the realtor's lockbox.

"Hello?" I walked out from the pool area, Larry in my arms.

A glamorous woman with enormous sunglasses stood next to a shining luxury sedan. "Are you here to let me in?"

"Yes, ma'am. Let me put him in the car and I'll be right with you."

"Blythe!" Another figure popped out of the passenger side of the luxury sedan.

It was Hannah's daughter, Jordan.

"You have a cat?" She bounced over and started cooing and stroking Larry's long tabby fur. "And he wears a harness? That's so cool."

"You want to hold him while I let . . ." My speech short-circuited as I tried to figure out how Hannah fit into this equation, or if she was in the back seat and I hadn't seen her yet.

The woman interjected. "Diane Greenfield. If you know my granddaughter, then I assume you're a friend of my daughter?"

Ah. So that was the connection. My brain sizzled and spat out the thought—*potential mother-in-law*. I quenched the thought and swallowed the nerves zapping through my system. Professional, I was a professional from the rental company. That was all.

"Yes, ma'am, I'm Blythe Fitzgerald. I work with Coastal Properties." I shook her outstretched hand. "Sorry about Larry. I should have already had him back in the car."

Five Months or Forever

Jordan had taken the cat out of my arms and immediately dropped to the concrete, where she could fully cradle his ample Maine Coon body in her lap.

"Nonsense. I adore cats. We had Abyssinians when Hannah was a child. I've always admired Maine Coons. Is it true they have doglike personalities?"

I looked at my new furry best friend. "Yep, seems like it."

She opened her trunk, and I bounded toward the car. "Here, let me get those." I grabbed the two large suitcases, not light packing for a long weekend, and walked ahead of her up the stairs. At the top, I opened the combination box to retrieve the key. "Ironically, I was looking to adopt a dog, but his write-up was hilarious. And they had him listed on the dog portion of their adoptable pets."

Hannah's mother smiled, and the dimples were the same as Hannah's. I could tell she was probably a bit of a tough customer, but I instantly liked her. I unlocked the door, pushed it open, and set her suitcases inside. "Why don't you take a look around and make sure it's to your liking. If there's anything we need to change, or anything you need, I can let them know right away at the office."

Jordan came up the stairs with Larry walking next to her on the leash. "It's so cool how he walks on a leash. I saw a really cute sweatshirt online that had a belly pouch where you could carry your cat. You need one of those, in case he gets tired."

I laughed at her exuberance. "Not sure a kangaroo hoodie is quite my style, but if it makes you feel better, I did get him a cat life vest for the boat."

"No way. I want to see that! I bet he'll love seeing the dolphins." She picked him up again, burying her face in his fur, then smooching the side of his face. He lived up to his hype, simply smiling and purring, even wrapping one paw around the side of Jordan's neck.

Diane reappeared. "Everything seems in order, however, could you please show Jordan how the heating and cooling system works? I'm a bit technologically challenged and this house is higher tech than one might expect at the beach. Here." She held out her hands to take Larry from Jordan. "I'll take him while you go look."

I walked to the kitchen, where the digital pad was installed. Behind me, I could hear Diane cooing to Larry. She couldn't be too high maintenance if she was willing to lug around a very furry cat while dressed to the nines.

Jordan stood next to me while I pointed out the various features on the thermostat. "Your grandmom seems nice," I said.

"She's awesome. She and Mom fight a lot, but we get along great. Did you really get him a life jacket?"

"I did. The people at the shelter gave me this book called *Adventure Cats* and said Larry was the perfect cat for an active lifestyle. I've already taken him out."

Jordan looked disappointed. "Oh."

"Don't worry, we didn't see dolphins yet. How long is your grandmother in town for?"

"Till Sunday."

We walked back out to the living room. "If you'd like, I'll take you guys out for a ride. With Larry, of course."

The door swung open and Hannah walked in.

We hadn't really spoken since the wedding dress day, but damn if all the buzzy feelings didn't come swarming in. My lonely heart obviously didn't care what my brain knew.

She stopped in her tracks and looked taken aback that I was there. "Blythe?"

"Yeah, hi. Ginny sent me to open the door. I didn't know it was your mom's rental."

Jordan grabbed Hannah by the hand. "Mom, come look! Blythe got a cat. His name is Larry, and he is seriously the coolest cat ever. He even rides on the boat and has a life jacket."

Hannah looked over her shoulder. I stood sheepishly near the door. Her expression was as confused as I felt.

Diane kissed her daughter's cheek. "Your friend has offered to take us out on the boat with this gorgeous feline specimen. I think that's something I'd like to see. A cat on a boat."

I edged toward the door. "We don't have to. I didn't mean to interfere with your family time."

"Mom, please. Can we?" Jordan steepled her fingertips and bounced on her toes. "I love going out on Blythe's boat."

Hannah faced me. "Are you sure?"

Was I sure? No. Being around Hannah was lighting up every part of me she'd lit up before. Hanging out with her and her daughter—and her mom—felt like more than friendship. But I wasn't going to say no.

"Absolutely. It would be my pleasure. Saturday? I've got work tomorrow."

Diane walked toward me with Larry. "Perfect. It's settled. Now, I will reluctantly return him to you." She held out her cat-filled arms.

I took Larry and hoisted him up over my shoulder, where he liked to ride. "Enjoy your stay. I'll see you on Saturday morning."

"With donuts?" Jordan bounced some more.

Hannah swatted her. "Jordan! Greedy."

"It would be my double pleasure."

I winked at Jordan, and when I caught Hannah's eye, I noticed her cheeks held the same bright flush from the last time I'd seen her. Maybe this wasn't a lost cause after all.

Chapter 15

HANNAH

Seeing Blythe knocked me off my mother game. I'd come up the stairs with my defense mechanisms locked and loaded, but now, after seeing the woman I had a massive yet unfortunate crush on, I felt vulnerable.

"She seems like a lovely person." Mom was pouring us large glasses of her favorite Kendall-Jackson Chardonnay, which we would both need as the night wore on.

"Yes. She's an architect. Right now she's on some type of hiatus and works with her sister at the rental agency."

"Blythe's cool." Jordan reached across the kitchen island for a handful of grapes. "Her new cat is amazing. When can I get a cat? You promised."

"We can't in the rental. Once we find a permanent place, I promise you."

"So, you're staying." Mom had *the* tone, and though I knew there was no getting out of a deep discussion about my 'mental health,' I really didn't want to do it in front of Jordan.

"At least until the end of Jordan's school year."

"Yeah." Jordan's hand stopped just shy of her mouth. "Four months, a little change, and we're out of here. Back to Asheville for something *more permanent*." She popped the grape in her mouth and watched me as she chewed, her eyes challenging me to say anything else on the subject.

I kept my face neutral, not letting my disappointment that the beach hadn't yet won her over show in my expression.

Thankfully, Mom turned her attention to Jordan and didn't press for details. "And your school?"

Jordan shrugged. "It's good enough. It's a charter school, so the kids are pretty motivated. But a lot of them have known each other a long time. I miss Tilda."

"Ah, yes. How is your best friend?"

As Jordan chattered about her life, I pulled out my phone and shot a quick text off to Blythe.

Are you sure you want to do this? I hate for you to give up your day for us.

She answered immediately.

I'm sure.

Well, I have to be honest. I'm really thankful. It will be nice to have someone around to keep Mom from using me as her scratching pad all weekend.

That bad, huh?

That bad. I hesitated a moment. ***Thanks, friend.***

I didn't want things to be weird between us. We'd left it that we would be friends but then she'd avoided me. And okay, fair enough, but I really did need friends. I loved my kid and my job, but I was human. I respected Blythe for knowing what she wanted, and I wouldn't step across that boundary again, but I liked her as a person. She was funny, kind, generous, and—from what I could tell—passionate and smart about her design career. Which might come in handy for my own career ideas. I needed to make her feel comfortable that we could hang out without it devolving into me trying to get laid.

Her response came in the form of a smiling selfie with Larry in her lap, her hand making him wave at me.

If we'd not discussed boundaries, I'd have answered with a simple **Nice pussy.** But I figured that'd be crossing a line, so I sent a smiling cat face instead.

"Something seems very interesting."

I flipped the phone over to find my mother looking at me over the top of her glass.

"Nothing like that, Mom."

She raised one eyebrow, but I changed the subject. "I picked up shrimp from the boat docks and stuff for salads. I can either boil it or sauté it in some garlic and butter. Do you have a preference?"

"Sautéed." Jordan hated salad for dinner, but I knew it was a regular thing for Mom. "And can we have pasta or something with it?"

I waited for the sniping comment from my mother about carbs and calories, but because Jordan had asked instead of me, she was silent on the matter.

"Sure," I answered. "I picked up some angel hair just in case."

In the kitchen, I put Jordan to work peeling carrots while I peeled shrimp. Mom sat at the island sipping her wine and began reminiscing about our old cats, Nepal and Everest. She was in a surprisingly peaceful frame of mind. I put a pot of water on to boil for the noodles. The night seemed almost normal. And I had to admit, being back in a regular-sized kitchen was nice. There was room to work.

After we ate, and Jordan had all she could take of adults, Mom and I decided to venture out to the hot tub.

"You look good." Even at sixty-eight, my mother could still rock a two-piece. She opted for a higher waistband to hold things in place, but the woman's boobs still sat up high—with a bit of surgical help, of course.

"And you look run-down."

I'd made the mistake of packing a faded one-piece Speedo that I used to wear for swimming laps at the YWCA, but I'd figured it didn't matter. Should have known better.

"Please don't start. I'm not that horrible."

"Of course you're not horrible. But you look haunted. Like there's something chasing you around behind your eyeballs and you can't get away from it. You're jumpy as a yard cat."

Though I wouldn't recommend drinking in a hot tub, when it came to hanging out with my mom, there was no way I was going out there without a glass of wine. I took a big sip.

"You're going to have to talk to me." Her eyes narrowed, and she looked at me over the top of her nose.

"Am I? Can my life not be my life?" I knew my tone was sharp and irritable, but at what point did I get to be grown-up and not have my mother grill me about my private life?

"When I'm dead, your life can be your life, but you'll still hear my voice in your head."

Guess I had my answer.

"I'm serious, darling. I would like to please know what is going on. Lisa was a fine woman. A bit standoffish, certainly, but decent. Is there something I'm missing? Some reason you pulled the plug on the big day?"

What should I tell her? That Lisa didn't want to be a parent, or that I'd chosen a partner without passion. I'd picked someone who ticked boxes but didn't light a fire in my soul. Certainly, the former was the easier excuse. Mom would be on my side. But it was more than that, wasn't it?

"You know how you and Dad knew the moment you laid eyes on each other that something was there?"

Her glaze clouded over with memory and a smile followed. "I sure do."

"I didn't have that with Lisa. And Lisa realized things

about our relationship that didn't work for her either. Things that hurt. That's why we called the wedding off."

Mom was quiet for a moment. Somewhere on the beach was the sound of a couple arguing and a dog barking.

Then, in a surprise move, she simply put her hand on mine.

It was almost worse than having her grill me about my private life.

Five Months or Forever

BLYTHE

Friday evening, after work, I went out and cleaned up the boat with Derrick and Isla, who helped keep an eye on Larry.

"Aunt B, can I put a hair clip in his hair?" Isla unsnapped a blue plastic clip with a butterfly from the end of one of her braids.

"Sure, but pay attention. If he seems irritated . . ."

"I know. You don't keep doing something to an animal if they don't like it. When Geepaw's horses put their ears back flat it means they're mad and you got to stop whatever it is you're doing to make 'em mad. Though some of them are just ornery."

"Well, Larry is not an ornery cat."

Isla already had the blue clip at the top of his head, and I couldn't stop myself from taking a picture of the two of them.

"How's y'all's horseback riding going?"

"I fell off Cherokee again." Derrick helped me scrub down the bow with sudsy water. "I don't think it's my thing. I'd rather play soccer. But Jordan was nice. She didn't laugh at me like Isla did."

Isla flipped the end of Larry's leash in a twirling circle. "Well, she should have. It was funny. You should have seen him, Aunt B. He was hanging under the horse, his feet still in the stirrups." Isla put a hand on her sassy little hip. "Amateur."

"Isla!" I scolded, even if it did sound pretty comical.

"What?" She held both hands out, dropping Larry's leash, but he didn't try to leave. "It's true. Me, though, I'm going to be a rodeo star. Geepaw said I could go with his riding club and ride in a parade." She picked up Larry's paw. "Would you like to go horseback riding, kitty?"

Derrick scoffed. "No way. Larry's like me. He'd rather dribble a soccer ball. Or maybe . . . captain a boat?" He looked at me hopefully.

"Sunday. Tomorrow I've promised to give Jordan and her family a tour. Then I have a night planned with some friends."

Part of me wanted to cancel the evening with Gia, her wife, and friend Jody. The plans were set, though, and it would be rude for me not to show, even if it were more of a house party than a blind date.

"Did you guys have fun with Jordan?" I figured if I was going to be spending the day on the boat with her, her grandmother, and Hannah, it'd give me something to talk about other than what her mom and I had almost been doing while she'd been cowgirling it up with my niblings.

"Yeah, she's cool. She's in a bunch of Tedrick's videos now." Derrick grabbed a rag and started drying the place he'd scrubbed to a white fiberglass shine.

"Oh yeah? Are they a thing?" This could be information to bring back to Hannah.

"No, BeeBee." Isla shook her head. "Tedrick likes a girl named Renee. But I think Jordan likes him or maybe she likes one of his friends. She didn't tell us because we're kids and she's in high school. But she looks sort of"—Isla stuck out her tongue and wagged her head, rolling her eyes in circles and panting—"like that in his videos."

I snort-laughed. What would my niece say about how I'd looked at Hannah?

"Okay, gang. Looks good. Can I buy you a pizza on the way home? Or do you want tacos?"

"Pizza!"

"Okay. Load up Larry and let's get going."

THE NEXT MORNING, I was true to my word.

"Let me have a dozen assorted, please." The kid working the donut truck handed me the bright red box, and I carried it carefully to Chester. On the short drive to the beach house, I had to hold Larry at bay as he mewed plaintively and tried to nudge the lip of the box to open it.

This felt like a next-level do-over. Nicer house. Add the mother. Know some of the backstory. But Hannah hadn't asked for this. She'd agreed to it after I'd made the offer. Plus, I hadn't known who I was meeting at the house. It was chance.

Or was it? Was it stupid to think that maybe there were bigger things at play here and I just had to be patient and wait them out?

Jordan grabbed Larry this time instead of the donuts. "Hey, Larry."

"Well, good morning to you too." I handed the cat over.

"Hey." Hannah smiled and took the box of donuts as Jordan disappeared with Larry. "I guess your donuts don't rate with her anymore."

She smelled fresh-out-of-the-shower clean, and her hair was still damp and slightly curled where it hung just over the top of her ears. I wanted to give her a hug hello—that's what friends did—but I hung back, knowing it would stir up a hornet's nest of feelings inside me.

I shrugged. "Even donuts can't compare to Larry."

Hannah placed the box on the kitchen island and turned toward me. My mind flashed to what she felt like pressed up against the wall in her hallway. Warm and soft with that honey-sweet hollow in the crook of her neck. The same electrical sizzle from that day scorched under my skin, despite the lack of skin-to-skin contact.

Jordan broke the wild energy hanging between us as she scolded the cat. "No, Larry."

She held a cereal-covered donut away from him. Then she glanced up, her mouth full. "Don't worry. I can handle both."

"Ugh. My child has no manners. I'm glad Lala's not out here yet to see that mouthful of gross." She turned back to me, and fortunately, my lustful thoughts had receded. "Can I get you a cup of coffee?"

"Sure, a splash of cream if you have it."

We sat at the kitchen island. I grabbed an apple cinnamon donut. Hannah passed.

"No donut?" I asked.

"If my mother comes out here and sees me eating one, I'll never hear the end of it."

"She's one of those, huh?"

"You can't tell by looking at her?"

I wrapped my hands around the coffee mug, repeating the words Hannah said to me on New Year's Eve. "I generally don't make assumptions based on appearance."

Hannah dropped her head onto the granite. "Oh, please. Someone here needs to be on my side."

This made me laugh and feel good at the same time. "Okay, if we're assuming a personality purely based on her car, clothing, and general coiffed appearance, then yes."

She put her hand on my forearm. "Thanks."

Traitorous goose bumps raised the fine hairs on my arm, and I hoped she didn't notice as she pulled her hand away.

She sat back. "You've never mentioned your parents."

"Dad's at a retirement village outside of Orlando. Busy golfing and flirting with available women. He comes up for big holidays. We go there a few times a year. Our mom passed away when Ginny and I were in our twenties. Freak car accident."

"Oh, I'm so sorry."

I took another sip. "Don't be. Ginny and I have learned how to live with it, even though we still miss her. It is part of why I moved here though. I want to be near my sister and her kids."

"That makes sense. If I had a sibling, I'd want to do the same."

"Are you still complaining about being an only child?" At some point Diane had entered the room. She wore tan corduroy slacks, a navy pullover sweater with tan accents at the cuff and collars, and a pair of Sperry boat shoes. Her hair was pulled back with a Hermès scarf.

"Well, don't you look elegant? My boat is not going to know how to react to such a finely dressed passenger."

I'd laid the suave cheese so thick, Jordan almost choked on her bite of donut.

But Hannah's mom lapped it up. She blushed just like Hannah, and her dimples deepened as a shy smile spread in response to my compliment. "You're a charmer, aren't you, Blythe?"

"No, ma'am. Just say the truth when I see it. May I take you for a boat ride?" I held out my arm, and Diane linked it with hers. When I glanced back to make sure Jordan and Hannah were following with the cat, I winked at Hannah.

I wondered.

Would I ever get the chance to make her blush again?

Chapter 16

HANNAH

Blythe had my mother so thoroughly charmed, she'd forgotten all about harassing me. Even Jordan left any bit of teenage snarl behind at the beach house. All I had to do was sit back, let the breeze lift my hair, and feel the sun kiss my face.

Kiss.

I wanted to kiss Blythe again.

Why couldn't I date? Was there some sort of statute of limitations about how and when you could move from almost marriage to the next thing? I had a colleague whose husband left her on a Sunday and she'd met another guy the following weekend. They were engaged now and seemed blissfully happy. There'd been no magical line in the sand. I understood Blythe wasn't into one-off sexual encounters, but that didn't mean she wouldn't be open to a monogamous dating situation. Besides, who went into dating 100 percent sure that the person was the one and forever. Blythe had to understand I'd be protective of Jordan and of my mama bear heart. Maybe if I could convince

Blythe that I wasn't strictly about the physical, she'd give me another chance. My brain circled back. What if you did know when you first met someone? Was that why I couldn't get her off my mind?

Jordan derailed my train of thought. "This is awesome." She plopped down next to me. "This is almost as good as hiking or skiing."

"You're having a change of heart?" I didn't catch the excitement in time to hide it from her.

She stiffened. "No. Just because I don't hate everything doesn't mean I want to move here for good. You promised, remember?"

I sighed into the wind. "I remember."

There was never a minute when I regretted becoming a parent. But it did complicate things that were easy for women who'd remained childless. Like dating when you weren't ready to bring your kid into it. Or keeping promises that didn't seem so great anymore.

Blythe slowed the boat when we got to a less populated area. "We'll probably see a pod of dolphins soon. They like these shallows for fishing. Keep an eye out."

Larry was sitting with my mother on the bow, his fur sticking out from beneath his life vest. He was really cute. And my mother, effortlessly chic as always, looked as excited as the cat.

"You see anything, Mom?"

"Not a thing." Then out of the blue, she turned to Blythe. "You do know my daughter just left a woman practically standing at the altar?"

"Jesus, Mom."

"What?" Mom's eyes grew round with innocence. "I wouldn't want this nice woman getting the wrong idea."

Blythe cleared her throat and shot me a look that I wanted

to kiss her for. It seemed to say, "Holy shit, if this woman were my mother, I'd want to throttle her." "Um, I don't have the wrong idea, ma'am. Hannah and I are just friends."

"Yeah, Lala." Jordan did a rapid look between her grandmother and us. "Mom was totally crying over her wedding dress the other night. She's still sad about Lisa."

That was a detail I would have preferred to keep to myself.

"Oh yeah? When was that?" Blythe's voice was weighted with concern.

I mumbled, "A few weeks ago." I couldn't look at her, knowing she was going to draw the line of connection between my tears and her leaving my apartment. "But I'm better now. Every day, I'm more certain it was the best thing that could have happened. Yes, I'm sad I didn't get to wear my beautiful dress, but no, I'm not sad we called off the wedding." I looked at my mother and spoke loudly enough that Blythe wouldn't miss it. "Lisa was not the right person."

My mother rolled her eyes. "Well if a woman like Lisa wasn't good enough for you, I doubt there ever will be one. You're too much like me. Picky and a perfectionist."

If I could have jumped off the boat and joined Ursula under the sea, I would have. My mother putting me in the same handbag with her was too much. I was not like my mother. I wasn't picky and I wasn't a perfectionist. If anything, I was a dreamer and my dream simply hadn't come along. I needed a partner who didn't make me have to fight for every single inch.

"Dolphins!" Jordan jumped up and pointed off to the left.

Sure enough, four or five fins arced up through the water. As my mom and daughter took turns with the binoculars Blythe brought, I whispered to her, "That was rough."

"Are you okay?" Blythe leaned into the captain's chair with her arms crossed against her chest. She was guarded. Thanks, Mom.

"I could use a drink. Is it bad to abandon my mother when she's only here for the weekend? Do you think you could concoct an excuse for me to get out of the house for a few hours? I need a breather from her criticism."

Blythe wore her thoughts on her face and something flitted across it.

"Oh." I tried to read whatever was going on behind her crinkled brow. "I swear, as friends only. Just a quick beer and a glass of wine. My treat. We could invite Ginny, too, if that would make a difference?"

"Actually, I, um . . ." Blythe looked at her feet, then looked up again. "I have plans."

Her blue eyes looked straight at me, and it felt kind of like a challenge and kind of like an apology, and then I got it.

"Oh . . . you have a date."

She swung her leg against the metal pole of her seat. "Not that formal. Just going to hang out with some old friends. And some new."

"Right. Yeah, of course. Why wouldn't you have plans? I'm sorry I brought it up."

She shrugged. "I would have said yes to the drink if that helps."

"If you didn't have something else." My brain said the words, but my gut reached up its hands to tangle with my emotions, and I made it sound too intense.

"Yes." Blythe was firm.

Awkwardness hung between us now, and I was mad at myself for creating it. Blythe wasn't here to be my savior. And I should be able to handle my mother on my own without running away.

Jordan pulled me by the back of my jacket.

"Mom, come look."

"Right." I smiled at Blythe and gave a little nod before turning away. It didn't stop the slow seep of disappointment.

She had all the hallmarks of an excellent friend.
Only I wasn't sure I wanted Blythe to fill that particular role.

BLYTHE

I'd planned to show Hannah and her family my possible piece of property, but our conversation left me flustered. My evening plans were not what I truly wanted to happen. When given the option of some random new woman or Hannah of the excellent kisses, to be ready for a relationship, the choice was simple.

It was obvious though, from the things her mother and Jordan had said, that she was still ages away from being ready for a relationship. I knew we'd established that, but the drink invitation threw me off my sturdy platform of understanding. Besides, Diane and Hannah's escalating bickering seemed too personal to include me.

I piloted the boat in the direction of the marina.

Diane pressed Hannah for explanations. "Why did you move here? Into that tiny apartment? Why not move home to Birmingham? There's a growing LGBTQ community. Or so I've heard."

"Mother. You could not pay me to move back to Alabama."

"Or me." Jordan shuddered. "I would die if I had to switch schools again."

"See?" Hannah brushed her hair back out of her eyes. "Jordan likes it here."

"Or back in Asheville, where we had friends."

"Exactly. Your daughter's right. You don't know anyone here." Diane looked at me. "Present company excluded, of course."

"No problem." I rolled the boat's wheel in my hands and tried to stay out of their family dynamic.

Hannah balled her fists by her side. "I know every painter who works on these islands. I know my boss. I know Blythe's sister and family. That's a good thirty people right there. Who needs more than thirty people in their lives?"

Diane adjusted her sunglasses in annoyance. "You know what I mean. You're hiding out while Lisa goes on with her glamorous life in that beautiful apartment you designed. And you've dragged my granddaughter away from her happy place."

Hannah put her hand to her heart. "Ah, for a second I thought you cared about me, as well as Jordan."

I worked hard not to laugh. They were definitely dramatic.

"You exasperate me." Diane crossed her arms and pivoted away from her daughter to look at the passing boats.

Off-kilter inspiration struck. It was a generous plan at best and a self-sabotaging one at worst. I slowed the motor as we cruised into the no-wake zone and turned to Hannah's mom. "You know, I'm going to a small gathering this evening with some very lovely professional women. I didn't invite Hannah because I knew you were visiting, but, if you want her to meet some non-painters, this might be a great opportunity. Though I'm sure you three have big plans."

Hannah's mouth dropped, which, I had to admit, was very much the reaction I was hoping for.

Jordan piped in excitedly. "Lala, we could binge-watch *Keeping Up With the Kardashians* or that Hollywood real estate show Mom hates."

Diane patted Jordan's knee. "You and me, huh? And we'll be rid of old grumpy pants?"

Hannah found her voice. "I am not old grumpy pants. But I would love to be rid of your deep examination of my flaws for a couple of hours."

"One day I'll be gone and you'll thank me for pointing out all the ways you became a better human because of me." Then Diane looked at me. "That's a lovely gesture. Please get her out of our hair for a few hours."

I turned the boat away from the marina, back out into open water, and roared the motor for one last loop. I knew if I spoke, my sheer excitement would unfurl like the massive advertising banners the planes pulled up and down the beach in the summer. But there was no way I could tamp down my grin.

THAT NIGHT, around seven, I picked up Hannah. I texted her from the car, telling her I was waiting. I didn't want Diane to see me with my casual linen oxford tucked into well-worn jeans, my black alligator belt, and a pair of black loafers on my feet. My hair was clean and slicked back with a soft-touch gel, and I'd put just the tiniest touch of cologne at the edges of my collarbone. Diane would take one look at me and her mother instincts would be ringing across six counties.

When I'd texted Gia, I'd said only that Hannah was a client of Ginny's, also a lesbian, and was new in town. Could I bring her to meet everyone? When Gia texted back with question marks, I'd simply answered, **She's a friend.** I wasn't closing myself off to any opportunity.

Hannah appeared at the bottom of the stairs, and that same swirl of excitement I kept trying to extinguish burbled up. She wore a mock turtleneck dress that clung perfectly to her gorgeous body, paired with knee-high brown boots. The few inches of skin between the bottom of her dress and the top of her boots gave my imagination a running start as I watched her walk to the car.

"Hey." She slid into the passenger seat. "You're crazy, you know that?"

I shrugged. "What? We're friends. You're new in town. I'm sure you want to meet some other queer women."

"But I got the feeling you were being set up." She paused and looked at me. "You clean up hot, by the way. She's lucky."

I felt the flush work its way up my face. "Thanks." I glanced at the smooth line of skin just above her knee and wedged my hand under my leg so I didn't do something stupid. "You clean up pretty nice too."

She turned to grab her seat belt but not before I saw the pleased smile on her face. "So," she asked, "where are we headed?"

"Gia and Sarah's house. Gia is the bartender at the Slippery Pearl, and her wife, Sarah, is a neonatal nurse. Not sure who else will be there, but it sounded like a group of about ten or so."

"Do you mind running me by my apartment so I can grab a bottle of wine? I hate to show up empty-handed."

"You don't have to. They'll have plenty."

Hannah tsked. "Blythe, Blythe, Blythe. I am a Southern woman. I cannot show up empty-handed to a stranger's house."

I laughed and pointed Chester in the opposite direction. "Yes, ma'am. And I have learned never to stand in the way of a Southern woman."

I pulled into her driveway, and Hannah unbuckled to get out. "Do you want to come in and see the paint job?"

My breath stilled and some emotion must have flitted across my face, because Hannah sighed. "I swear, only to see the paint job. It looks great and you did do a fair amount of the work."

Yeah, before we almost slept together, I thought.

But I got out of the car and followed her inside.

"Go on back and look at Jordan's room while I grab the wine."

I walked down the hall and peeked my head in. They'd finished up the room, and it looked bright and fresh and clean. Jordan had a new set of bedding, and there was a compact desk and coordinating chair in the corner covered with schoolbooks.

As I walked back up the short hallway, I paused at Hannah's door. The infamous dress was gone.

She appeared at my side, the bottle of wine in her hand. "It was pretty though, wasn't it?"

Apparently she'd figured out why I stopped for a look. I knew I should express some sort of sympathy or recognition, but I was having a hard time thinking with her standing so near. I wanted to reach out, wrap my hand around her waist, and pull her in snug next to my side in an expression of caring. But if I touched her, I was going to turn to face her. And if I turned to face her, I was going to kiss her. And if I kissed her, my hands were going to find that sliver of skin below the hem of her dress and work their way slowly and gently upward, and . . .

She cleared her throat. "Right, well, that's that. We should go."

"Yep, right. Go." I backed carefully out of the doorframe so I didn't bump even an elbow against her. I took one backward glance and realized I hadn't answered her. It had been gorgeous. But only because I knew she'd look devastating in it.

Chapter 17

HANNAH

An electric air bounced between the driver's and passenger's seats. The chemistry between us hadn't disappeared. If I wasn't trying to be on my best behavior, the moment in the apartment might have turned into a chance for something more.

Instead, we were driving toward Charleston so Blythe could meet another woman. Someone who'd been deemed more appropriate or more available. Probably one who didn't have a child and recent baggage. But that's what true friends were for, right? To know where they stood and support each other in finding their best life? I didn't want to be her wing woman, but here I was. Might as well embrace the role.

"I'm—" looking forward to meeting your friends, is what I was going to say, but Blythe spoke at the same time.

"I didn't answer you back there. Your dress was beautiful."

"Right dress, wrong woman." I clutched the bottle of red. At the rate I was going, this once-in-a-lifetime case of wine was going to be gone before the month was out. "I donated it to the hospice thrift shop."

"Wow. That's a generous donation." Blythe paused. "Marriage is out for you?" She looked straight ahead, eyes on the road, as she waited for my response.

"Gosh. That's a big question."

"Oh, I—sorry, you don't have to answer."

"It's okay. Of course, I want the fairy tale. I want to meet the person who's going to love me with all my flaws and love Jordan with all of hers. I'd like to have a true partnership. Does it have to be marriage in the legal sense of the word? No, I guess not. Not all women would want to take on two people in such a binding way. But I guess if I'm being totally honest, then yes. I would want that. But I figure for now, Jordan and I will keep chugging along like we always have. The last thing I want is to get three years into something only to find out the other person has only been tolerating my daughter. What about you? Have you ever been close to marriage?"

Blythe turned on her blinker, and we drove into an older neighborhood with rows of pastel-painted bungalows surrounded by mature oak trees. She cleared her throat. "It wasn't federally legal until near the end of my relationship with Constance. By that point, I'd already figured we were a ticking time bomb. There's been no one since then who I've felt serious enough about. But yeah, I grew up with Disney too. Figure one day I'll find my Cinderella."

My imagination's vision of Blythe in a perfectly fitted tux standing at the end of a flower-strewn aisle was too perfect. I let the image linger.

She parallel parked in front of a pale green house with a large covered front porch.

I flipped down the visor, tucked a stray hair behind my ear, and fluffed my bangs. When I pushed the visor back in place, I smiled and turned to Blythe. "Well, Princess Charming, let's go see if we can find your true love." I wanted to scream, "It's me. I'm Cinderella. Right here. Beside you."

Blythe led the way up the uneven red brick walkway. She tapped on the door, and a dark-haired woman with beautiful watercolor-style tattoos running up both arms welcomed us. "Hey, Blythe." She gave Blythe a hug. "You're looking well." Then she checked me out. "And you must be . . ."

"Hannah." I extended a hand, but she bypassed and came in fast for a hug. "Oh, okay, so we're doing this." There was no easy way out, so I gave in, accepting the circle of her arms.

She pushed back but kept her hands on my shoulders. "I'm Sarah. We're so glad you could come. Welcome to the Low Country. Where'd you move from?"

"The Asheville area."

"Gorgeous." She released me, then put an arm on my waist to guide me into the house behind Blythe. "Mountains versus beach is a proverbial question, isn't it?"

"Yes, exactly." The shock of her full contact hug wore off. Sarah's warmth was genuine, as was the laughter echoing out from the end of the hallway. In the kitchen, she showed me where to put the bottle of wine, then led me away from Blythe into the den, which opened to a large screened back deck. Women, and a couple of guys, milled in and out. Someone called her name. She put her hand on my shoulder. "Oh, sorry, honey. Will you be okay for a minute?"

"Sure."

Sarah excused herself with a smile. I looked around to see where Blythe had gone.

Across the den, Blythe was being introduced to a woman. An attractive woman with close-cropped curls, envy-inspiring skin, and an incredibly curvaceous body.

Bubbles of jealousy fizzed in my veins. I shook my arms to make them go away, but it wasn't much help.

The woman's smile spoke volumes as she looked up from the ottoman where she sat. There was no doubt she found Blythe every bit as attractive as I did if the way she crossed her ankles and shifted her hips ever so slightly meant anything.

The woman introducing them saw me watching, left them talking, and came over. "Hannah, is it? I'm Gia, Sarah's wife. Come on, let me get you a drink and introduce you to some folks." She led me away toward the deck. When I looked back, the woman had patted the edge of the ottoman next to her, and Blythe sat down. Blythe glanced up, caught me looking at her, and winked.

My mind tumbled into confusion. What the hell kind of wink was that? Was that a "Hey, wing girl, look at this fine peach" wink or a "Don't worry, I felt our chemistry too" wink? Or had there even been a wink at all? Maybe my mind was playing tricks on me.

"Here you go." Gia handed me the glass of wine I'd requested, then introduced me to her next-door neighbors, Walter and his husband, Alexander.

We made the obligatory small talk about the weather—cool and thank goodness for these deck heaters—to where I was from—oh have you been to the Grove Park Inn?—to work.

"Williamsons? That little mom-and-pop paint store out near Folly?" Walter asked.

"Yes. That's the one."

Alexander reacted. "I adore that store. When Zachary was there, we went in all the time for projects I was working on. He had an immaculate eye for color."

Walter laughed. "Alexander really liked his immaculate ass."

I laughed, but my interest piqued. "What do you do?"

"I'm an interior designer. Walter makes large custom mirrors."

"You should come back sometime. I'm the new color person. My ass may not be quite as immaculate, but I'd love to help out if I can."

Alexander leaned around so he could get a peek. "Girl, that ass is divine. And you are in the right place to find someone, besides us, to admire it. Are you married? Partnered? You are gay, aren't you?"

"Yes to the latter, nope to the former two." I shrugged. "But I am the mom of a teenager and newly out of a relationship."

"That's never stopped any lesbian I've ever known." Alexander looked around. "Let's see. Nope. Nope. They're all with someone. What about her?" He pointed out an athletically built woman with short dreads in an animated conversation with Gia and another woman at the end of the deck.

"She looks sporty and I am decidedly not."

"Doesn't mean she's not good in the sack."

"Alexander." Walter shook his head. "You have literally known this lovely woman for all of five minutes and you're already getting her into bed with someone?"

"Sounds like I'm interrupting something."

Blythe appeared at my shoulder.

"Ohhhhh. Now this could work," Alexander whispered.

Little did he know.

BLYTHE

"I see you've met the neighbors." I smiled at Hannah and tried to gauge her frame of mind. Was she okay? Should I have brought her? The way she held herself close made me think I'd made a mistake, but I couldn't ask her. I turned to the guys. "How you doing? We met once before."

"The architect." Walter shook my hand. "And you two know each other?"

"We sure do. Hannah is my new neighbor. Sort of. I figured it'd be good to introduce her around. And I'm glad she met you. She's changing over from an education career to a design career."

Alexander put his hand on his hip. "You are five minutes late on that conversation. We know her whole life story. More important, have you seen her divine ass? Why would you introduce her around? If I recall, you were single and ready to mingle the last time we hung out." He grabbed Hannah's shoulders and turned her toward me, then did an up-and-down gesture with his hand as if he were showing her off. "Right here. This one."

I didn't waste the opportunity to ogle her perfectly formed derriere.

Walter took the rocks glass out of Alexander's hand. "Baby, you've gone one bourbon too far with that. I think we need to get you some water."

Hannah dropped her forehead into her hand, but her shoulders were shaking with laughter.

"I can't disagree with you there. She's definitely beautiful," I said.

"Well then, I don't understand." Alexander wouldn't let it die.

Hannah cleared her throat. "I'm just out of an engagement and not really clear about my future."

"Well, get clear, queer. Look at this one." He put an arm over my shoulders and planted me in front of Hannah, using the same gesture to show me off. "Those eyes. Those amazing shoes." He pulled back. "Where did you get those shoes, by the way?"

I waggled my foot. "These old things? Remember that designer discount place off Elm Street?"

Alexander threw his hands in the air. "Yes, child. The bargains they had."

With the subject changed, I took a deep breath. Jody was waiting for me to return with a glass of wine, and though she was very attractive, our ten minutes of conversation revealed that she didn't like the beach, hated boats, and was allergic to cats. We were definitely not a match, but I didn't want to be rude after Gia had worked so hard to make this meeting happen. I grabbed a beer and refilled Jody's wineglass.

Walter and Alexander had moved a few steps away to have a low-toned argument about the amount of liquor Alexander had ingested. Hannah stood with her hands clasping her drink. She reminded me of a middle school girl at her first dance, sort of forlorn and uncomfortable in her own skin as she waited for something to happen. "Are you okay?" I hesitated before going inside.

Hannah nodded. "Sure. You go. It's nice to be away from my mom for a couple of hours."

"You should come in and meet Jody. You have things in common."

"That seems awkward."

"No, of course not. Come on." I tilted my head in the direction of indoors. "Besides, you look like you're freezing out here. I promise, it's fine." Part of me wanted to tell her that she had no competition from Jody, that I was still very much crushing on her. But there was another part that wasn't above using a smidge of unnecessary jealousy to further my cause. Lord knows it sure worked on me.

"It is getting chilly. Let me refill my glass, then I'll be right there."

Inside, Jody stood and took her drink from me. When Hannah came in, I introduced them. "Jody, this is my neighbor, Hannah. She and her daughter just moved to the area from Asheville. I thought she might like to meet some other women in the area."

Jody looked between us, obviously trying to get a handle on the situation. "You two came together?"

Hannah sputtered. "Oh, no, nothing like that. We're just friends."

Jody looked at me over her wineglass, then at Hannah. "Okay."

From across the room, Gia called, "Blythe! Over here."

"If you two would excuse me for a second." I was glad for the distraction because I wasn't sure what else I had to say to Jody.

"What's going on over there?" Gia leaned against her kitchen island and watched Hannah and Jody strike up a conversation. They'd obviously found something in common, because they were both smiling and laughing, and Jody had even reached out and put her hand on Hannah's forearm.

Then let it stay there as they talked.

"A backfire" is what I wanted to say. Obviously, Alexander was right. I was a dumbass. I brought a beautiful, single lesbian who, though maybe not certain about any sort of real relationship, seemed more than certain about flirting and putting herself out there.

"Jody is a nonstarter."

"Geez, woman. What's the reason this time?"

"She's allergic to cats. I just adopted an awesome cat."

"Yes to one kitty, no to the other."

I laughed. "Something like that."

We hung out in silence for a second, both of us watching the interaction between Hannah and Jody, which now involved Jody moving her hand from Hannah's forearm up to her bicep and leaning in to say something to which Hannah threw back her head, exposing that gorgeous skin on her throat as she laughed out loud.

"And her?" Gia asked, referring to Hannah.

Jody pulled out her phone and typed. Then Hannah pulled out her own phone when a text came through and nodded before typing in something. Great. Now they were texting each other. I hadn't even gotten Jody's number.

"Obviously, just friends."

Gia cocked her head and raised one eyebrow. "You sure about that?"

That was the question of the night. Because no, I wasn't sure about that. Why couldn't I just hang out and have some fun with Hannah? We could do it in a way that Jordan didn't have to know, if that was a concern for Hannah. My heart had been battered and bruised enough times that I would know how to handle it when Hannah inevitably realized she'd moved from one thing to another too quickly and cut me free.

"She's cute, isn't she?"

"Ah. So you do like her. What's the catch? She allergic to cats too?"

"It's complicated."

Gia waved as a couple walked to the door, saying goodbyes. She turned back to me. "The complicated ones are usually worth it. But I wouldn't wait around if you're thinking about it." She nodded over to where a couple of other women had joined Jody and Hannah in their conversation. "The sharks are circling."

I drained my beer but stayed put, even as Gia moved away to join some other guests.

Now who was the wallflower stuck at the dance?

Chapter 18

HANNAH

I could feel Blythe's eyes on me as I talked to Jody. Maybe that's why, when Jody put her hand on me, I didn't move my arm away. Let Blythe think I was making a play. Let her think this was more than two women who realized they had a really good childhood friend in common. It turned out Jody had briefly dated my first high school girlfriend and had even lived in Birmingham for a couple of years. We'd made plans to have lunch one day so she could show me and Jordan around downtown Charleston, but that was as far as it would ever go.

When a couple of other women came over, including the sporty woman from the patio who was obviously interested in Jody, I excused myself.

"She's really awesome." I leaned next to Blythe. "I can see why your friends wanted you to meet her."

Blythe grumbled. "She's allergic to cats."

"You seem pretty upset about that."

"Are you ready to go? I'm ready to get out of here." She set her beer bottle down and turned away from me.

Oh my goodness. Blythe was acting jealous. And she was a total baby when her feelings were hurt.

"Aren't you going to say goodbye to our hosts?"

Blythe turned around and caught Gia's eye and waved. "There. Goodbyes said. You're welcome to stay. I'm happy to get you an Uber."

"You're being kind of silly." I followed her through the door as she stomped toward the car. "Blythe." I grabbed her arm. "Would you stop and look at me?"

She stopped but kept her eyes to the ground. I reached out and lifted her chin with my forefinger. She glared in return.

"You are being a brat. Are you jealous that Jody and I hit it off?"

She looked away from me.

"Oh my gosh. You are." I held her out so I could look in her eyes. "Blythe, stop. She's not my type either. We had a friend in common, that's all."

Finally, Blythe met my gaze. "You're not going out with her? I saw you exchange texts."

"I am going to lunch with her. But it's not a date."

"Oh right, another 'just friends.'"

"Yes. Except with Jody, I want it to stay just friends."

She inhaled. "Versus?"

I took a step closer. "Not staying just friends."

"What are you saying?"

"I'm saying I respect whatever it is that you want and need. Which means I'm happy to be your friend." I paused. I don't know if it was the wine or the realization that I'd both gotten jealous and was happy about Blythe getting jealous—something Lisa had never done—but I went ahead and spit out what I'd been thinking all night. "The truth is, I really want to be more than just friends." What I didn't spit out was the promise I'd made to Jordan.

Blythe swallowed. "You do?"

I took another half step closer. "I do. And my brain is seriously trying to convince me it's ready for another relationship."

"It is?"

"It is." This would be the moment to tell her I might be moving back, but anything could happen in the interim, right? We might find out we weren't a fit. She might change her mind about me. It might be nothing but hormones.

We stood for a few seconds, our breath hanging in the cool night air.

Blythe did the hair thing. "Now what?"

"Well, we could stand here, freezing on this sidewalk all night trying to figure it out, or we could go back. Your house is empty and so is mine. Or you could take me back to the beach house and drop me off. Why don't you surprise me?" I walked toward the passenger door of her car. Blythe was obviously caught in the crosshairs of her own feelings, but we were never going to get anywhere at the rate she was moving.

"Right, right." I heard her footsteps behind me, and then she unlocked my door. I didn't look at her or hesitate, just slid into the car and buckled my seat belt waiting to see what happened next. When we turned left before crossing the bridge to Folly, I figured out her decision. We were going to her place. I felt frothy again, but this time with anticipation.

She pulled under a tall condominium unit.

"It's not much. But it's home." She clicked three times before managing to unhook her seat belt.

We walked up the stairs to her corner unit. From the deck, you could see the twinkle of house lights on Folly across the dark marsh. She fidgeted to get her key into the door.

I took a deep breath. We were doing this. Doing something anyway.

Inside, Blythe flipped on the lights and Larry meowed a welcome from his perch in the window.

"Wow." Blythe's furniture ran toward modern and architectural, and her house was immaculately clean, which, to be honest, wasn't what I was expecting based on her car. "This is gorgeous."

"Thanks. Can I get you another glass of wine? Or something else?"

"Water. How about a glass of water?"

"I can do that."

She stepped into the kitchen, and I stepped over to the perch affixed to the window. Larry rolled over so I would pet his belly, and his loud purr made me smile. "He seems at home here."

"I've gotten very attached to him. He's the first cat I've ever had, if you can believe that."

"You picked a good one."

She returned and handed me the glass.

I took a big sip. "So . . ."

"I'm legitimately scared, Hannah." Blythe shoved her hands in her pockets.

"That's real." I set the glass down.

Blythe paced between her seating area and her dining table.

"Hey." I walked to her and grabbed her arm. "Shhhh. Nothing has to happen here. We're talking, right? Friends, right?"

"But you said . . ."

"I know what I said. I meant what I said. But my reality hasn't changed. I can't change it. I'm still newly out of a long-term relationship. And I'm still a mom with a daughter who comes first. You can walk me right back out the door and take me home."

"Fuck."

I wasn't sure how to respond, because the word sounded as

much like desire as a curse, and come to think of it, I rarely heard Blythe curse.

"Well, I mean, if you want." Joking might ease the tension.

Blythe laughed. "Can you stop being so damn cute for a minute while I sort this shit out in my head?"

"Did you say sort this shit out in your bed?"

"You're incorrigible." But she pulled her hands out of her pockets and laced her fingers into mine.

I looked directly into the turquoise swim of her eyes and spoke my truth. "I can't promise you anything right now in terms of what this is. That wouldn't be fair to either of us. But I can promise you complete transparency with my feelings. Right now, I'm feeling like this chemistry is real. I'm feeling like you're an amazing human being who I want to get to know better. And while I'm happy to do that as your friend, we're going to keep bumping up against this tension. What would be the harm in seeing where it takes us?"

"What about Jordan?" Her hand moved to my waist, the touch raising chills on my skin. It was a concession on her part, a step closer to taking us somewhere.

"Jordan is the child. I'm the adult. She doesn't need to know anything until there's something she needs to know."

"And that will be okay?"

"It will be fine. Though she is always my focus, sometimes I need to focus on me, the best me, the things I want that are going to make me shine."

Blythe leaned in and pressed her lips to the side of my neck. "Is this one of the things that will make you shine?"

I arched toward her, a month's worth of want exploding on the surface of my skin. "Yes." The word was a rush, a whisper, laced with desire.

"Don't break my heart, Hannah." Blythe's voice reverberated on my skin as she moved her lips along the edge of my jaw toward my mouth.

She didn't let me answer though. In one swift move, she pulled my dress up and off, leaving me standing in the middle of her living room in nothing but lingerie and knee-high boots.

BLYTHE

Hannah was going to destroy me. I could feel it. But I'd been dreaming about taking that dress off from the moment I saw her in it.

"You. Are. Magnificent."

Hannah's black bra edged with lace and her black lacey boy shorts did her every sort of favor. They showed off strong thighs, an ample ass, and skin that begged to be touched. The boots were like the bow on a package made just for me.

I took her in my arms, spreading my fingers out against the warmth of her back and pulled her close. It was a melting. A closing of the gap. Inevitable.

My mouth met hers and our lips collided. It took a moment to shift from fury to finesse, but soon we were kissing in a way that pointed toward one inevitable conclusion and all I could think was, *finally*. We were a tangle of lips, tongues, breath, and I wanted to inhabit her.

"I'm not so scary," she whispered.

"No." I pressed my face to the side of her neck and breathed her in. She was right. She wasn't scary. But closeness was. I was—if only to myself. I wanted to race to the finish line. Bed her, then wed her. How could I have all of this without scaring her away? What did she want?

Hannah answered by reaching behind her back and unbuckling the clasp of her bra.

She let go of me long enough to let it fall to the ground. When she took my hands, and placed them upon her gorgeous breasts, I almost forgot what to do. Thank the stars above for lesbian auto-pilot. Soon she was practically crawling up me, one booted leg wrapped around the back of mine, her hand pulling the back of my head into our kiss, her body arching into me.

"Take me to bed." She nipped at my lower lip and smiled.

Part of me didn't want to move. I wanted to freeze this moment. Pretend this was the beginning of all my tomorrows even though, somewhere deep in the shadowy folds of my mind, a scared voice was whispering concerns. But I couldn't let the lady down.

"Yes, ma'am."

I walked her backward, careful not to let her stumble over fallen clothes, toward my bedroom. Once there, I settled her onto the comforter and cradled each leg as I carefully unzipped her boots.

"Are you still scared?" She propped on her elbows.

"Terrified." But it didn't stop me from crawling onto the bed, straddling her, and pulling off my own top. I leaned forward, scooping my body so that we met, all soft curves and secrets. The exquisite feeling of skin on skin made me shudder.

Hannah grabbed my hand and whispered, "Don't be scared," as she guided it down her body.

This wasn't what I was afraid of. This is what I'd been dreaming of since she'd kissed me that day in the parking lot. Hell, maybe even from the moment I'd first laid eyes on her.

Never had I been happier to love women. Hannah, the way she moved, felt, tasted, was tailor-made for me. I hoped she'd realize the same.

"Blythe."

My name on her lips was like the wind picking up shimmers of stardust over the rising tide. I followed its current along her body, lingering in spots to memorize each eddy, each dance of moonlight. I found places that made her cry out and fill her hands with my hair, my skin, my want.

My own arousal throbbed as we melted into each other, crying out, stilling, our breath hitching and calming until we found our way back to fire and fury.

Hannah's heat and sweet saltiness cast a spell upon me. I became a part of her. I didn't know where Hannah began and

I ended. My body shuddered against the sheets as she surrendered, as I surrendered, both of us giving in to the release, the pleasure, the joy.

I opened my eyes and looked up the length of her body. Her head was thrown back and she was so free, so open, so willing. She looked satisfied, but I didn't want to let her go, not yet.

"Again?" I whispered.

She didn't open her eyes, but a little smile played on her lips and her fingertips danced across my hair in invitation as she opened her legs wider and hummed something that sounded like an affirmation.

I took my time, alternating touch and speed as she gathered beneath me. When her hands grew tight again on my shoulders, I abandoned finesse and soared with her, my own body pressing upward in stroke after stroke after stroke.

Hannah's body convulsed.

She exploded against me, the vibrations stronger than her earlier climaxes. I worked to memorize every pulse, every flutter, every breath until her body stilled.

Eventually we pulled apart and I crawled to join her on the pillows. She wrapped me in a tight hug, kissed me, then fell back. "That was incredible. Wow." She laid her arms out to her side. "You're amazing."

I let my fingers flow in circles over her skin. "That honor goes to you. You didn't even have to touch me to take me over the edge."

She flipped onto her side and pushed me onto mine. "You didn't give me the chance."

"Another night." I pulled her by the hip toward my body. "Your family will start to worry about you if I don't get you home soon. And if we start again, we may be here till dawn."

"That sounds like a dream." She nuzzled her nose against mine. "You promise there will be another night?"

"As many nights as you'll give me." Because that was the truth. There was something about Hannah that sparked a furious need inside of me. Not just physical. But if physical was all I could get for now, then that's what I'd take. I prayed I wasn't going to end up totally devastated at the end of this.

"Oh, I don't want to go." She nestled her body into mine, and our curves and planes lined up without even a fraction of space for light to slip through.

I traced my hand down the line of her back to the fullness of her bottom to the place where her cheek met the top of her thigh, and I had to stop myself from caressing the gentle skin of her inner thigh to see if I could arouse her again.

"We'd better get going, or I'm going to end up on your family's bad side."

"But my good side." She flopped over onto her back and stretched. I looked at her and took a snapshot for my memory. I wanted to be able to visually call her up, just like this, until we found another opportunity to be together. "Okay, I'm getting up." She stood, naked and beautiful. "Bathroom?"

I pointed to the door and watched her walk out to the living room, then return with her bra and dress. She scooped up her boots and underwear and disappeared into my bathroom.

I couldn't wipe the grin off my face.

Or the terror in my heart.

Chapter 19

HANNAH

I woke up with Blythe on my mind, replaying every delicious moment. Oh, if only I could start the day the way my night ended. I sent her a text.

***Woke up thinking about you.*128**

She texted back immediately.

You don't even know. When can we see each other again?

This was where things got complicated. I didn't know. Mom was leaving today so there was that, but then there was Jordan, and I didn't want to tell her anything yet. I wasn't dragging my kid into the mix with the wrong woman ever again. No matter how awesome she seemed to be on the surface. Besides, she'd only freak out if she thought someone might bind us to this place she didn't love.

I'm not sure. Don't freak. Remember? I'm honestly not sure.

Yeah, I figured it'd get complicated. But I'm at your mercy. Name the time and place and I'm there.

Soon. I promise. I won't be able to go without seeing you again for very long.

She sent me heart eyes in return.

I've got to help my mom clean up before checkout. How about I call you later?

Sounds good. And hey, last night was amazing. I can't stop thinking about you. All of you.

I deleted the text stream, just in case, and got up to start breakfast. Mom was already in the kitchen. "So, how was your evening? Have you gotten past your need to be away from your dear mother? Meet some other woman to transfer all of those issues to?"

"I don't have those kind of mother issues, Mom."

She poured me a cup of coffee and put it and the creamer in front of me at the island.

"Thanks." I fixed it the way I liked it, one shade lighter than black, and took a big sip. "Ah." I had to be careful not to let my thoughts drift to Blythe, because my face would give me away. But damn, that was difficult.

"You know." My mother had a realty brochure in front of her. "I've quite enjoyed my weekend here. Maybe I should buy a condo. You could live in it, if you stay, and I could pop over every so often to visit."

"What happens when I do find the woman I marry? She might not be so keen on a live-in mother-in-law."

"Ah, meet someone on your night out?"

I got up from the island and went to the sink. The giant cat who ate the canary was taking over my face. I turned on the water and rinsed out my cup before I'd even finished. "No, Mom. Not so lucky. But I might one day. And as much as your offer is generous and kind, I'd like to keep my options open. Plus, you filled me with more than a shred of independence. I'd like to think I could figure out how to buy my own place and not have to rely on my mother at this age and stage."

"Suit yourself. But if you're not going to move home, I may as well move to you. I'm not getting any younger. And I like this better than Asheville. It suits my sensibilities."

I knew this was a serious conversation. One that I should carve out a moment of real listening for, but I was daydreaming about Blythe's lips, Blythe's hands, Blythe's beautiful eyes looking down into mine. "Yep, uh-hum."

Jordan appeared from the hallway. Her hair was smushed up on one side and down on the other. "Morning, sweet pea." I smiled broadly, and Jordan scowled at my out-of-the-ordinary enthusiasm.

"Are there any donuts left?" She pushed past me and fumbled with the box on the counter. The box that had been in Blythe's hands yesterday morning. The hands that had been on me, and in me, last night. My cheeks turned hot, and I imagined they matched the red of the cardboard. I took a deep breath. I needed to get it together.

"I'm going to go strip the beds and gather the towels."

"Aren't you going to eat something?" My mother twisted on her stool to look at me.

"Not yet."

"You certainly seem ready to be rid of me. I thought we'd have a nice breakfast, enjoy the pool, and then I'd take you two out for lunch before I drive home."

"Yeah, Mom. We decided last night." Jordan slumped onto a stool with her donut and a glass of almond milk. "I want to hang out here longer. This house is way nicer than our apartment."

I blew out a breath, slowing myself down. Getting rid of my mom didn't get me any closer to seeing Blythe again. "Okay, you're right. I'm sorry. Eggs?"

"Over medium. With one slice of pumpernickel." My mother closed the real estate pamphlet.

Jordan nodded. "Same, but with bacon, and two pieces of toast."

I got up and moved around the kitchen, gathering what I needed to get started. As I stood over the frying pan, I imagined Blythe sneaking up behind me, wrapping her arms around my waist, and kissing the side of my neck. My body responded to my daydreams with tightened muscles and a flutter that threatened my balance. The butter popped in the skillet, and a hot droplet landed on the back of my hand.

"Ouch." It snapped me out of my fantasies and back to the current reality.

After the breakfast was eaten and the dishes cleaned and loaded in the dishwasher, we prepared the house for checkout. Finally, it was time to change into our swimsuits. I shut my bedroom door and locked it, taking my phone into the bathroom with me.

It rang once, twice, and then, "Hey, beautiful." Blythe sounded sexy as hell on the other end of the line.

"Hey. I've only got a minute but I wanted to hear your voice."

"Would you like me to tell you that I can't stop thinking about you? The image of you standing there in those boots is burned into my brain."

"In a good way, I hope." My body image wasn't horrible, but what girl didn't want to fish for a little compliment now and again?

"In an incredible way."

"That's nice to hear." I hoped she could feel my ridiculous grin through the phone. From outside my door, I heard Jordan yell, "Mom, we're going down to the pool."

"Listen, I probably won't have another chance to talk to you today. I'm doing stuff with Mom and Jordan for a few more hours, and then Jordan and I have to get ready for the week, but maybe you could come see me for lunch tomorrow? I only get thirty minutes, but it'd be nice to see your face."

"You sure? I don't want to get you in trouble with your boss."

"I'm sure." I paused. "I'd really love to see you again."

"I'll be there, then."

I felt as if I were in middle school the way I clung to the phone, my clenched hands pressing it to my ear, my stomach in excited knots. "Okay. Bye, Blythe."

"Bye, Hannah."

When she clicked off, an involuntary squeal sounded from my lips.

Tomorrow couldn't come fast enough.

BLYTHE

Every time my phone buzzed in my pocket, I pulled it out to check. Unfortunately, Hannah had been spot-on about not having time to be in touch. I hadn't heard from her since the morning.

"What are you doing? You're acting like you're the realtor the way you're checking that phone of yours."

I'd managed to throw Ginny off the scent by making my jumpiness, stupid smile, and constant phone checking about the lot deal.

"I know. But I went back by the lot today and I'm excited. I can see a house rising from the land, and you know how it is when something starts to take shape like that. You want to run with it."

"Don't you need to see their house rising from the land first?"

"Well, yeah, of course."

I sucked in a breath. I had an email from the Smith-Itos.

"Listen to this." I read it out loud to Ginny.

"Hello Blythe,

We spent the weekend talking about our walk-through, looking at your portfolio, and reading over your ideas. We would very much like to proceed with you doing the general contracting work for us. If this is still amenable to you, we'll have our attorney send over a contract within the next couple of weeks. As we hash out the details of the work required in exchange, and the lot restrictions for your build, along with required timeline, please feel free to call us with any concerns or adjustments that need to be made."

"Oh my gosh! That's awesome, Blythe. That means you're staying."

I looked up from my phone. "What? What is that supposed to mean?"

Ginny put down the book she'd been idly reading. "I don't know. When you moved back here, I didn't think it would last. I thought you'd just had your heart broken by Constance and that this was a break from reality. I figured eventually you'd miss architecture and bigger city life and leave again. But if you're getting into designing here, and designing a house that will clear out your storage shed, maybe it means you're not going anywhere."

"Of course I'm not going anywhere. You're here. Todd's here. My niblings are here. I'm absolutely clear on that one. This is my forever home."

"I still think you need more. I wish you'd meet someone."

Larry stretched and meowed as if to say "She found me, human." Which was perfect timing on his part because my sister laughed at him without noticing the dreamy look on my face. I'd found not only Hannah but Jordan too. Maybe, with the appropriate amount of time, I'd actually get to realize what it was like to be a parent.

THE NEXT DAY—MY see-Hannah-on her-lunch-break day— the morning to-do list took forever. I watched the clock, begging the minute hand to move faster. At my last house, I used the bathroom sink and brushed my teeth before heading to Williamson's. When I pulled up, I could see Hannah helping a customer at the register, so I waited in my car till they left. I checked my hair in the mirror. I blew my breath into my hand again. I ran a chapstik across my lips and mushed them together. Finally, the customer came out and I got out of my car.

Hannah saw me as I pushed open the door, and her face flushed and her dimples deepened. Then she crooked her finger in that universal come-hither gesture. I didn't have to be asked again.

"Are we alone?" I glanced behind her to see if Joel sat in his office.

"He left to deliver some paint to a client."

"Then it's probably okay if I do this." I stepped behind the counter, and she turned toward me. "And this." I stepped forward and put my hands on her hips. "And what about this?" I leaned forward and put my lips on hers.

She immediately brought her hands up to my hair, tangling her fingers there before pulling back, laughing. "I feel like I'm sixteen. I wanted to doodle your name on notepads all morning."

"I couldn't stop looking at my watch. Minutes were hours."

We stood for a second, both of us with grins that wouldn't quit.

"Come on," Hannah said. "I have an idea."

She grabbed my hand and walked me back into the aisles of paint. "We'll hear the door if anyone comes in."

At the end of the aisle, we turned and she nudged me back against a wall with the strength of her kiss. Her body met every inch of mine as she pressed into me and showered my lips, my cheeks, my jawline with kisses.

Public places were not my thing, but she felt so good. This felt so good. When she slipped her hands under my shirt and traced my skin, I felt myself go hot, my breath labored.

"Hannah, what if . . ."

"Shhhh," she whispered into my ear as she traced her tongue over the soft hollow just below it. "We're alone. Besides . . . it's my turn."

She found the button of my jeans and undid it with a quick twist of her fingers.

I gasped and went rigid against the wall. I knew this was definitely some people's fantasy, but she was pushing the wrong button with me. My brain triggered into panic and took me back to the stockroom where Constance had thrown herself at me the first time and I'd let her do just what Hannah was doing. As the memory of the door creaking open and the face of the startled intern flooded in, I grabbed Hannah's arm. "Stop."

She froze. "Oh. Is that not okay? You don't like to be touched?" Disappointment etched her features.

I pulled her close and dropped my face against her shoulder. I didn't want to cause her to question herself but I needed to be clear with my own boundaries if the two of us were going to work out. "I like to be touched. It's not that. It's just . . ." I looked around. "We're at your job."

"I promise you. Nobody's coming in. This time of the day is dead. The door has a big old bell on it, and I promise you, I will stop if it jingles." She pressed closer and whispered against my neck. "I've been thinking about nothing but you for the past thirty-six hours. I'm not sure when I'll be able to see you again."

Okay, so she had a point. But I'd gone this long without someone's hands on me. I could go until a proper time and place for me to relax into the moment. "Hannah . . ."

She was quick to back down. "I know. I know. I'm sorry. Damn pheromones. Dopamine thrown in now too. Kissing? Is kissing allowed?"

I nodded, and my panic subsided as she placed feather-soft kisses against my jawline. She may as well have been touching me in other places—the gentle graze of her teeth and tongue forged a direct path to where I imagined a more intense caress and my body shuddered with want.

The bell on the door rang. I jumped in surprise.

"Shhhh," she said, and slowly edged out of my arms. Then she popped up on her toes and, with her hands on my shoulders, kissed my forehead and whispered, "You're really beautiful when you're nervous."

Then she yelled to the front of the store. "Be there in a second." When she turned back to kiss me on the cheek, she wore an enormous grin. "You look stunned."

"I thought I was here for lunch."

She whispered, "That's not what I was hungry for. Don't leave, okay? Let me see if I can get rid of them."

As she walked away, I did a quick body check. Pants buttoned. Shirt down. Hair in one piece. I touched the top of my head. Nope, that was a disaster. But what a small price to pay for the moment we'd just had.

Holy hell. Hannah was amazing. And though there were traces of the Constance situation, we'd worked through it. Like adults. I'd told her what I needed and she'd respected me.

I think I might end up liking Blythe 2.0.

Hannah? Well, that was a no-brainer.

Chapter 20

HANNAH

I gloated as I walked to the front of the store. The look on Blythe's face—shock, satisfaction, and, okay, maybe a bit of puppy love—had me feeling powerful and sexy as hell. She'd freaked out momentarily. I'd worried I crossed a line—again. But then she'd relaxed and we'd found a new way.

"Well, hello there, beautiful. You are looking absolutely radiant if I must say so."

It was one of the guys from Saturday night's party. The drunk one who'd shown off my ass.

"Oh, hey. Alexander, right?" I met him on the floor by the color sample cards. "Are you here on a job, or just saying hi?"

"Both, darling." He pulled out an iPad and opened up a design schematic for a home he was working on. "I'm looking for some excellent creams and a warmer soft blue as an accent. What do you have?"

I glanced toward the stock aisles. There was no way I was getting him out of here quickly. Poor Blythe. I'd left her hiding in the back like a secret. Which she sort of was. I pulled out my phone, pretending to source some stock numbers and shot her a quick text.

It's Alexander from the party. He won't be quick. Just come on out.

Then I pulled some cards from the racks and spread out various colors on the design table for him to compare.

Blythe managed to slip around the cash register counter without him noticing, but she didn't make it to the door.

"Well, hello. If it isn't the architect."

Blythe did not have a poker face. She looked at me, looked to the ground, turned beet red, then waved. "How are you doing?"

"Oh." He looked between us. "Oh my. Have I just interrupted a little daytime dalliance?"

I was too quick with my answer. "What? Of course not. This is my job. Blythe shops here all the time."

Alexander rolled his eyes. "Sure, sugar, and I was born under a turnip truck. But don't worry. Your secret is safe with me." He turned to Blythe. "And you, I'm glad you took my advice and stopped introducing this one all over town. You two seem good together." He paused, assessing us. "You are together now, correct?"

I glanced at Blythe, who couldn't figure out where to look or what to say. "Correct," I said. "Well, as together as we can be in less than forty-eight hours."

Alexander guffawed. "That's like forty-eight weeks in lesbian time."

He had a point. But my daughter didn't know, my boss didn't know, and I didn't think Blythe's sister knew, but I didn't mind that Alexander knew. If I let myself believe in fate or knowing or whatever else had transpired between us upon meeting, I was going to have to also believe Blythe was okay dating a single mom. The only way to truly figure that out would be to, you know, actually date and hang out with other people.

Blythe's smile in response to my answer was worth the risk I took admitting it to Alexander. She stepped closer to the table and took my hand in hers, giving it a gentle squeeze before letting go. Of course, Alexander's quick eyes didn't miss a thing, but all it did was elicit a smile before he returned to the color samples. As he shifted them and made a few selections, he paused. "Why don't you two come into town this weekend? Have dinner with me and Walter. We can talk shop, and I promise I won't overdo it on the whiskey."

"Blythe?" I asked, and waited to see if she was open to it.

"I can, if you can."

I wrote Alexander's paint choices down as I answered him. "We'd love to." Then jokingly, in a sugar-sweet Southern accent, I said, "Blythe, honey, why don't you get the address and see what we can bring for this soiree?"

"Oooh, child." Alexander nudged Blythe's elbow with his own. "The way she called you 'honey' ought to have your toes curling in your boots."

"And they're steel-toed at that." Blythe winked at me, and my own toes curled because her look spoke of unfinished business and another opportunity to be together.

Eventually, she had to leave to go back to work. I excused myself from Alexander and walked her out to her car, which I now knew was Chester. "Thanks for stopping by."

"Yeah, I don't even know what to say to that. Thank you?" She reached out and tugged on the corner of my jeans pocket. "So, we have a date for Friday night. Is that going to work out with Jordan?"

"Jordan's old enough to stay home alone for a couple of hours. Though I don't want to make a habit of it."

"Can I talk you into running by my place tonight?"

"I wish. Oh, how I wish."

"No worries. I understand how moms think. I actually have work to do. On a project I'd planned to tell you about . . . if you hadn't tried to seduce me in the stockroom."

"Oh." I shrugged my shoulders and held out my hands. "Sorry? Not sorry?"

She smiled and shook her head. "Don't worry about it. I much prefer what *did* happen during lunch today. I'll tell you all about the project the next time we talk. Deal?"

"Deal. Look, I've got to . . ." I motioned to the door.

"Yep, go do your thing. And Hannah . . ."

"Yeah."

"Don't forget."

"Forget what?"

She leaned in and kissed me, then whispered, "I desperately want you to touch me." With that, Blythe opened the driver's door and slipped inside her car, leaving me standing with weak knees in the parking lot.

BLYTHE

The week went by at a snail's pace. Even though I was happily busy drawing out ideas for my new clients, going back and forth with the attorney to get the details of the contract agreeable to us both, and dealing with some frozen pipes in rental units after a surprise drop in temperature on Tuesday night, I hadn't been able to see Hannah for more than a minute in passing, and it was making me anxious.

When the temperature climbed to the low 60s on Thursday, I couldn't wait any longer.

How about I take you and Jordan for a ride in the boat after work? We'll have about an hour before we lose the sun. I can show you the thing I've been working on.

I saw her typing a response. The bubbles disappeared. But no text came through. Then bubbles again. I tried not to fret. Not to let insecurity rear its ugly head. She said she'd be honest, and so far she hadn't said we needed to end it. But maybe this was the moment. Maybe this text was going to be the last. My phone pinged, and I took a deep breath.

I think I'm going to have to say no this time. Jordan can't know yet. About us. If that upsets you, I understand. But I don't want either of us to have to lie to her and I'm not ready to tell her. I'm sorry. But I'm still on for Friday if that helps.

I blew out the breath I'd been holding. We still had traction—that was good. Might as well flirt while I had her texting me.

You don't think I can keep it together when you're around?

I'm more worried about me.

That put a relieved smile on my face.

We've got this. We're adults. Pretend your mom's

still on the boat with us. Ignore me. Don't you want to see me?

The last comment was bold, but why the hell not? There was a pause in the texts again. Maybe a customer, but maybe she was thinking about it. Finally, she responded.

Won't it be weird? To be not together when we've been so, you know, together?

She was giving me an opening.

Hannah, you promised total honesty and you've given it. I 100% understand where you're coming from with Jordan, and honestly I agree. But it's a pretty day. She likes my boat and my cat. And I want to show you what I'm so excited about. Meet me at the marina after you get off. I'll have the boat ready to go. Then I'll buy y'all tacos.

No way. Tacos on me.

That's what she said! ;)

Blythe!

See you later.

I was still laughing when I walked into the realty office.

"What's so funny?"

"Nothing, just something I saw online." I felt bad I hadn't told Ginny about me and Hannah. She wouldn't care. But as a mom, she might care about Jordan's reaction to our sneaking around. And I had to admit, even though I understood it, even though I agreed with it, it still felt wrong. Like maybe we should have just waited to act on this crazy chemistry between us. We were the adults in the room.

"Did you get the pool shut down at Blue View?" Ginny turned her attention back to whatever she was working on at the computer.

"I actually left it running because of the freeze warning. Figured Diane's payment more than covered the cost of the extra heat. Did you cut your hair?"

"You like it?" She pivoted in her chair, showing me the 360 view of a slightly shorter and blonder style.

"Looks good." My sister had a way of being both approachable and put together.

"Thanks." She blew me a kiss. "As far as the pool, it's all good. I have new people checking in on Sunday, and they were super excited to find out it might still be up and running. It sealed the deal. The owners were fine with it for one more rental."

"Great." An idea percolated, a way for Jordan to not be left at home on the night of our dinner with Walter and Alexander. "Maybe your kids would want to swim Friday night? I bet Jordan would babysit."

"Is she a lifeguard?"

I plopped onto the edge of her desk. "I hadn't thought about that."

Ginny poked my side with the end of her pen. "I love you, sis, but you don't think like a mom. It's a great idea though. Todd and I will take them. And Hannah can bring Jordan over."

Well, that didn't work out like I'd hoped. But I still didn't want to let Ginny in on the whole story. "Yeah, I bet they'd love that. You should ask."

Ginny cocked her head. "You sure you don't want to ask?"

"Sorry. I've got to run over to pick up some air filters. No time. Just send her an email."

"God, you're frustrating."

I blew her a return kiss and walked backward out the door. Then I shot Hannah another text.

Ginny's going to ask you and Jordan to come swimming on Friday night. Tell her you're going to a new friend's house for dinner and that Jordan's staying home.

That is what's happening.

I know. But we're leaving me out of it. I haven't told Ginny about us yet.

So we're both keeping secrets.

Fair. Ginny will extend the invitation to Jordan once she finds out you're not going to be home. She'll have fun and won't be stuck in the apartment.

That's sweet.

You're sweet. See you this afternoon.

HANNAH AND JORDAN arrived at the marina a little after five.

"Hey, you two. We've got about forty minutes before we lose daylight. All aboard." I turned on the motor and let the boat idle while Jordan helped me with the ropes. Hannah took Larry, and we did our best not to smile like fools whenever we looked at each other.

"How come we're going for a ride?" Jordan took the cat from her mom, then held him up to her face. "Not that I mind, since I get to hang out with my buddy, Larry Styles."

"That's clever." I laughed at Jordan's addition to the cat's name and reversed out of the slip. "We are going for a ride because I realized you two hadn't seen sunset from the water. It's a gorgeous day and my philosophy is, Any winter day when it's sunny and above fifty degrees, I'm taking out the boat. Plus, I'm excited about something and I wanted to share it with my fellow adventurers."

"That is an excellent philosophy."

Hannah smiled at me and I felt as if I could float high above the boat. Why was I like this? I knew that the step we took last week was foolish. I knew I was going to fall too quick. But if I never took a risk again, how would I ever find what I was looking for?

"Did you hear that, Larry Styles?" Jordan stood and put

her hand to her forehead, peering out at the water. "We are mighty adventurers."

This time I smiled at Jordan. She was a good kid. Funny and goofy. It was heartwarming. It made me sad to think that Hannah almost married someone who could take Jordan or leave her.

I powered up the main waterway until I got to the smaller channel that led to the lots. When we reached the edge of my future property, I turned the boat back around so the bow pointed west. I idled and let the gentle lap of the current push us to and fro.

"Sun headed down."

"Wow. Look at the colors of the sky." Jordan moved to sit cross-legged on the bow, the cat in her lap. I desperately wanted to wrap my arms around Hannah's waist and pull her back toward me. I could picture it, us, a happy little family of four. We could spend every sunset just like this.

"This is beautiful," Hannah whispered.

Yes, you are, I thought.

Yes, you are.

Chapter 21

HANNAH

I tried to be nonchalant while driving home the next day with Jordan. The whole outing the day before had gone perfectly. Jordan had been content and happy sitting and watching the sunset. Blythe and I managed a few special glances but nothing Jordan noticed. Blythe even impressed Jordan when she'd told her about the piece of land she'd be getting and how she'd been saving materials to build a more sustainable home.

And, let's be honest, I was impressed too.

Blythe was great with my kid. Genuinely great. She'd even run with the whole Larry Styles thing, which made Jordan insanely happy.

And Jordan seemed to like her too.

I was tempted to tell my daughter about my date.

But.

"Do you miss Lisa at all?" Jordan was scrolling on her phone as we left the paint store after work.

I sat up straighter. "Of course. We were together for three

years. You don't just turn that off like a faucet." Then I asked, "How about you? Do you miss her?"

"Not as much as I thought I would. You're not so stressed out anymore. And she's not constantly telling me to clean my room."

"That was within her right."

Jordan huffed out a breath. "Whatever. You're my mom. You can tell me stuff like that. But it bugged me when she did."

I laughed. "Pretty sure it bugs you when I do too."

"That's different."

Jordan put her phone on the seat next to her leg. "I wasn't always sure she liked me. She kind of talked down to me. Like how Lala does to you sometimes."

I turned onto the highway, torn between heartache for Jordan and elation at this show of insight and maturity. "Have you been thinking a lot about this?"

"I don't know. You don't talk about the breakup and you seem really chill lately. Like maybe you're happier."

I itched to jump in and ask if she was happier, if she'd turned a corner about wanting to go back, but I sensed she wasn't finished talking yet.

"You don't seem to miss Lisa much even though you cried about the dress." She paused, and when she spoke again her voice had dropped. "It makes me wonder how people decide to be together."

I glanced at Jordan. She was purposefully looking down and away from me, picking up her phone and flipping it over again. Huh. Maybe this conversation wasn't about me or Lisa or staying at the beach at all. Which, damn. Now would have been the perfect moment to tell her the whole truth. It was something she should know. Not all women wanted children, and that was okay. I think, given what she'd just said, that even if her feelings were hurt at first, like mine were, eventually it would sink in and make sense. It was important that she know she could make any choice she wanted in her adult life. But right now, it seemed as if she needed answers to an entirely different question.

I thought about what to say for a few seconds. "I suppose it depends. Some people swear there are instant connections based on attraction. And then there can be slower ones, where people are friends first and then over time they look at each other in new ways."

"Do you think that second one really happens?"

I laughed. "My poor child. You grew up with a lesbian mom and all of your lesbian aunties. Queer women move fast. We often think we've fallen deeply in love. Sometimes it's true, like with Flora and Hazel, or Smyth and Daria, but then other times it isn't. Like me and Lisa. As we got to know each other, it turned out we were pretty different and maybe our relationship was built less on love and more on convenience. We prioritized different things. If you're lucky and get to know someone over time and make your moves slowly, you might have the possibility of creating something long-lasting."

"You don't think there's such a thing as love at first meeting?"

Jordan had no idea how weighted her question was. It was my nightly grapple. Was this thing with Blythe real? Or was my sex drive simply making a midlife comeback? I went with an honest answer. "You know, I really hope so."

I watched my daughter's cheeks flush as she typed into her phone. I bit my tongue, not wanting to spoil the moment but at the same time dying to know who she was texting. But I'd learned that if I waited for her perfect moment, eventually I'd find out.

With Jordan preoccupied, my mind wandered. Was I letting attraction and libido trick me into thinking that Blythe and I had something more than chemistry? Blythe had been excited talking to Jordan about the house she was going to build. She'd figured out a good balance between work life and real life. She'd never said anything to make me feel less than, a trait I avoided in all partners after eighteen years with an overdirective mother. She seemed to genuinely love kids, even mine. She was down-to-earth and 100 percent real. She was the kind of person you could imagine waking up slowly with, then making pancakes together, and laughing when one hit the floor. She was the kind of person who would do anything for you once you were her friend.

As I turned into the apartment driveway, I thought, *Oh shit, I'm seriously falling for her*.

AT SIX-THIRTY, I dropped Jordan off at the same beach house Mom had rented. "Have fun. Tell Ginny and Todd I said hi." She walked through the wooden gate to the pool. Todd waved and I waved back, then I backed out of the driveway. It took less than fifteen minutes to get to Blythe's condo.

She was waiting for me in the parking area underneath, wearing the tailored look that suited her so well. She slipped into the passenger seat. "You look gorgeous."

I wrapped my arms around her. "I've missed you. What are you doing down here?" Disappointment filled me at the cellular level.

She kissed me softly. "I was worried if you came upstairs, we'd never make it over to their house for dinner."

I pouted. "You're no fun. Alexander already thinks we're the queens of quickies."

"I'd rather have the long slow burn later."

"Oooh, are we going to feign an excuse to get out of there early?"

"Let's agree to say no to any after-dinner drinks."

"I love your devious plan."

Blythe pointed to a road ahead. "Take a right up there." Then, "Thanks again for coming out with me yesterday."

"Are you kidding? I'm the one who has to thank you. Jordan couldn't stop talking about the house you'll be building. I think you're her new idol."

Blythe's hand drifted across the console, and she played the tips of her fingers against my thigh. I tried to ignore the tingling sensations that radiated in all directions. She didn't seem to notice the effect she was having on me as she kept talking. "Ah really? That's cute. She's a good kid. I'm happy to let her ride along when I get a call about salvaging building materials."

"As long as it's Insta worthy, she's in. I swear, lately I can't get her off her phone. I actually think she might have a crush on someone."

"Like mother, like daughter?" Blythe's hand slipped toward the inside of my thigh.

"We might be talking crash instead of crush if you keep that up." I took Blythe's hand and moved it to the console. "But yes." I traced my finger inside her palm. "Like mother, like daughter. Except I think Jordan's strictly into boys. At least, that's been historically true."

"Derrick and Isla may have said something about her liking Tedrick. Or maybe one of his friends? Anyway, I wouldn't worry too much. All those kids he hangs out with are pretty straitlaced and intellectual."

"Did you ever question your sexuality?"

Blythe shifted to look directly at me. "You're kidding me, right?"

I shrugged. "We all have a story."

"No. Gold star. I've been queer since the womb. I have fallen into the trap of straight women, but that's the closest I've ever gotten to being straight. And you?"

"I've never questioned my sexuality, but I did sleep with a

couple guys in college, just to make sure I wasn't missing out on something."

"Were you?"

"Nothing that can't be done more expertly by a woman." I turned my head and winked before returning my gaze to the road.

With that, Blythe seemed to run out of things to talk about.

BLYTHE

Alexander and Walter fell completely under Hannah's spell. She gave them perfect compliments about their home, their portfolios, their choice of menu, and the rich zinfandel they poured in her glass. Yet at the same time, she did it with such ease and an utter lack of pretentiousness. I loved watching her and listening to their banter.

"You did not love Britney." Alexander put his hand over his heart.

"What's not to love about Britney? The dance moves. The hair. The lack of hair when she had *the* moment. And I've been so worried about her."

"Right? Being held captive by her dad and fed too many mood stabilizers . . ."

"Hallelujah for that judge who finally gave her freedom."

Walter leaned over to me as Hannah and Alexander dove deep into Britney Spears conspiracy theories. "Who are you working for these days? Still choosing not to do design work?"

I'd shared my move-from-Atlanta story at a party where we'd first met.

"Actually, I just picked up a home design project for a couple out of D.C. They have similar philosophies about land and material use. Should be a fun design challenge."

"Oh really? You know, we should talk more seriously. Alexander and I want to create a full-spectrum home service for people not interested in builder models. We need an architect on board. He'd do the interiors. I'd expand into doing custom furniture pieces and specialty built-ins. And though Alexander sometimes has to be pulled toward recycle and reuse, I really love your ideas."

I was flattered. "That's quite a proposal. But I'm not sure I'm ready to go back to it full-time. I'm managing okay without it."

"But don't you miss it?" He didn't wait for me to answer. "Anyway, think about it. We can set up a time to talk more."

I took the napkin from my lap and placed it on the table. "Restroom?" Standing up was the first step toward being able to leave and being able to hold Hannah in my arms again.

Walter pointed me in the direction of the hall.

When I returned, the three of them had moved to the living room and were settled onto chairs there. Alexander showed no signs of letting Hannah, or me, slip away. I tried to catch her eye, but she was engrossed in their conversation.

Alexander sat back and crossed his leg over his knee. "Be bold, girlfriend. Have Joel add a kitchens and bath division. There's always a demand for renovations, and it's the kind of work that you could do without any sort of design degree. You have an eye, and there are plenty of people in this world who do not."

Hannah leaned forward on the edge of the rich raspberry-colored sofa. "You think so? I actually love doing that kind of work."

Walter motioned for me to come over and sit. I resisted and stood near the archway between the two rooms. I hoped that Hannah would get the cue and we could head back to my place. She looked toward me. I stood up straighter and shifted slightly toward the door.

But she didn't seem to catch the hint. Or if she did, she was ignoring it. She was way more interested in what Alexander was telling her.

Her voice lifted. "That would be a perfect fit for me. The job at Williamson's is good, but I do need more. Maybe if Joel is interested, he will let me spearhead it." She smiled up at me, her eyes shining, and I got a little irritated she'd totally forgotten about our plan to head out early. It brought back memories of Constance latching on to the firm's partners at parties I'd invited her to. How she'd flirt and laugh and fawn over their ideas in an effort to ingratiate herself, all while totally forgetting why she was even at the party in the first place.

Hannah tried to draw me in. "Blythe, you know Joel. Has he ever talked about growing his business?"

Planning an expansion for someone else's business seemed more like conjecture than useful conversation. "I have no clue. We're friendly, but what he wants . . . ?" I shrugged, still irritated. "I've always had the impression he likes his low-key mom-and-pop paint store. He's already got enough competition from the big-box stores without honing in on their kitchen and bath departments." Then I tilted my head toward the door and did a hard sideways look with my eyes, hoping she'd get the message.

Hers narrowed, but that didn't stop me from tipping my head again.

This time her mouth straightened into a line before she looked away, refocusing on Alexander.

Eventually I gave up and accepted Walter's offer of a glass of rye and settled in one of the luxurious dove-gray leather armchairs.

After another hour of chitchat about Charleston and home design shows and the death of gay bars and me drinking one too many glasses of excellent whiskey, Hannah stood up. "I hate to cut this short, but I need to make sure my daughter is okay."

"Well, we loved having y'all over. It was a real joy." Alexander stood up and gave Hannah a kiss on each cheek.

Walter shook my hand. "We'll be in touch."

"Sounds good." I handed him the crystal rocks glass I was holding.

Outside, the air had turned a bit cooler, and when Hannah rubbed her arms against the chill, I wrapped my arm over her shoulder, feeling warm from the last double shot of whiskey. "You were spectacular in there."

Her body stiffened, and she stepped out from under my arm. "I'm sorry we stayed longer than you wanted, but they're both so interesting. It was good for me to have some new adults to talk to."

Something about the way she said it stung. Maybe I was being overly sensitive, but maybe she was too. We'd said we were going to leave early. All I'd been doing was giving her hints to say goodbye. Inside the car, she pulled out her phone and sent a text to Jordan before driving off. Her phone lit up immediately with the returning message.

"Shoot." She looked at me. "Jordan's home and kind of freaked out I've been gone so long. I'm going to need to drop you off and head to the house."

"Yeah. Sure. I get it." And I did. Something had cooled between us. Like the rollicking conversation she'd been having with Alexander made her realize I wasn't the most exciting catch in the Low Country. Throw the first fish back because there might be a bigger one waiting. Or something like that.

On the way home, I was quiet and she turned on the radio. Occasionally, she'd make a comment about a song that came on, but something was definitely up. For both of us. When she pulled into my driveway, she didn't even turn off her engine.

"I enjoyed tonight." I leaned over the console and she met my lips, but her kiss was perfunctory and preoccupied. If we'd been seeing each other for any real length of time, I would have asked what was wrong. But we weren't even a thing to anyone who mattered. And she had Jordan waiting at home.

I could rationalize all I wanted, but it would still trip my anxiety button.

"I really do have to run. I'm sorry."

"No need to apologize. I understand." My head was buzzy

with the whiskey, so I kept my mouth shut before I said anything stupid.

As she backed out of the driveway without so much as a lingering look in my direction, I had a sneaking suspicion tonight had been a turning point in the wrong direction.

I only hoped I'd get the opportunity to find out where we'd gone wrong.

Chapter 22

HANNAH

As I drove away from Blythe's condo, I replayed the evening. We'd been having such a good time. The dinner was fantastic, the conversation fun. And yes, I'd agreed we'd leave early, but we weren't teenagers anymore. Surely Blythe could sense I was enjoying myself and wanted to stay. When she cut my dreams off at the knees before I'd even had the rest of the weekend to fantasize about them, it pissed me off. My mother had criticized me since birth. I didn't need a new girlfriend who wouldn't at least allow me five minutes of career fantasy. Did she think I was stupid? I knew it was a long shot for Joel to get on board and that it was out of my control. But she'd talked to me as if I were an idiot and then acted rudely over-the-top about trying to get out of there.

Her, of all people. Someone who dreamed of building a gorgeous home out of scraps and cast-off building materials. I guess only her dreams mattered.

I unlocked the apartment door.

Jordan was giggling and video chatting on her phone. She looked up, then quickly said, "I gotta go. Bye."

"Who was that?" My current mood extended to my daughter, who no longer seemed panicked about being home alone.

"Tilda."

I could tell she was lying by the way she forced herself not to blink. But if I pushed her on it, we'd end up in a fight, and I still wouldn't get the truth. I grunted and then walked to the tiny kitchen and poured myself a glass of wine. "I'm going to bed. Don't stay up too late."

In my small room, I set the wineglass down on my bedside table and plugged my phone into the charger.

There was a text from Blythe.

Hope you made it home safe. I enjoyed seeing you so excited about Alexander's idea. Let me know if I can help with the pitch to Joel.

I reread it. Then took a sip of wine.

I replayed the conversation from earlier in my head to assess if I'd overreacted. Maybe she hadn't been implying I was an idiot. Should I give her the benefit of the doubt? She was obviously trying to be supportive now.

I took a few more sips of wine and thought about texting her back.

I'd wanted to stay. I could have simply told her and she'd have been fine. Instead, I got pissy and let myself become the victim. It was a pattern created in childhood. It was what I'd allowed myself to believe after Lisa told me what she needed. That it was her fault. I didn't want to create the same pattern with Blythe.

I could let her know I'd made it home in one piece.

I'm home. Thanks.

Then.

Jordan seems fine, by the way. Sorry to rush out on you.

Bubbles appeared, then disappeared on my phone. I waited but there was no follow-up text. I changed out of my clothes, then slipped into a worn flannel nightshirt and got under the covers. The wine was warm going down my throat and the tension slowly eased. It wasn't Blythe trying to criticize. She'd obviously been ready to leave and didn't want to deep dive into my career strategies. We'd even pre-agreed to head out before those glasses of whiskey.

Poor thing. She'd looked incredibly dashing standing there under that arch, her body angled against the casing, her head not-so-subtly tilting toward the door. I thought about what could be happening in this very moment if Jordan hadn't panicked and I hadn't gotten all up in arms over nothing.

I put the glass down and grabbed my phone.

Are you still awake?

Bubbles, then, ***Yes***.

Meet me for a walk in the morning? Public beach? East Ashley?

Then, because I didn't want her to worry.

I'd love to see you, and Jordan will sleep until noon if I let her.

This time, her response was quicker.

Sure. 10 am? I usually head over to Ginny's to hang out around lunchtime.

Perfect. See you then. My fingers hesitated, then I added, **Sweet dreams.**

THE NEXT MORNING, I wrote a note for Jordan and slipped out the door. It was too far to walk, so I took the bike. Blythe was already there when I wheeled in behind Chester.

"Hey." I leaned the bike against the wooden beach stairs and locked it.

"Hey." She wore faded boy-cut jeans, her hands shoved

into a blue puffer jacket, and a Crosby Fish Company ball cap on her head. In other words, she looked hot as hell.

"Let's walk." We took the steps down to the beach and headed into the wind. Pelicans flew along the shoreline, and a few plovers dipped their long beaks into the sand.

There was no sense in avoiding the conversation, so I jumped right in. "I think I need to apologize to you."

"Oh yeah?" Blythe's hands were still in her pockets.

"Yes. You see, I was flattered by the things Alexander was suggesting, and I saw you asking for us to leave, and I ignored you instead of simply telling you I wanted to stay. But then I thought you were kind of curt with me about the idea for Williamson's and my feelings got irrationally hurt."

Blythe stopped walking. "I didn't mean to hurt your feelings."

"I figured that out. But you have to understand, one of my flaws is that I often view things people say as criticism, even when that's not the case."

"Cause of your mom?"

"Yes. I'm not great at speaking up for my needs."

Blythe took her hand out of her pocket and reached for mine. She laced our fingers together. "I wasn't being critical. Just practical. I figured without Joel in the conversation, there was no point in speculation. But I can see how I should have gotten excited with you. And okay, maybe I was irritated that you changed your mind about wanting to leave early."

"Irritated?" My eyebrows rose a notch.

"I know. Not a pretty look on me. But all I could think about was getting you to my place and feeling you in my arms. And I'm sensitive, too. When you said that thing about hanging out with other adults, I thought maybe you don't find me as interesting as those guys."

I grabbed her other hand so we were facing each other. "Blythe. Stop. You're incredibly interesting. And kind. And thoughtful. And smart. And believe me, I've chastised myself repeatedly about missing out on the real dessert last night."

She scuffed her toe in the sand. Without looking at me, she said,. "I really like you, Hannah. Otherwise it wouldn't have mattered."

I swung our linked hands and felt the giddy rush of what she'd said. "I like you too." I leaned my head against Blythe's shoulder. "Are we good now?" I asked.

Blythe put her arm around my waist and pulled me close. "We're good."

Then I took a deep breath and thought the words out into the wind: *I think I might want to marry this woman.* But I could never say them out loud, because look where it got me last time.

BLYTHE

Hannah gave me the perfect opportunity to tell her everything about the Constance incident, but I didn't want to ruin the moment. Telling someone you even fleetingly worried they might be using you for a career boost is definitely a character dig. Did I really think Hannah was a repeat of Constance? On a heart level, no. But on some reptilian level . . . maybe? What was it going to take for me to shake this relationship trauma for once and for all? I decided to lean into it. With trust and openness instead of suspicion.

"Maybe you could come over tonight and I can help you strategize talking to Joel?" I leaned against Chester, and Hannah leaned into me. It was nice to be with someone so utterly comfortable with her sexuality.

"You're sweet. But I think it's too soon to talk to him. I haven't even been working there long enough to get vacation time. Besides . . ." She tilted forward and kissed the tip of my nose. "I doubt that's what we'd end up doing."

I pushed my hands farther down into the back pockets of her jeans and gave her bottom a little squeeze. "Would that be so bad?" Now that we'd talked through our misunderstanding, I desperately wanted more time with her.

"Oh, it'd be terrible." She stepped a little closer and whispered into the side of my neck. "Awful." Her breath tiptoed across my skin, and I had to restrain myself from pulling her hips tight against mine.

"Could you?" I asked. "Sneak away? Make a grocery store run?" I put my mouth to the side of her neck as she'd done to me and growled, "Do something awful?"

"So needy." But her tone held a smile.

I pulled back, not because I thought she was serious but because I didn't want her to ever feel pressured. "Like I said. I like you. Not just the chemistry, but you. I mean, I'm happy to come to your place and hang out with Jordan as well, but I understand you're not ready to bring her into this."

"Let me see what I can do. But no promises. I left her last night, and right now she's being a little cagey about something. We'll have tons of nights. Eventually, I'll tell her."

"That sounds promising." I knew I was looking at her like one of those cartoon animals in love, but I couldn't stop myself. This living, breathing, beautiful woman had waltzed into my life when I had stopped looking for love. And even though the circumstances were not ideal for her, she seemed open to us. I hoped she was really in this thing. If she wasn't, my heart would tatter. All of my big internal talks about how I could handle it were steaming piles of malarkey when it came to how I felt about Hannah.

WHEN I GOT to Ginny and Todd's, the niblings immediately pounced. Derrick jumped on my back, and Isla pulled on my hand. "You promised us a boat ride, Aunt Blythe. You said you'd take us out." Isla nodded vigorously. "You did. You promised."

"Kids. Leave your aunt alone. Let her at least have something to eat." Ginny clapped twice, then swatted Isla on the bottom. "Come on, leave her be."

"It's okay. Do you guys really want to go out? It's a little cool today."

"Really. We really want to go out."

I looked at my sister, who shrugged. "They're impervious to the cold. Besides, Todd had to go into work today. It'd be fun to have something to do instead of housework."

"Okay then. Why don't you two pack up some sandwiches and we can head out?"

The kids ran inside to the kitchen.

"Don't make a mess!" Ginny yelled. "I just cleaned those countertops." She shook her head.

"Sorry about that, sis."

She linked her arm with mine as we walked up the stairs onto the front porch. "Don't be. I love when they get excited about helping. How come you couldn't come to the pool last night?"

I didn't want to tell her I'd had dinner with friends, because it was too closely aligned with what Hannah had told her, so I did something I rarely did—I lied to my sister.

"Stayed in. Watched my favorite *Schitt's Creek* episodes. Cuddled with Larry." Really only the first part of this was a lie. I had rewatched David and Patrick's wedding about four times after my awkward text exchange with Hannah. Larry had provided solace while I cried a sad tear or two, thinking the relationship was over.

"Ew." Ginny twisted her mouth in a perfect David impression.

"Ha ha."

"Honestly, though, that's a pretty lame excuse for not hanging out with your favorite family at a swank heated pool. Jordan joined us. Apparently, Hannah had other plans. Jordan said she thought her mom had a secret date. Saw her using some fancy body lotion that she only uses for special occasions. I have to admit, I'd kind of hoped it was with you."

Well, this was news. Both that she'd put on special body lotion for me and that Jordan was onto her. I desperately wanted to tell my sister, but I couldn't risk Jordan finding out before her mom broke the news to her. And what if Hannah did decide to detour after a few more weeks? What then? It would make things weird, and technically Ginny was Hannah's landlord. I didn't want Ginny to hold anything against her, even if she did end up breaking my heart.

"Nope, not me. But lucky someone. So how was Jordan?"

"Sweet. She was very tolerant of these two being annoying PIAs."

Isla looked up. "What's a PIA?"

Derrick smirked.

Ginny held up a finger and wagged it at him. "Don't."

I intervened. "What kind of sandwich did you make me? Frog's ears with lemon tart toenails? Or jam and earthworm bellies?"

Isla giggled. "Gross." Then her eyes narrowed as she thought of her comeback. She held up a peanut butter and jelly sandwich in a baggie. "I made you a mud and blood."

I rubbed my tummy. "Yummm, my favorite."

Derrick threw some potato chips into the bag. "Jordan's cool. And pretty."

"Oooooh," Isla sassed. "You like a girl. That means you're a lesbian, like Aunt Blythe."

Ginny started laughing.

I shook my head. "Remember how you said I didn't think like a mom? Well, this explanation is on you."

Ginny was still laughing when Derrick called foul.

"I am not. And I don't like Jordan. Anyway, she's dating Tedrick's friend Robbie. She told me at the pool that she had a boyfriend."

Now *this* I would share with Hannah. I guess her hunch had been right.

"Come on, guys. Grab your coats and a warm hat. The day's wasting. There are dolphins to see and crab traps to check."

They tumbled out the door in front of me and Ginny. She grabbed my arm before I walked down the stairs. "I hope I didn't hurt your feelings when I said that, about you not thinking like a mom."

"You can't hurt my feelings with the truth."

"Well, I want you to know, you would have been a great mom. I hope you still get the chance one day."

I nodded. "Thanks."

And I realized, I hoped I did too. Or at least the chance to be a great stepmom.

Chapter 23

HANNAH

Blythe opened the door with a wicked smile on her face, a bathrobe hanging from her broad shoulders.

"Oh, I . . ." I was speechless is what I was.

She grabbed my hand and pulled me inside, allowing the robe to fall open so I could see that the only thing underneath was a pair of navy-blue boy shorts.

"Damnit, Blythe. I'm supposed to be running out for ice cream. I literally have thirty to forty minutes tops."

"If you've been thinking about me the way I've been thinking about you, that's all it will take." She pulled me toward her and lifted my hoodie and athletic tank over my head so I was equally naked from the waist up.

"This is ridiculous," I said, though to be honest it's exactly what I'd hoped would happen when I decided to stop by.

"No more ridiculous than you trying to get jiggy with me at the paint store." Blythe cradled my chin in her hand and looked into my eyes with a deeply sexy smile that made me want to open up my chest and hand her my gift-wrapped heart. "Don't tell me about ridiculous."

"Fair." I pushed the robe off her shoulders. All I wanted was her.

We fell onto the sofa. Each kiss ricocheted through me, bouncing from neuron to neuron, lulling me into sublime happiness. I could do this, and only this, all night, except . . . I writhed on top of her, my "Mom snuck out of the house" clock was ticking, and I still had my pants on. "Please. Pants. Off."

Blythe flipped me over and wriggled me out of my leggings. I tilted my head back and closed my eyes and let myself get absolutely lost in the sensation of her mouth on me. Her breath vibrated electric currents across my skin as she whispered, "So beautiful." My inner goddess woke up. The way her hands glided over me. The way she delved deeper. I'd never felt so adored by a lover.

If only I could hold myself back for hours but I'd been thinking about her, about this, too often. As she found a perfect rhythm, my body sent up a prayer. This. Her. Yes. Now. As she took me fully, my body, blood, and nerves came together in a rush and waves of emotions racked me. I pulled her tight, loving not only the way she made me feel but this closeness. Blythe. My Blythe.

"Your Blythe," she answered.

I hadn't realized I'd said it aloud. My body, or rather my mind, threatened to betray me and knock me out of the moment, but Blythe whispered sweet nothings against my skin and I quickly slipped back into the sublime sweetness of her adoration.

Her own gentle whispers and cries grew louder as she relentlessly explored and caressed me. The tender sound pushed me beyond the present. I grew rigid beneath her. My fingers curled into her hair and I cried out, my body spasming intensely.

She made her way up to my mouth, a slow trail of kisses from belly to breasts to lips.

"Your Blythe, huh?" Her smile lifted in a wry expression.

I felt my cheeks burn hot. "I, um, didn't mean to say that out loud."

She kissed across my eyebrows. "You did. I liked it."

I pulled her to me, loving our closeness, loving the connection we were creating. But I wanted more. I flipped onto my side, pulling her with me. "My turn. Please?"

She nuzzled against my neck in response and guided my hand to the hem of her boy shorts.

I eased them off. My body rippled with anticipation as I began this long-awaited exploration. I wanted to know her. Every fold, every crevice, every way she responded to touch. Feeling her react, hearing her subtle sounds, learning her impatience when I backed off, I knew I was getting in deep in more ways than one.

When Blythe bucked hard against me—"Jesus, Hannah, now, please"— I did as she asked. She groaned and grabbed my back, quivering against me as I held her tight until she stilled.

Afterward, we lay on the couch, holding each other, our hearts beating into the other's.

She laughed. "You make me feel like a teenage boy."

"You make me feel so beautiful. And powerful." I knew it was bad to compare her with Lisa right now, but I couldn't help it. Lisa had always needed to be in charge when it came to our rare sex. Directing and orchestrating. There was never the kind of wild abandon and relinquishing that Blythe had just given me in our lovemaking. I could get used to this kind of reaction.

"Me?" She ran her fingers lightly on my arm as she looked into my eyes. "You definitely win all the awards."

"Queens of the quickie? Isn't that what you called us?"

She groaned and pulled me closer. "Don't say it. Please, don't say it."

I brushed my fingertips lightly across her jawline and pressed my lips against her mouth. "You were the one who started this, Ms. Meet Me at the Door in Nothing but a Robe and Boy Shorts."

She grinned and her blue eyes twinkled in the little bit of light coming from the hallway. "It's what I'd hoped would happen after dinner at Walter and Alexander's. You said you were stopping by. . . . I didn't want to miss another opportunity." She sat up and allowed me a moment to really take in the beauty that was Blythe in the nude. I think that's the thing I loved most about masculine women. It was all a facade once they took off their clothes.

"This view is way better than the marsh."

She blushed and started to cross her arms over her chest. I shook my head. She dropped her arms back to her sides.

"Perfect," I said. Then I got up, totally naked, and retrieved her robe from the floor before I reached for my leggings. "But now I do have to say it."

"I know." Blythe slipped on the robe and tugged the sash into a loose knot. "You need to get home. I think I have some ice cream in the freezer you can grab to save you time."

I kissed her cheek and sighed after I'd gotten dressed. "I wish I could stay."

"I wish you could too." She kissed the tip of my nose.

Larry yawned from his window perch. I laughed. "He seems bored with us."

"Well, he's the only one." She pulled me to her and spoke low into my ear. "Think of all the things we still get to explore."

The timbre of her voice, the way her mouth moved against

the fine hairs of my neck, the strength of her warm hands on my hips, all of it threatened to have me tearing off my clothes again and walking the hall to her bedroom for another round.

I pulled away with a groan. "Stop. You're killing me."

The only response she gave me was a wicked grin.

BLYTHE

When I wasn't thinking about Hannah, I was thinking about the Smith-Itos' design. But mostly I was thinking about Hannah. We were on our fourth week of clandestine visits and steaming hot sex, we'd even managed a romantic dinner for Valentine's Day, and though I wouldn't have traded any of it, I did long to simply hold her through the night. Wake up with her. Bring her coffee in bed. I was trying to be patient. I understood she was a parent and that her daughter came first, but a part of me also grew frustrated.

I liked her. Really liked her. And if I was honest with myself, I might even use the word *love*. But how could I fall in love with Hannah without Jordan even knowing about us? Warning bells subtly rang in the less-evolved part of my brain.

"Let me see." Ginny plopped down on the edge of the desk and peered at the piece of paper under my hand.

Normally I did my design work in the second bedroom of my apartment at night. I had an old-school drafting table along with a big computer monitor set up for CAD work. But today, I was sneaking in some quick sketches at an extra desk in the office. Tuesdays were notoriously slow, as they were not a common check-in or checkout day for renters.

I flipped the paper around to show Ginny an idea I'd had for the east–west orientation of the house on the land. "This way they can capture both the sunsets and the sunrises, but I'll use the north side of the home as the entry."

"And where will you put your house?"

The site plan I was working from had my lot on it too. "Here." I pointed to the modest swell of land that was the only possible place for a house, no doubt the reason they were willing to make the trade. But it would give me a nice southwestern exposure, and I could build a dock for my boat.

My phone buzzed with a text. Ginny was holding the maps

and looking at my sketch, so I did a quick check. Hannah had sent me a string of emojis. Fire bursts, water droplets, and the smiling one with the hearts floating around it. I typed quickly.

Ditto. And a kiss face.

But though I got the immediate ping of excitement that always came with any sort of communication from Hannah, this time there was also something else. The best way to describe it would be a smidge of heaviness.

"Sis."

"Yeah?" Ginny looked up from the papers.

"I think I need your advice."

She shook her head. "Looks like you're making excellent progress here. They're going to be thrilled with where this is headed."

"No, not about the project."

"Oh?" She looked up, concern lighting her eyes. "What then?"

I looked around. A couple of the sales brokers were at their desks, and this was a private matter. "Can we maybe take a lunch walk?"

"Of course. Let me switch shoes real quick. Meet you out front."

Outside, I leaned against the brokerage's iron railing. The sun was high, and a hint of warmth radiated from the metal. Ginny walked out the office door, concern still on her face.

"I don't have cancer."

"Thank God. I was freaking out."

Ever since our mom died, both my sister and I had a hyperawareness of death and all the ways it could find us. Though we did a super job keeping it in check around everyone else, with each other we knew it was where our worries landed first.

We headed across the parking lot toward the nearby neighborhood, where we could avoid traffic as we walked and talked.

"If you don't have a potentially fatal disease, which is great news, what's going on?"

"Girl problems."

"What? You didn't even tell me you were seeing anyone. Or is it that someone won't see you?"

I hadn't planned on telling my sister about us until Hannah had told Jordan, but Hannah had made no moves in that direction. I needed to know if I was being unreasonable. I needed to shut down the alarm bells so I didn't back away for fear of the broken heart I'd been so sure I could handle.

"I've been seeing Hannah."

"Shut up." My sister stopped walking. "Why didn't you tell me? She's awesome. We love Hannah. And Jordan. Look at you, sly dog. When did this all start? But wait, you said problems. What problems?"

"It's been going on for . . . a little bit." I didn't want Ginny to know I'd bold-faced lied to her about the night we were at Alexander and Walter's house. I sighed. "And I really like her."

"Ah, sissy. You've got the puppy face. You haven't had that in a long time."

"Right? And you know me. How I am."

"True. Honest. Beautiful. Loyal."

"Gullible," I added.

"Gullible to what? Hannah seems to have it together."

"She hasn't told Jordan we're seeing each other."

"Oh." Ginny was quiet for a few steps. "I mean, is that so bad? I think I'd be protective of Derrick and Isla if, God forbid, I ever had to date someone new."

"But it makes me feel awful. The only time I get to see her is in these stolen moments."

"She hasn't told Jordan she's dating? I mean, I can get not revealing who until you guys know if you're serious, but to not even explain that 'Mom has a date'? That I don't get."

It really wasn't my business to share the details of Hannah's life, but this was Ginny, and I needed a sounding board. "That's the complicated part. I think you know she's recently out of a serious relationship."

"Yeah, but it's been what . . . two or three months now? Long enough to go on a date."

"There's more. Her ex told Hannah she didn't want to be a parent."

"Oof. Ouch. Can you even imagine?" Ginny shook her head.

A car breezed past us, then a work truck loaded with rattling ladders and construction scaffolding. When the noise quieted, Ginny asked, "How serious were they? Was the ex Jordan's other mom?"

"Hannah had Jordan on her own, but they were with Lisa for three years. Engaged for one. The truth came out just before she moved here. She called off their wedding plans and hightailed it out of town."

"Oh wow. Better to call it off than make a mistake. But picking up and leaving . . . .that's kind of intense."

"Yeah." We walked a bit in silence before I blew out a deep breath. "I'm scared, sis. I really like her, but if she's not willing to tell her daughter about us, then I'm not sure the feeling is mutual. And it's hard, because I know I should talk to her about my feelings, but I don't want to push her into doing something she's not ready to do just because I'm dealing with ghosts of relationships past."

Ginny nodded. "That is a conundrum. But it seems legit on her part. Not nefarious. There's nothing in the world I want less than you getting hurt, but I also see where she's coming from. Maybe give it a bit more time? She'll figure out that you would be an awesome plus one for her daughter."

We turned to head back to the office.

Ginny stopped and put a hand on my forearm, her voice excited. "What if I invite her over again on a Sunday? I won't tell Todd y'all are seeing each other and I swear I won't act like I know. But it would give you time with Jordan and vice versa, in a low-pressure kind of way. It's a no-brainer that you're great with kids."

It was a solid idea. "Yeah, okay."

My steps felt lighter. Ginny didn't see red flags. She liked Hannah enough not to immediately jump into overprotective sister mode. And she was going to help me figure out a way forward.

I loved my sister.

And I hoped I'd find a way to quiet my nervous heart.

Chapter 24

HANNAH

Ever since Jordan had talked to me about knowing when you liked someone—and okay, ever since I'd started sneaking around with Blythe—she'd become increasingly private about her school and social life. So when Ginny called out of the blue to invite us for another swim date, I said yes without asking if my daughter wanted to go.

I knew it was past time to tell Jordan I was seeing someone, but part of me was embarrassed. What kind of lesson did it teach my daughter that I jumped from one relationship into another? What was I going to say? "Oh by the way, darling, we're going to give Blythe a try as mommy number two." It seemed cruel. And selfish.

Plus, there was the whole uprooting bit. It hadn't escaped my notice that Jordan had hung a wall calendar next to her desk. Or that she'd steadily crossed off the days leading up to one in early June that said "Back to Asheville" in bold black marker. I knew it was past time for a serious talk about my promise, but I kept holding on to hope that one day she'd wake up and change her mind on her own.

"Swimming? On a Sunday? But I don't want to go." Jordan stopped her geometry homework and threw the pencil down on her desk.

"Because you have something else?" Maybe at least she would tell me why she'd been so shut down around me lately.

"Yes. We have a planning meeting for this protest thing we're going to do."

"And you were getting there how?"

"We're doing it virtual. But I need to be here, where I have Wi-Fi."

"You don't want to swim at that house again? They don't have tenants this week, and I know Derrick and Isla are excited to see you."

My cagey brain didn't miss the alternate possibility. I could tell Ginny that Jordan had a thing, which would be true, and I could go lounge with Blythe all day instead. But then that put me back at selfish. But which was more selfish? Not letting my daughter attend her planning meeting, or letting her and then spending all afternoon in bed with my secret girlfriend?

Maybe it would be good to spend time with Blythe and her family. I was seeing her, secret or not, and if I truly believed we had something special, seeing her around Jordan and Jordan seeing Blythe around us might nudge me past residual fears.

"I'm sorry, hon, but I already said we'd go. You'll have to catch the next meeting."

"That's not fair."

"You're right. But sometimes that's how things work out."

She growled in frustration, and I chose to ignore it. Then she slammed her geometry book.

I stepped out into the hall. "Be pissed all you want, but we're going over there after lunch." I pointed to her book. "Finish your homework this morning."

"Whatever." She slammed the door to get rid of me.

Before I could fuss at her for the outburst, the phone rang. This could only mean one thing on a late Sunday morning—my mother.

"Hi, Mom."

"Dear. You sound frazzled."

"Jordan's being a teenager."

My mother absolutely cackled on the other end of the line. "Turnabout is so sweet. That child has been far too easy on you."

Leave it to my mom to think more about her delight in parental karma than any hardship on me. "You're right. She's great. But lately she's been kind of withdrawn and secretive. I think she may have a boyfriend, but I don't understand why she won't tell me about him."

Which, okay, pot meet kettle. Hello. But it was not the same. I was a cool mom. She should be excited to tell me if she was falling for someone. And it wasn't like she broke off an engagement and had to be concerned with proper timing. I wouldn't care. I'd be excited with her.

"Anyway, it doesn't matter. Hi, Mom. How are you? Did you have a good week?"

"Delores Crosby died."

My mom was only in her sixties, but the past couple of years she'd had more friends and friend's husbands die than ever before. I knew it was getting her down. Especially since she'd chosen not to remarry after Dad died.

"I'm sorry. I didn't realize you guys were still close."

"I saw her once a month for book club. And we used to play tennis together years ago. But it's the principle of the thing. I need younger people in my life. I need you."

"Mom." My heart twisted in my chest. Yes, we had our disagreements, and yes, she could be harsh as hell, but she had always been there in a pinch. Her forthrightness made me feel like shit.

She kept talking. "I know you won't move back here, and I don't think you should. But we never finished our conversation about a condominium there. I've decided I'm serious about it. You scout out the area. Find me a good community that's safe, with a pool, pickleball courts, and a view. I won't live there full-time. Not until I'm too decrepit to drive, but I'd like to spend more time with you and Jordan. There's no huge rush. And I won't even bother saying we can all live together."

"Mom, when you can no longer drive or walk to get your glass of Chardonnay from the fridge, I promise I will take care of you. But you're right, until then we need our own space, which I need to remind you might be in Asheville."

"We could vacation at the beach, best of both worlds."

She had a point.

"You're in luck, then. I'll be seeing Blythe's sister, Ginny, this afternoon. She's a realtor. I'll give her your specs and see if she knows of anything."

We talked for another twenty minutes, or rather she talked and I listened, and as she talked I thought about Jordan and how she was being so secretive. I realized I was doing the same thing with my own mother. Maybe she'd have good advice.

When she took a breath, I lowered my voice to an almost whisper, though I could hear music coming from Jordan's room, so chances were she wasn't eavesdropping. "Can I ask you something?"

"Me?" Mom sounded legitimately surprised.

"I know. Shocker. But I'm serious."

"Of course, dear. Anything."

"Do you think it's too soon for me to be dating again?"

"You mean, seeing as the date of your cancelled wedding has barely been crossed off of my wall calendar?"

"Never mind." Approaching my mother as a confidante may have been the dumbest idea I ever had. Jordan probably got her stupid calendar from the source.

"I'm sorry. That was insensitive of me."

Now I was the one shocked. My mother rarely apologized —and admitting a flaw? Forget it. I could hang up and be happy for the rest of my life. Except, I did want to know what she thought. I might as well just spill it.

"Remember Blythe?"

"Of course! The boat captain. I tried to warn her about you."

"Well, it didn't work. We've been seeing each other."

Mom was quiet, waiting for me to go on.

"And I know it's going to sound crazy, but I really like her. Like, really, really like her. She's smart and funny and kind. And even though she has ideas and things she wants to do, she cares about other people's ideas too. She's generous and beautiful and . . ."

"Okay. You've made your point. And I don't disagree. She came across as an absolutely lovely human being. And attractive in a very handsome sort of way."

"You don't think it's bad?"

My mom sighed on the other end of the line before she spoke. "Darling. Life is short. Delores could tell you about that if she hadn't died. Besides, who among us can say when timing is right or wrong? It just is. And if we're getting all deep and honest, I always thought the last one was a bit uptight for you. And Jordan."

I'd circle back to that factoid at another time. "What I'm hearing is you don't think it's weird I'm already seeing someone new?"

"Your life is your life, and as long as she's not a bad person, I want you to be happy."

I blew out the breath I didn't realize I'd been holding. "Great. Now you're going to have to help me figure out how to tell Jordan."

All I got in response was a long peal of laughter.

BLYTHE

When I got to the house, Hannah's car was already there. I was nervous about seeing Jordan. Before, I hadn't been trying to impress her because it didn't really matter. But now . . . I wanted her to like me. I wanted her to like me enough that dating her mom would be seen as a positive in both of their eyes.

Laughter sounded from the pool area as I walked underneath the house to the lower patio.

"Hey, hey, hey." I opened the wooden gate and made a concerted effort not to look at Hannah first.

Todd slapped me on the back. "What's up, sis?"

"Not much. Just came to see your ugly mugs."

Derrick bonked me with a wet pool noodle. "Who you calling ugly?" He stood in his board shorts and nothing else, pool water streaming off his legs. "Come swim with us, Aunt B."

"Unreal. It's February and you bozos are running around like it's August. There's no way you're talking me into getting in that water." Which was untrue. Derrick and Isla were totally capable of talking me into getting into a pool in the dead of winter. Thank goodness it was heated.

I did a quick glance across the pool deck toward the seating area. Hannah sat cross-legged on one of the loungers, a cute pink ball cap on her head, her mirrored sunglasses covering her eyes. Ginny was on the lounger next to her, and they were laughing about something.

There was a tug on my hand. Isla stared up at me.

"What's up, chicken?" I tweaked the tip of my nibling's nose.

"I'm not a chicken. But you need to come Chicken Fight with us. I'm riding on Jordan's shoulders, and Derrick can ride on yours."

"Let me go say hi to your mama first. Then I promise I'll get into this freezing pool just to keep you two quiet."

"You promise?"

"I promise."

She ran off and cannonballed into the deep end while yelling "Aunt B's coming in!"

I walked over to where Hannah and Ginny waited.

"Are you really getting in?" Ginny shook her head. "They have got you wrapped around their little fingers."

"Wasn't that the point of today? A pool party. Aren't you getting in, Hannah?" I tried to keep any special trill out of my voice. Because now that Ginny knew, even if she was being hush-hush about it, she would be paying close attention to the two of us.

"I am already deep on Jordan's shit list. If I got into the pool and tried to interact with her right now, I might find myself floating on the bottom. Ginny and I are hitting the hot tub. You should join us once you've gotten good and frozen in that pool."

Though getting into a hot tub with Hannah sounded heavenly, it sounded a lot less so with my sister present.

"We'll see." But the barely contained smile snuck onto my face anyway, and I had to turn away before my sister examined it too closely.

I pulled off my hoodie and cargo pants to reveal my nonswimsuit swimsuit: an old pair of running shorts and a shelf bra tank. It'd been a few years since they'd seen any running action. "Look out!" I yelled. "Here I come!" I cannonballed into the pool, sending up a huge splash all over Derrick, Isla, and Jordan. When I emerged, they were ready for me, their hands batting the top of the water so I was surrounded by the spray.

"Okay, okay, okay. Gah! Enough!" I held up my hands to

keep the water out of my eyes. "Are we playing this game or what? I've got a hot tub with my name on it."

Derrick jumped on my back. Another six months and there'd be no way I could carry him without busting a disc. Isla scrambled up on Jordan's back.

"Okay." I looked at Jordan. "They're going to try to get each other, but be warned, I'm going to try to get you." I angled my shoulders back and forth and bounced on the balls of my feet.

She narrowed her eyes and grabbed on to Isla's legs. "Not if we get you first."

"Ooh, a competitor. I like it."

Derrick got into position, and Jordan and I started bouncing around each other. Isla clucked from her perch aboard Jordan's shoulders, and Derrick cock-a-doodle-dooed. I made a quick lunge toward Jordan, shifting my right shoulder, and Derrick swatted at his sister. But Jordan had the advantage of lightness—she bounced easily out of our way and came in fast toward our left.

I sidestepped away from her, but Isla grabbed Derrick's arm and tried to pull him backward off me. She almost got him.

"BeeBee. Pay attention." Derrick latched on to my head.

I hunkered down and came at Jordan, scratching my feet on the bottom of the pool like a chicken scratching the dirt.

"Oh no you won't." She scratched back at me.

We circled. We parried. We charged in. And out. Then, in a move neither Derrick nor I saw coming, Jordan ran straight at me and Isla held her hands out, making contact with me instead of Derrick. I went down like the middle-aged woman I was.

When Derrick and I emerged from the water, they were hooting and hollering and Jordan's face was lit up with her inherited dimples. I glanced over my shoulder to see Hannah smiling the same smile back at us.

"Did you see that?" I yelled. "What a tactic."

"Again, BeeBee. Again."

"One more time. Then it's the hot tub for me."

Our second round ended up very much like the first, but I didn't care. I'd made Jordan laugh, which was a delightful thing. Whatever had happened between her and her mom seemed to be better now. My job here was done.

I climbed out of the pool, squeezing water from my shorts and pushing my hair back flat against my head. When I glanced up, Hannah looked at me with a soft expression.

Maybe we'd get to take the next step.

Chapter 25

HANNAH

Ginny was deep in discourse on brining versus not brining when her sister slipped into the hot tub. It was hard to listen to tips on baking a chicken—prompted by the pool game, of course—when Blythe's proximity absorbed my focus. A flush of desire rushed up my spine when she brushed against me, and I wished I could magic everyone else away so it was the two of us, in each other's arms.

"Have you tried it with a brine soak?"

"What? Oh, no, I haven't. I'll definitely try that, but to be honest I usually pick up a rotisserie chicken." I hoped she didn't notice the lag time in my response.

I turned to Blythe, trying not to touch her again. "Looked like you guys were having fun. Thanks for getting Jordan out of her funk."

"She having a teenage moment?" Blythe propped her arms on the back of the hot tub and crossed her leg over the other in a feminine version of a man spread. I guess it was her way of keeping us a proper distance apart with her sister present. She must have felt it too.

I put my hands in my lap where they'd be neat, contained, and obedient. "She wanted to do something with her friends, but I didn't want her to stay home alone again. I basically had to force her to come."

We both looked toward the pool. Todd was in the water now, and a new game of Chicken Fight was on.

"Looks like all's good now." Ginny shouted, "Get him, Jordan! Take that big guy out!"

Jordan shouted back, "We're working on it!"

"He's a nice guy," I said.

Ginny smiled. "He's the best. Now if only my Blythe could find someone. Our little family would be complete."

Blythe's eyes turned to saucers and she wouldn't look at me, and I thought she might kill her sister. It made me think about the stuff my mom said that day on the boat. Which made me think about my earlier conversation with her. I stepped in to save Blythe from her current embarrassment. "Oh, speaking of families, my mom asked me to keep my ear to the ground for a deal on a condo in the area."

Ginny snapped into realtor mode. "Oh yeah? She's going to move here? You must be thrilled."

"Well." I glanced at Blythe, who stared intently at the pool and away from both of us. "Thrilled might not be the adjective I'd use. But she is retired, and she seems to think that if she puts down roots here, then I will too."

"Oh?" Ginny hit the button to lower the jets' force. "Are roots hard for you?" She seemed super intent on my answer.

I'd never told Ginny about my life, but it seemed like today would be a good moment to begin. "Generally, no. I worked at the same school for ten years. I have lifelong friends. But I did recently end an engagement. It's why we moved here." I paused, wondering if I should mention my promise to Jordan, but Ginny moved on to a new line of questioning.

"And your mom thinks you're unstable in relationships?" Again with the pregnant pause.

I thought of how Mom had reacted to the news of me seeing Blythe. "Maybe when I first told her. She definitely thought I was unstable picking up and moving like I did. But no, now that we've talked, she understands I was in the wrong relationship." I let out a laughing breath. "She actually told me she'd always thought my ex was too buttoned up, something she never said when we were together."

Blythe uncrossed her legs.

"But now that Mom's been here. Now that she's met some of the locals and seen the area and received the message that I'd always dreamed of living down here permanently, she's just as charmed as I am. In a weird way, this place might even be healing for our relationship. She's seeing me as someone who could actually be there when she needs me."

I felt the water move as Blythe shifted to rejoin our conversation, though it was obvious she'd never stopped listening.

Ginny's eyes softened. "Ah, that's wonderful. You're lucky to have her."

Blythe turned toward me. "What's she looking for in a condo?"

I shared what Mom had told me. Ginny nodded and mused about potential properties.

Blythe cleared her throat. "You know. You said she's not in a hurry. My condo will be available eventually. There's no pickleball court, but there's a pool, great marsh trails for hiking or biking, and a kayak landing. I'd even rent it back from her if she wanted to buy it sooner and didn't plan on living here yet. That might help me with my construction costs on the new place. I mean, if it was her cup of tea, of course."

"Oh!" I sat up, thinking about how perfect that could be.

"She would love your place. She'd be blown away by the view." As soon as it was out of my mouth, Blythe's eyes did the saucer thing again, and I realized what I'd done. I backpedaled. "I mean, I'm assuming that's the view on your social profile. Because, um, you told me it faced the marsh."

A strangled noise came from Ginny to my right. "Oh, goodness, sorry. Bug in the windpipe." She coughed over laughter.

I'd be freaking about a bug in my windpipe. Not laughing. "Oh my gosh. Let me get you a bottle of water." I crawled out of the hot tub, glad my face was red from the steam. That was close. I'd almost blown our cover. Though I wouldn't really care if Ginny knew. She was a mom, so she'd probably understand where I was coming from with Jordan. But Blythe needed to be the one to share the news. And beyond Jordan, I understood Blythe's reluctance to tell her. Until I was a sure thing, there was no sense in dragging her sister into it.

Jordan trotted over. "Can I get in the hot tub? I'm freezing."

"Your lips are a little blue. Go jump in for a minute. Then we'll go home and dry off." I figured we'd gracefully make our exit before I could get myself in any more trouble. "Here, take these for Ginny and Blythe." I handed her the bottles and grabbed my towel from the deck chair. After I'd wiped off, I threw on my hoodie and sweats.

Todd came over and fished a hard seltzer out from the bottom of the cooler. "You want one of these?"

"Brrr. No thanks. I'm thinking hot shower and a hot tea."

"Ginny told me about you and Blythe. Made me happy."

"What?"

"Yeah." He cracked open the can and took a swig. "About y'all seeing each other on the sly. Don't worry, we won't say anything to Jordan before you. But we hope you'll tell her soon. My kids sure like hanging out with her, and I know Blythe thinks she's a cool cat. It'd be good to have y'all around more often."

Something in my face must have given me away.

"Shit. You didn't know we knew." He rubbed his hand over his chin.

The bug thing made sense now. Ginny was literally swallowing her laughter over my slip up. I shook my head. "No, Blythe didn't tell me she'd told y'all."

"Well, technically she told Ginny, and I suppose Ginny maybe wasn't supposed to tell me, but she tells me everything, so here we are. Hope I didn't get B in trouble."

I took a deep breath and looked over at where my daughter was laughing and talking with Ginny and Blythe in the hot tub. "No," I said. "She's not in trouble."

Not at all.

BLYTHE

"So, you're not mad?" I lay on my sofa, showered and clean after a day at the pool. Moonlight bounced across the water outside my window, and Larry Styles kneaded biscuits on my chest as I talked to Hannah.

"Not mad. Surprised, but not mad."

The cat's purr rumbled against me. I shifted and put the phone closer to my ear. "Yeah. I hadn't planned on telling Ginny, until, well, I didn't know when I was going to tell her. It sort of just happened. I needed to talk to somebody about us."

"Was it because you're worried . . . about me?"

"Honestly?" I hesitated because once it was out of my mouth, there was no taking it back. "Yes. Because you haven't told Jordan. Because you don't know when you're going to tell her. I haven't wanted to pressure you because, believe me, I do get it. I really do. But it also scares me. I worry you're using Jordan as an excuse, and keeping us secret is a way to keep me around without you having to enter into a relationship again. And though, don't get me wrong, I do love being your booty call, I also want more."

She laughed, which I took as a good sign.

"You are my favorite booty call. In fact, I wish I were paying you a booty call right this very moment." She paused for a second. "But thank you. For your honesty. It's one of the things I love about you. You're really a great communicator, Blythe."

"But you don't want more."

"Why would you say that?"

"Because you made it clear early on that this was a no-strings sort of thing. I agreed to it, so I'm owning my part. But now I'm not sure where I am is where I want to be. I want more, Hannah. I want a relationship. With you."

"I want more, too, Blythe. But I have a daughter and there

are commitments I've made to her. Don't get me wrong, I'd love nothing more than to be at your house every night with my naked body pressed against yours, but I can't snap my fingers and make it magically happen in your perfect time frame. I'm not there. Why can't we just date for a while? See where we end up?"

Whew, talk about immediately feeling the consequences of my truth. "You're saying I'm too much for you?"

She took a beat before responding. "Blythe, that's not what I'm saying. I understand you have an enormous heart and want to share it with me. Which is amazing. But you have to hear me too. Even though there are many things I love about you, pushing me to tell Jordan before I decide the time is right is not going to make me feel good about us. You have to trust this, Blythe. I know that's hard for you, but I'm not Constance. I'm not sure exactly what went down between the two of you, but I don't have some secret agenda by not telling my daughter about us. I want what's best for me and her. If that's you, time will tell. Can you support me around that? Can you add a big dash of patience to the beautiful creature that you are? If we're meant to be together, we'll figure it out."

A part of me still felt panicked and scared, but I pushed it down. She was right. She'd had a huge blow. We hadn't known each other very long, and all she was asking for was an expanded timeline. "I can try."

"Thank you," she said.

I didn't want her to hang up, and something she said buzzed around the edges of my happiness. "You said you love many things about me?" I was kind of teasing but kind of not. I wasn't without the need for a little reassurance.

"Do you want to hear them?"

Hannah's voice went soft, and I could picture her on the other end. She'd be curled up on the bed, wearing tattered boxer shorts and a soft loose T-shirt in coral or raspberry, two colors I'd noticed she wore often. Her hair would be hanging in her eyes, and the longer tendrils around her ears would be messy and slightly curled. Her toes would be painted a nude pink, and her legs would be soft and smelling of the woodsy lotion she liked.

"Sure," I whispered, my voice catching as I thought about wrapping myself around her, talking through our disagreements and misunderstandings face-to-face like an actual couple.

"Let's see." Her voice was a caress. "I love your genuineness. I love the way you love the water and the things of the sea. I love how your eyes are the clearest blue but get slightly darker when you're turned on. I love the little smile lines that curve at the corners of your mouth. I love your creativity and the way you listen and respond so carefully. I love how sweet you are with your niece and nephew and Jordan, even my mom." She hesitated, then added, "Don't be worried about us, okay?"

"Okay."

"You swear you won't worry?"

I laughed. "I can't promise you I won't. My history of falling hard for the wrong women has left me a little mentally self-destructive."

"I'll try to be more sensitive to that. And I'm not the wrong woman. Our timing is just a little off balance. But we'll sort it out."

"How did I find you?" It wasn't so much a question for her as an observation for the universe.

"You were in my driveway, remember?"

This made me smile. "Oh, believe me, I remember. Like the clouds parted and the sun lit you up in Technicolor."

"Not true."

"Actually, it is. I had a feeling about you that day. Now I guess I just have to wait for timing to play out and prove me wrong." I paused, and this time she filled in with the right response.

"Or prove you right."

"Or prove me right," I echoed. "Good night, Hannah."

When we'd clicked off, I put the phone down and gave Larry Styles the attention he deserved.

I hoped the wait wouldn't be too long, not that I wouldn't give Hannah the time she needed, but when you find the woman who makes you forget all of your previous heartaches, you don't want to spend another night without her.

Chapter 26

HANNAH

I'd thought a lot about the conversation Blythe and I had on the phone Sunday night. Was it fair for me to keep things under wraps if I was truly serious about her? Which brought me to the next thought. Was I serious? Jordan loved me. She'd want me to be happy. And it was obvious she liked Blythe, Ginny, and family.

Lisa had never invited Jordan along to so many things at the beginning of our dating life. It'd been adult focused from the get-go. So why was I hesitating about letting my daughter know I was dating again?

I closed my eyes and tried to push everything out of it for a minute of mindful thought.

Giving my subconscious room to appear revealed the no-brainer that lived there. I was as scared as Blythe. But unlike Blythe, I wasn't being honest about it. I was going along all la-di-da, let's just see where this leads, have mind-blowing sex, not talk to my daughter about it, and worse, not be honest about the fact we might not stay here. The realization that it was time to come clean hit like a thunderclap. I opened my eyes and texted Blythe before I left for work.

Can I see you tonight?

If there was one thing lesbians could do, it was process. Blythe wanted my assurance this was the real deal, but maybe I needed the same assurance. Why would someone like her choose a single mom with a career in limbo? How did I know she wouldn't eventually want another big-haired, big-breasted flashy femme who loved nights out on the town and calling her Daddy? Okay, I didn't know that her exes called her Daddy, but I could imagine.

I'd love it.

Great. I'll bring dinner. We'll have a real date. Not a booty call.

I mean, okay, but really? Not even dessert? She added a wink to her text.

Well, I am powerless when it comes to your advances, but yes, dinner first.

I'll be good until dessert then.

I put the phone in my pocket and grabbed my car keys. "Ready?"

Jordan mumbled her way to the front door with her backpack up on her shoulder. When we got in the car and were backing out of the drive, I casually said, "I have plans for dinner with someone tonight. Will you be okay at home without me?"

Her head pivoted to look at me. "Like a date?"

"I mean, no, maybe. It's dinner with a friend. But can I leave it at that for now? I promise I'll be home by ten and I'll keep my cell on if you need me."

"Yeah, sure. Whatever."

Her nonchalant response wasn't what I expected. I expected pushback and "Isn't it kind of soon?" or something about how it was supposed to be just the two of us now. But when I glanced her way, she'd already moved on and was busy typing into her phone. Okay. That was kind of anticlimactic.

At work, Alexander showed up again. "Hello, love." He kissed both of my cheeks as I came out to the paint color area to help him. "Did that handsome girlfriend of yours tell you about our meeting later today?"

"She did not. But I'm seeing her tonight, so I guess I'll hear all about it then."

"You should bring her a bottle of champagne. I think she'll be celebrating."

"Oh yeah?"

"Yes. Okay, I'll spill." He acted like I'd twisted his arm. "We're starting our company and we're hoping she'll come in as a partner and be our architect. I'm pretty sure it's an offer she won't be able to refuse."

Though I was excited for Blythe, it also concerned me. Part of my big talk for tonight was going to be about us becoming an actual thing, even if it meant Jordan and I were long-distance. With the hope, of course, that Blythe might move too. But if she had a job like he described, she wouldn't want to move. Eventually Jordan would go to college and my life would be more flexible, but that was three long years away.

Joel came out from the back. Alexander looked at him, then winked at me, before he said, loudly, "And if you get to transform this little paint store into the cutting-edge design center I know it can be, we will source all of our future clients here." He turned to Joel. "I hope you know what a fabulous resource you have in this woman. I won't go to anyone else for color decisions in my design projects. You should let her run with it."

Joel nodded. "Oh, I know. I got real lucky when she stumbled in here that day."

Alexander pulled out a chair at the table and whipped out a digital tablet. "Let me show you what you should do with this old place." Within seconds he'd sketched out a new facade for the store and pushed out the paint area to create an area for clients who wanted design help that went beyond a gallon of primer. Joel, to my delight, seemed interested in the idea.

"What do you think, Hannah? If I did something like this, I'd sure need to know you were staying on."

And here we were, back at my personal crossroads. All the current excitement in my life pointed to me being right here. But my daughter . . . her life mattered more.

THAT EVENING, I left Jordan with a big bowl of grilled chicken salad and a hefty slice of cheese bread and loaded the rest into bags to take to Blythe's. "Are you sure you're going to be okay?"

"Fine, Mom. I have homework and then I promised Tilda I'd call her later."

"Okay. If you need me . . ."

"I know, your cell will be on."

I lingered for a second, making sure she was truly comfortable with my going out.

"Are you going?" She spoke through a mouthful of greens.

"Fine."

I stopped and bought a bottle of champagne on my way to Blythe's. If she was full of news of a new opportunity, tonight might not be the best night to address my fears or my ideas. But if we were going to take next steps, like telling Jordan, I'd have to put all my cards on the table.

She was waiting out on her deck when I pulled up. She came down the steps and helped me with the bags. "Looks like you brought enough to feed an army. And what's this?" She looked in the store bag with the champagne.

"Alexander came into Williamson's today and he may have slipped about a potential celebration?"

"Oh, he did, did he?"

I followed her up the stairs and noted the muscles on her forearms that showed themselves under the weight of the grocery bags. This could be my life. All of the mundane tasks made better by having a special someone, besides my child of course, to share them with.

I really hoped it would be Blythe.

BLYTHE

I put the bags down on the island and turned to take Hannah into my arms. It had been too many nights since I'd held her.

"We can't," she said as I traced a line of kisses down the side of her neck, my thoughts going red hot in an instant with her nearness. I ignored her and put my hands on her waist, then inched them up little by little. My mouth moved from the side of her neck to her clavicle, to the hollow spot at the base of her throat while my hands positioned themselves high enough that with a simple shift I had my thumb exactly where it wanted to be.

"Blythe, holy hell," she exhaled, her head tipping back as I started to push her shirt up and off her delightfully sensitive breasts.

"I'd be your devil if you let me." I grinned, but her dimples didn't shine for my bad pun. When she pushed me back a few inches, I dropped my hands instantly, worried I'd overstepped. "Too much? I'm so sorry."

She put her hands on my jawline and pulled me forward for a fast but full kiss. "No, never, nothing to be sorry about. I want that too. But I would like us to have conversation first. And food. I'm starving."

This was definitely a new turn of events, but the food, the champagne, the way her body responded to me so immediately, all allowed me to send my overworked relationship anxiety to the quiet corner of my mind.

She stepped out of my arms. "I made salad and have grilled chicken. And there's cheese bread on good homemade sourdough I found at the little bakery near work."

"Sounds great."

Hannah pulled the food out of the bags, and I grabbed bowls and small plates for the bread. As she served up the food, I set the table rather than us sitting at the kitchen island. I lit the candles that normally collected dust, then dimmed the lights so we could see the reflection of the water. A warm swell of happiness washed over me. I loved each new moment with her.

"Should I open this?" I held up the bottle of bubbly she'd brought.

"That depends on if you feel like celebrating."

"Any night with you is a night worth celebrating."

She groaned. "So cheesy."

"But true. I mean it." The cork came out with a gentle pop, and I filled two flutes. Bubbles spun to the top of each glass. "Here you go." I handed one to Hannah. "To us."

"To your new opportunity?" She tilted her head with the question.

"Yes," I said. We gently tapped the glasses and took a sip. Then we carried plates and glasses to the table and sat down across from each other so we could talk.

"Are you going to tell me about it?" Hannah sipped champagne and took a bite of salad.

I tried to ignore the worry line running across her forehead. "Not much to say that you probably haven't already heard. The guys are starting a business and they want me to come in as the architectural partner. For now, it's more of a part-time thing, but it could turn busier. I'll be able to work from home a fair amount of time. Which is good. I like the flexibility, so I can get out on the boat. I'll be happy getting back to design work. I'm getting tired of unclogging plumbing and fixing lock combinations." I stopped talking so I could take a few bites of the bread. "Mmm, this is delicious. I feel pretty spoiled by all of this."

"Right. Your boat. I bet not having that easily accessible would be super hard." Hannah smiled, but I could sense there was something going on beneath the surface. The past me might be worried to bring it up, but the now me wanted to know what was going on.

"What's the occasion for all this?" I motioned to the spread.

"Can't a girl cook for her girlfriend?"

"Of course she can." Then what she said hit me. "Girlfriend?"

She drank a big swig of her champagne.

"Is everything okay, Hannah?"

A shine that looked like tears glistened on her lower lid. I jumped up and went around to where she was sitting and put my arms around her. "Shhh, don't cry. Talk to me. Tell me what's going on." My heart raced. Panic tiptoed up behind me.

"It's just . . ." A single tear rolled down her cheek. "You know it won't be like this." She turned toward me. "I'm a mom. We won't have candlelit dinners and sex in the living room. You've never dated a woman with a child before. You keep asking if I'm really in this thing, but what about you? I have a plus-one that's non-negotiable." She cried more, so I pulled her up from the dining room table and walked her over to the couch so that I could hold her while we worked through this.

I nudged my own plus-one out of the way. "Get down, Larry."

I wrapped my arms around Hannah and pulled her in tight as she shook with tears. This felt like so much more. And though it was scary, I absolutely loved being the one she was turning to, letting in to what she was feeling. "Hannah," I whispered into her hair. "I want this. I want you. Which means all the parts of you." I pushed back and wiped stray tears from her face. "I'm not Lisa. Though, yes, it's you I want to be with, I won't look at the moment Jordan leaves for college as the start of our relationship. I love you so much. I love Jordan. I love the idea of both of you being in my life." I held back from saying "my family," though those were truly the right words.

"You love me?" She wiped at her face.

"I love you," I said again, and leaned forward, pressing my lips gently against hers.

"I love you, too," she whispered as we kissed. "So, do you want to be my girlfriend? Even if it means I have to put Jordan's needs first?"

I kissed her again and pulled her into a tight hug. "Of course."

We stayed locked in each other's embrace.

I couldn't believe this moment. Hannah. She was mine. I was hers.

"Come on." I stood up and held out my hand.

She stood to face me. "Where are we going?"

I kissed the tip of her nose. "To prove we are girlfriends rather than friends who are girls."

She laughed and followed me down the hall to my bed.

Chapter 27

HANNAH

I lay back on the cool cotton sheets, Blythe's comforter tangled around my ankles. She was propped on her elbow, looking at me, trailing her fingertips over my skin.

"You are so incredibly beautiful." She leaned down and placed gentle kisses along my cheekbones. "I'm sorry you were worried."

"You know, it's weird." I tilted my head to look into her kind eyes. "Here I was thinking I was so strong and absolutely right in my decisions. I never doubted ending my engagement. I felt resilient and strong and capable of conquering anything. Then you were in my driveway, like some sort of backlit vision, challenging my determination to never get involved with someone again."

Blythe's fingertips drew lazy circles along my rib cage. "I wish I could say I was sorry I made you have to deal with your feelings, but I'm really not."

I flipped to face her and snuggled in so our naked bodies were pressed against each other. "I thought you were the one freaking out, but really it was me." I kissed her. The warm fullness of her lips was always such a welcome surprise. "I'm going to tell Jordan this week. My mom was right. There's no time frame on knowing when something is worth pursuing. I'd rather teach my daughter honesty than sneak around behind her back."

"Then we can be official."

"Girlfriends."

"But maybe we can have one more night of sneaking around?" Blythe's grin was devilish as she reached a hand beneath the sheets.

I fell onto the pillow, ready for all the places she would take me, when her phone buzzed from where it sat on the charger.

She ignored it. My body flooded with warmth and happiness.

Her phone buzzed again.

My knees fell together.

"You better check that."

Blythe remained propped on one elbow, touching me, a smile on her face. "No way." She whispered kisses against my jawline. I reveled in the way my body responded to her lightest touch.

Her phone rang this time.

I groaned and put a hand on her wrist. "This is going to go nowhere if you don't check your phone. It's messing with my mojo."

"Ugh. Fine." She slowly pulled herself away from me and reached for the phone. "Shit."

I sat up with her. "Who is it?"

"Ginny. There are a bunch of texts from her too."

"Call her back. Make sure everything's okay."

She called the number back. "Hey, sis? What's up?"

She held the phone out so I could hear Ginny talking.

"Have you checked your texts?"

Blythe winked at me. "No, I was busy. Just heard the phone ring."

"Well check your texts and then call Hannah. Or wait. Is she there?"

I shook my head no. I wasn't ready yet for Ginny to know every intimate detail of our lives.

"No, she's not."

"Well check your texts, call her, then call me back."

Blythe hung up and clicked open her message app.

"Uh-oh."

"What?"

Blythe flashed her phone toward me. It was Jordan in a hot tub with an unknown boy. Tedrick had posted a boomerang video of the two of them making heart hands. It wasn't any old hot tub, though. It was the one at the beach house. The beach house that we were not renting anymore and did not own.

"Crap." Then, "We've got to go get her."

Blythe called Ginny back. "We'll handle this."

I threw on my clothes and raced out the door. How could this happen? The first night I'd been honest about meeting someone for dinner and Jordan had snuck out behind my back. Why would she do that to me? This would never have happened in Asheville.

The same way it felt fated I'd met Blythe, this felt like the reverse omen. If Jordan was going to go rogue on me, could I really do this? Was I that scared of being alone that I had to jump into another relationship with the first woman who came my way? Especially if it meant my daughter was going to spiral out of control?

"Are you okay?" Blythe knew I was too upset to drive and backed Chester out of the parking spot.

"I don't know. I can't believe my kid is trespassing on somebody else's property."

"Take some breaths. We don't know the whole story."

But maybe I did.

Maybe the story I'd created about me and Blythe was all wrong and I'd be a lot better off not imagining fairy tales. If Jordan was going to act out, I was going to hightail it back to where she, and I, had support from old friends and colleagues. My romantic notions would have to wait.

BLYTHE

Hannah's eyes were wide. With each mile, she scooted closer to the passenger door away from me. Her voice, when she spoke, came out tense, her words stilted.

"This is my fault. If I hadn't been sneaking out, leaving her alone, this wouldn't have happened. Who is that boy anyway?"

I remembered what Derrick had told me. "I think his name is Robbie. He's Tedrick's friend."

She drummed her fingers on her thigh. "Can you not go faster? What if he's trying to have sex with her? I mean, I know one day she'll have sex, but there's more I need to tell her about all of that."

I put my hand on Hannah's forearm.

She flinched away from me.

I ignored the flair of self-protection and pressed on. "She's not having sex. Tedrick is obviously there, and I bet some other kids are too. They were making two halves of a heart with their hands, very innocently, and wearing bathing suits. They were probably announcing that they're together to their friends. You said she'd do anything for the 'Gram."

Hannah stopped drumming. "Thanks. You're right, I'm freaking out. But she's trespassing and it obviously happened because I told her I was going out for the night. Why couldn't she just ask me if she could go on a date? Why did I think sneaking around and leaving her would be okay? We should never have moved here. I should have listened."

"If you hadn't moved here, I wouldn't have met y'all." Hannah seemed a little dramatic. But it wasn't my place to say so. Besides, what did I know about having a daughter?

She crossed her arms. "Stop. I'm serious. This is exactly what I've been worried about, which is why I went along with the promise."

"What promise?"

"She didn't want to move here, so I promised her we'd stay until the end of the semester, then see."

"See what?" The question escaped me, though I had a hunch I might not want the answer.

"If we were staying."

"What?" My body came to a standstill, though I managed to keep Chester on the road. There was a possibility they weren't staying? What the hell?

Hannah's hand came to her mouth. Maybe it was the realization she'd let something slip that she shouldn't have. "I told you Jordan was my priority. You said you understood."

Yeah, I thought, *but you never said anything about leaving*.

I took slow, even breaths. This moment was not about me. I needed to be her calm in the storm. I needed to keep my head together and handle this well. There must be some reason why she'd chosen never to mention this detail. I had to trust in the things we'd said to each other earlier.

"Look, Hannah, I know you're panicking, but please don't get so upset about this that you get upset about us. The things we said before, those were all real, right?"

Hannah took a deep breath. "Of course they were real. Look, can we put what I just said on pause? I'm flipping out right now. What am I even going to say to Jordan? If I barge in there like a lunatic, she's going to hate me."

I took my own deep breath. Pause she wanted. Pause she'd get. I could do this. I could be the bigger woman. Not about me. It's not about me.

"No problem. You want me to handle this? I do work for the rental agency. And Tedrick is my sister's nephew. I'm happy to be the bad cop in this situation."

"You would do that?"

"Of course." The words came out of my mouth, but tiny pinpricks of fear ran through my veins. I kept breathing.

We got to the house a few minutes later, and I was

surprised to see Todd's car there along with Tedrick's. Guess Ginny wasn't convinced I could handle it.

Hannah followed a few steps behind me as we walked under the house to the pool area.

"What's up, guys?" I said as I walked into the lights on the deck. My brother-in-law was sitting at the table drinking a soft drink. The hot tub was empty now, and there were five teens in the pool, including Jordan.

Todd waved as if the two of us showing up was the most normal thing in the world. "Hey, you two. Tedrick heard about the pool and asked if I could supervise for a night swim for him and some buddies before the next renters arrive. They roped Jordan in."

"You haven't talked to Ginny?" I held up my phone.

"Naw. She had a late showing and this was a last-minute decision. Phone's in the car. Didn't want it to get wet. Is everything okay?"

I gave him a thumbs-up and shot a quick text off to Ginny so she'd stop panicking, but Hannah fumed. "Everything is not okay." Then to her daughter: "Jordan!?" It was less of a question and more of a "Girl, you are in so much trouble."

"Mom?" Jordan glanced at the boy next to her as she treaded water.

"You were supposed to be studying." Hannah stood by the pool with her hands on her hips.

Jordan scowled. "You don't tell me stuff. Why should I tell you everything? Besides, you didn't answer your phone because you were on some mystery date." Hurt tinged the last word as she spit it out. Then she paused, looked at me, then back at her mom. "Wait. Did you take the food over to Blythe's? Is she your mystery date?"

I looked at Hannah. This wasn't my announcement to make. Besides, after the things she said on the ride over, I wasn't sure where we stood.

Hannah stumbled getting the words out and sounded more like a teenager than Jordan. "It's not like that, Jordan."

I tensed as Hannah stepped away from me to deal with her daughter.

Jordan scowled and treaded away from the side of the pool, glaring at her mom. "What about the whole you and me, happy Lorelai and Rory thing? You want me to tell you everything when you tell me nothing." With that, she turned and dove under the water.

The boy kept treading. "Um, hello, Ms. Greenfield. I'm Robbie, Jordan's boyfriend."

Hannah kept staring at the spot where her daughter was swimming along the bottom of the pool. "Hi, Robbie, it's nice to meet you. Listen, I'm going to go home now. Can you and Todd have Jordan home in thirty minutes? Can you do that for me?"

He nodded.

Hannah turned to me. "I'm going to walk home."

Her face twisted in an unreadable canvas of emotions. My instinct shouted to grab her hand, but my fear held me back. Besides, I didn't want to upset Jordan any more than we already had.

"I'll drive you."

She shook her head. "No, I need to be alone right now. Please give me that."

I teetered on the verge of hyperventilation. We'd just said I love you. We'd just called each other *girlfriend*. Were a few hours all I got of finally feeling happy again? "Hannah." I reached for her, and she stepped sideways.

"No, Blythe."

I dropped my arm as bile rose in my throat. Fine.

The beginning of a hairline crack snaked across my heart.

Here I was again.

I took a huge breath and turned away from her.

This time, though, I was not going to be too much. I was going to let her walk away from me and I would be fine.

Chapter 28

HANNAH

Cold air buffeted my senses as I walked the quiet streets to our apartment. My mind tangled with thoughts. I'd let Jordan down. I'd never been totally honest about me and Lisa. Or with how I'd handled Blythe. I'd been awful with how quickly I'd made assumptions based on Ginny's texts. She barely knew Jordan, but I knew it wasn't like my daughter to trespass on private property and sneak out with a boy. Jordan tried to reach me, and I'd been too damn busy with my own needs to be there for my kid. I was a horrible fucking mom.

Once inside the apartment, I slumped on the couch. What a mess I'd made of everything. I glanced at my phone. Nothing from Blythe. But who could blame her? I'd been pretty clear about needing space. And the bombshell I'd landed about the five-month promise? That needed to be dealt with as well.

My stomach growled through the nausea. We'd hardly eaten the beautiful salad I made. I thought about the things we'd said. In the moment, I'd meant them. But now? How could I do this to Jordan if what she said at the pool about wanting it to be the two of us was true?

I heard a car pull in. I wiped the tears off my cheeks and sat up.

Jordan walked in, her hair still wet from the pool, but she wouldn't meet my eyes.

"You must be cold. Go get into something warm and dry. I'll make you a cup of hot cocoa."

She blew out a breath, her eyes shooting skyward.

"I'm not trying to bribe you. I want to talk."

"I'm old enough to have a boyfriend." She dropped her bag on the ground.

"You're fourteen. Too young to date. But Robbie seems nice. Please go put on something warm."

She picked up her bag and disappeared. I went to the kitchen and made two cups of hot cocoa and sprinkled them with extra marshmallows. She reappeared wearing sweats and the aqua-blue Folly Beach sweatshirt we'd bought the first weekend we were here.

She sat cross-legged in one of the chairs and wrapped her hands around the mug.

"First, I want to apologize if I embarrassed you in front of your friends. You did try to reach me and I wasn't there for you and I'm sorry."

She shifted, and I knew I had her attention.

"I'm also sorry for not being up-front about Blythe. But the reason I wasn't up-front is layered. Do you think you're mature enough to hear me out?"

She nodded.

I took a breath. "You were right when you made those observations about me and Lisa. Remember when you asked me about love at first sight?"

She nodded again.

"I've always wanted to believe in it. I didn't have it with

Lisa. I liked her. A lot. Like you said, she was responsible, smart, self-sufficient. But we weren't passionate."

"Gross." Jordan pulled her sleeves over her hands, then clapped them to her ears.

"Not like that . . . I mean, yes, like that, but also we weren't passionate about each other inside. I'm a mom. I love being your mom. Lisa, well, being a parent wasn't something she wanted."

"I figured." Jordan pulled on one of her curls.

"You did?"

"Well, yeah. She tolerated me, but I could tell she mostly wanted to hang out with you and her other friends." She picked up her mug and let the steam drift onto her face. "Why didn't you tell me about Blythe?"

I glanced at the ceiling. I'd never been so open about my heart with Jordan. I took a deep breath. "Because I've been a little embarrassed. It's awfully fast for me to be dating again."

"Do you like her?"

"I do."

Jordan was quiet for a moment. "Like love at first sight?"

I shrugged, but the silly smile escaped onto my face.

Jordan rolled her eyes. "Oh my gosh, seriously?" She took a sip of her hot cocoa, then questioned, "Sooooo, if I let you date Blythe, will you let me date Robbie?"

I grabbed a pillow and bopped her knee. "Nice try, kiddo." Then I grew serious. "When I decided to move us here, it was to have a fresh start. You know, I was here on vacation when I took the pregnancy test that said you were coming into my life."

"You never told me that."

"It's true. This place is really special to me. But I realize it probably isn't to you. I don't want you to feel any pressure to stay here. The promise I made holds. If Blythe and I are meant to be, then we'll make it work wherever we're living."

She didn't respond right away, but finally she asked, "What do you want?"

I pulled her up into a hug. "I want you to be happy and to feel valued. That's all I want in this world."

Anything else would be gravy.

BLYTHE

Hannah finally called me near midnight.

"Is it too late?" she asked.

"No. I was hoping you'd call. Is everything good now with Jordan?" I got off the sofa and walked to the window to look in the general direction of their apartment. The past few hours had been difficult. My internal thought processes weren't the greatest conversationalists.

"Yeah. She's sleeping. We had a good talk."

"That's good." I cleared my throat and spit out what I'd determined since I last saw her. "Maybe we should press pause on this relationship."

"What?" Hannah's voice rose slightly.

"Look. I get what you've got going on with Jordan, and I respect you. But we've only just started, and just like Jordan comes first for you, my decision to be near my sister was a permanent one. I don't want to fall deeper in love only to have you move away in a few months."

The hum of the refrigerator started in the background and grew loud as I waited for Hannah to respond.

When she finally did, she sounded shocked. "Wow. Okay. I thought we'd be able to work through this. Asheville's not that far. Jordan will be off to college in three years. People date long-distance."

"I wish you'd told me this was a possibility." The parts of me where anger lived felt itchy, but I tuned them out. I didn't want to get angry. I also didn't want a long-distance relationship. I would have kept my walls up if I'd known.

"I get that. I'm sorry. I held off because I was hoping Jordan would come around to staying put and it would never be an issue. I would have told you once I saw how Jordan reacted to us dating."

"And? How did she? React?"

Hannah laughed, and something inside me eased ever so slightly. "She tried to bargain for a boyfriend in exchange for allowing me a girlfriend."

"Clever girl."

"She likes you, Blythe. In fact, I think her exact quote was, 'It'd be cool for you to date somebody who can teach me how to drive a boat.'" She took a breath, then continued with her thoughts. "I'm okay with hitting pause—well, that's not entirely true. I don't want to hit pause, but I will if that's what you need. This is a big detail about our lives. We still have a few more months to go, and no final decision has been made. I can't promise you she's going to be okay staying. But I can promise that if we go, I'll do everything in my power to be the mom Jordan needs and the girlfriend you desire. I love you, Blythe. That hasn't changed. We can make this work."

I was glad she wasn't here. It would be hard to stay strong and clear on what I needed most in my life. Pause or no pause. I saw advantages to both. With one, my heart could begin to patch back up. I could focus on my new job and the houses I was designing. With the other, I'd fall deeper into both Hannah's and Jordan's lives and maybe I could help show Jordan how awesome this place was. But I got it. She'd had friends, a home she'd loved, a life she'd been yanked away from. If she wasn't happy here, they would both leave. And I'd be left with decisions I never wanted to make.

"I need time to think, Hannah. I hope you can understand."

"I do. Take all the time you need. My heart isn't going anywhere. I believe in us. I think you can too." With that, she said good night and the phone line went quiet.

I sat for too long watching the reflection of the moon shimmer off the sound.

Five months? Or forever?

Which was it going to be?

TWO YEARS LATER

BLYTHE

I paced the floor of the condominium and checked my phone again. Nothing.

Larry curled around my legs, sensing my anxiety.

Finally, I heard the thunk of a car door closing and footsteps coming up the steps. I pulled the door open.

Jordan stood in a raspberry-colored dress, a huge smile on her face.

"Do you think she knows?" I asked.

"No clue."

"Okay good. How do I look?"

Jordan stepped back and swished her finger for me to turn. "Like Princess Charming."

"You look beautiful too. Your mom's favorite color."

Jordan laughed. "I stole it from her closet. Figured it'd look good in pictures." She reached into the pocket and pulled out a little raspberry-colored bow tie. "For Larry Styles." She picked up the cat and slipped it over his neck, then put him in his harness and leash.

TWO YEARS LATER

I straightened my vest and my raspberry-colored shirt one last time. "Let's go."

The drive over to the lot was interminable. I'd never been so happy to let a teenager take the wheel.

As we pulled onto the gravel lane, I saw Ginny, Todd, Isla, and Derrick setting up a picnic on the dock. Hannah was there too, standing by Diane's car in our newly created driveway.

"Are you sure about this, kiddo?"

Jordan rolled her eyes. "B. How many times do we need to go over this? Just don't be gross around me."

She parked and we got out. Hannah had loved when Jordan concocted a fancy sunset picnic to celebrate breaking ground on the new house and Lala buying my condominium. But it didn't seem like she'd caught on to the real reason for this event.

After the confessions of the pool-incident night, we'd started over again. I'd chosen to be vulnerable. And Hannah chose to be open with everyone about everything. The sexy times were fewer, but the family times were more. Jordan fell in first-love with Robbie, and wild horses couldn't have dragged her back to the mountains, which meant we were never faced with the long-distance decision.

Both of us spent less and less time sifting through the memories of our past hurts and focused on the moments of our now. We had stepped fully into our careers. Together. We had become family. With Jordan's help and permission, I was going to make it official.

I reached down and felt the box in my pocket.

Robbie showed up, his camera bag at the ready. Jordan kissed him, and I grabbed his shoulder. "Thanks for this, man."

"It's cool. Thanks for including me."

I walked over to Hannah and put my arm around her, leaning in to kiss her cheek. "Hey, babe. You look beautiful."

TWO YEARS LATER

"I can't believe Jordan did this. It's fun, isn't it? And you guys coordinated."

"We sure did." I winked at Jordan as we walked to join the others on the dock.

Once there, Todd handed each of us a glass of champagne. "To the new house."

"Hold on," I said.

Jordan nudged Robbie, who pulled out his camera.

The sky was turning shades of rose and orange and lavender. I looked at Jordan one last time. She nodded.

"I'd like to make a different toast."

Everyone gathered around. I handed Ginny my champagne glass and reached into my pocket. Her eyes grew wide and a broad grin grew on her face as she realized immediately what was about to happen.

"Two years ago, on a day a little chillier than this one, a mom and a daughter pulled that green car into a driveway. I'd given up on love. I'd given up on ever getting to be a parent. But all that changed. Because I fell in love. With both of them." I moved to stand in front of Hannah.

She looked at my hand as I withdrew the box, realization dawning. "Is this . . ."

I nodded. My sister clapped. Diane let out a happy sigh.

Hannah put her hand to her mouth, then pulled it away, her deep dimples on full display as an enormous smile overtook her face. "Hold this, Mom." She held out her champagne glass to Diane, who winked at me as she took it from her daughter.

"Hannah." I took her hand and put my other over Jordan's shoulder. "Jordan." Then I let go and dropped to one knee. "Will the two of you be my family? Will you marry me, Hannah? Will you let me be your stepmom, Jordan?"

I opened the hinged velvet box. Inside were two rings. A gold band set with gorgeous diamond and ruby stars for

TWO YEARS LATER

Hannah. A simple gold crescent moon on a slender gold band for Jordan. My moon and my stars.

I held the ring toward Hannah's finger. Tears rolled down her cheeks. "Yes," she whispered, and I slipped on the band.

Jordan fist pumped. "Yes!" She picked up Larry Styles. "Finally, I get a cat!"

Her mom pulled the other ring from the box and slipped it on Jordan's finger. Then the four of us, Larry Styles included, squeezed into a hug.

"I love you."

"I love you."

"I told y'all not to be gross."

Through happy tears and laughter, we pulled apart and stood arm in arm, watching the sun slip down to the western horizon. Then Isla yelled, "Look! Dolphins!"

Sure enough, a pod came cruising by the dock. Fins crested the surface, and several of them rolled as they swam. The largest of the pod stopped mid-roll, and I swear . . . it winked at me.

I squeezed Hannah's hand and knew.

We'd found home.

About the Author

Jaye Robin Brown is the critically acclaimed author of books for young adults. This is her first novel for adults. She lives in North Carolina with her wife, dogs, cats, and horses. When not writing you can find her riding one of her horses.

Click here to sign up for my newsletter!

You can find information about me, my books, and other tidbits at my website:

www.jayerobinbrown.com

Also by Jaye Robin Brown

Young Adult Novels

No Place To Fall
Georgia Peaches and Other Forbidden Fruit
The Meaning of Birds
The Key to You and Me

www.ingramcontent.com/pod-product-compliance
Ingram Content Group UK Ltd.
Pitfield, Milton Keynes, MK11 3LW, UK
UKHW041209180426
11947UKWH00025B/1953